MASSACRE
ᴬᵀ SUNDOWN

MATTHEW DAVID EVANS

MASSACRE
AT SUNDOWN

ARMORA PUBLISHING

This one's for Michael Wayne.

Prologue

T HE CIRCLE OF CLOAKED figures could be seen only by the light of their torches. *They still use the torches? Of course they still use the damn torches.* The children that they had kidnapped and taken to the old factory on Progress Street were bound and gagged and staring at their captors with pleading, terrified eyes. They couldn't understand what was happening. The black cloaks spoke in a language that none of the children could understand.

A man stepped forward from the circle and removed his hood, revealing an old face with thin white hair that hung to his shoulders. He looked at the children who would be his offering, and then he looked to the sky and raised his hands.

"Our lady," he said, speaking in English for the first time that night, "We bring before you six chosen as an offering. Take them from this world and fold them into your soul, we pray. Accept this offer of innocence and bless your servants accordingly, as you have promised in your sacred word."

"Hear our prayer," the circle chanted.

Jasper Gunne watched this happen from the roof of the factory building. This group was gathered in what had been the back parking lot because it was blocked from the road. They did not want to be seen by passing cars—especially the kind that had red and blue lights.

Jasper had followed this group for days, waiting for the right moment to strike. If he could have come sooner, he would have. This was the only way to account for all of the children taken.

Six children vanished within two weeks. He had watched the story on the News and that (as well as that certain feeling that he got that drew him to his enemies) brought him to the quiet town of Stetson, Michigan. He hadn't been in the state in years. In fact, he tried to avoid it because of the things he had experienced there. But he wouldn't let that keep him from saving children from the clutches of a demonic cult.

From his vantage point he counted all six children. Now all that was left to do was kill the robed people and get out of town before the cops could show up.

A gun would make quick work of the job at hand, but Jasper needed silence. He would not draw any attention to what was happening until well after it was over. That was his way. It was how he had learned to operate after fighting this war for nearly a century and a half. For the task at hand, Jasper had a dagger hanging from his belt.

As the warlock who removed his hood began to speak, Jasper drew the dagger, listening to the familiar sound of the steel scraping against the leather scabbard. There were twelve black cloaks. Not a large number and easy work for someone like Jasper. With luck, they'd all be dead before they had a chance to react.

"Hear our prayer. Hear our prayer. Hear our prayer." Their leader began speaking in that strange language known only to those within his cult while his followers chanted in English for their god to hear their prayer. Jasper listened to the leader's voice get harsher and faster and he decided that it was the best time to act. He leapt from the roof, twisting and flipping in the air like a high diver, and descended onto the crowd. The leader's chant was cut off when Jasper landed on him. He died instantly from the impact.

Jasper was on his feet by the time his enemies realized what had happened. He swung his dagger and cut one across the throat. It was a clean strike and a fatal cut. Two were dead instantly, and Jasper Gunne was moving onto his next victim.

There were ten others in the circle. *Twelve,* Jasper reminded himself. They pulled knives from their robes. These blades were sharp and jagged, and Jasper recognized them as the darkblades. These were not normal knives. These could hurt him.

He had known that they would have the darkblades. They all had the darkblades. Even the cults that broke off from the Order (even the ones that didn't believe in the existence of Jasper Gunne) carried the darkblades. It was the only way to properly do the ceremony and ritual. It was the only way to offer the victims to Valayra, the demon that these fools called a goddess.

Jasper stepped backward to avoid a man who sliced at his chest. He moved forward, brandishing his dagger and his foe backed away. Jasper drove the dagger into the man's skull. He withdrew it and turned on the remaining nine who attacked him simultaneously.

And that was when Jasper showed his skills.

The nine in black robes were practicing witches, but they were not fighters. Without adequate time to weave their spells, they were easy victims for a man who was stronger and faster than all of them. The dagger slashed, and the blood sprayed. There were cries of pain and shouts of rage.

Jasper cut through a woman and turned her scream into a gurgle of blood when he stabbed her throat. *Probably didn't think that was how this night was going to go.* Jasper drove the dagger into another cloak after that, driving the point of the blade through his left eye. *Memories,* he though. He withdrew the dagger, dodged and deflected the blades that were slicing through the air above and around him, and chopped off the hand of one of the cultists.

Six left. The man with the missing hand had fallen to his knees and Jasper had finished him with one strike. The last six were grouped together with their hoods off now. Three women and three men.

The children were all staring at what was happening, wide-eyed and terrified. "Can you kids get up?" Jasper asked.

None of them made a reply other than a whimper. Jasper glanced down and saw them all bound together. He moved quickly, stepping toward them and swinging the dagger. The rope was cut.

"Untie the others," Jasper told the girl he had released. She could not have been more than ten years old. "Untie them and run!"

The six remaining cultists just stared as Jasper let their offering go. There was nothing they could do.

"Looks like Old Valayra goes hungry tonight," Jasper said.

There was no reply from the group of six who still held their knives.

"What?" Jasper said. "Nothing to say? Valayra is not here to help you, you know. She might have better things to do. Being a vile monster is a tough business."

There was still no reply. Jasper was disappointed. He wanted to insult them. He wanted to anger them. It was so much more satisfying to kill his enemies after he worked them into a rage.

"She's a false goddess. A pretender. Not even as powerful as Satan and that's saying something."

"She's real!" one of the men said. He was the youngest of the group. Jasper guessed his age to be no more than twenty-one. "She's real and she'll make you pay!"

"Boy," Jasper said, "she hasn't made me pay in the hundred plus years I've been hunting you people down."

Hunting these fanatical witches had been the focus of Jasper's life for over a century, and it was the only way he could deal with the guilt of living. His own immortality was a curse that could never be fully avenged. Each strike of the dagger had decades of pain behind it. Each fallen enemy was another splash of blood staining his soul. Jasper craved it though. He never felt more at peace than when he had his hand at his enemies' throats.

"We are Valayra!" the boy shouted. "We are Valayra!"

This is new, Jasper thought. *Never heard a group call themselves by the demon's name before.*

"Valayra is not mocked!" the boy shouted.

The children were gone and Jasper no longer had a reason to keep the last six cultists occupied. The boy was talking again, spouting his nonsense about Valayra and how she'd make the unbelievers tremble.

"Enough," Jasper said in a lazy voice. He crouched and leapt, landing in the midst of the six. His dagger slashed in a circle, killing one of the three women and wounding a man on his hand. Jasper then drove his dagger into that man's chest and punctured his heart. He swung the blade again, decapitating the other man, leaving only two women and the boy who had been so defiant. Jasper jammed an elbow into a woman's face. The blow was powerful enough to kill her. He stepped back and raised the dagger...

And that was when he was wounded.

The killing had taken place so fast that the six had barely any time to react. They merely stabbed and slashed with their knives wildly. The boy had been lucky when he had stabbed the darkblade into Jasper's side. He and the woman backed away, astonished that they had managed to wound the man that had come to kill them.

"He's hurt," the woman said. "Finish him!"

"The knife's still in him!" the boy said, panicking but proud of himself.

It was too. He had left the darkblade in Jasper's stomach. If they had attacked him at that moment, they could have won. They hesitated though. Jasper had time to fight through the excruciating pain coursing through his body and grab the hilt of the darkblade. He pulled it from his stomach and dropped it on the concrete.

The woman and the boy backed away and then broke into a run. Jasper growled and pursued. He overtook the woman first, grabbing her by her right shoulder and throwing her on her back. He drove the dagger into her chest. *Another witch dead.* He then threw the dagger at the fleeing boy who had so bravely tried to defend his grotesque religion. He fell with the dagger lodged in the back of his head.

Jasper grunted and put his hand on his stomach. He was bleeding and he would be in for a painful night. He walked to the corpse of the final cultist he had killed and pulled his weapon free from his skull.

Fool. How could you let this little shit hurt you?

But it was over, at least. It had been another victory for Jasper Gunne, and he walked away from that old factory knowing that he had saved the lives of the innocent and taken the lives of the guilty. It was what he did. It was his life. It had been that way for longer than almost anyone on Earth had been alive.

———◦———

LATER, AS HE STUMBLED back to his car, one of the children he had saved approached him. "Hey," the girl said, "mister."

Jasper looked at her. She was the one who had untied the others after being cut free. African American with thick dark hair tied behind her head. A brave girl. Many children would have run after being cut free and left the others behind.

"What?" Jasper asked. His hand was pressed to his stomach in an effort the staunch the wound that he knew wouldn't close for hours.

"Hey," she said again. "Thanks. Thanks for saving us."

"You need to call the cops," Jasper said.

"We can't. They took our phones. Can I use yours?"

"I don't have one," Jasper said. He had never owned a cell phone. Travelling the world like he did, alone, he never had a reason to call anyone. It wasn't as if he had friends that he needed to talk to from time to time. He'd had friends once. It didn't end well. He looked around the street where they were standing. There was a gas station not too far ahead but it was closed. Jasper narrowed his eyes and thought he saw something in the parking lot that would help them.

"Kid," he said, "where are the others?"

"They're a little ways back," the girl said. "I'm Kayla, by the way."

"Okay, Kayla. Do you see the gas station?" He pointed to it.

"Yeah," she said.

"Against the wall, unless I'm wrong, there are payphones."

"Payphones?"

"Before there were cell phones there were payphones. Dial 911 there."

"Really?" she sounded as though she didn't believe him.

"Do it!" Jasper said. He sounded angry and impatient, but it was the pain talking.

"Okay," she said.

"You shouldn't need any quarters," Jasper said. "But call the cops. They need to get you kids to your families."

She ran off and gathered the other children. Jasper continued hobbling to his car. The pain came in waves, and it nearly knocked him over. That was always how it happened. *Lucky punk. Damn lucky punk bastard.*

The car was unremarkable. A twenty-year-old Buick with scratches and dents. The stereo didn't work and the driver's-side window had long ago been smashed. But it ran. Jasper got behind the wheel, started the engine, collected himself and pushed through yet another wave of pain. Then he began driving. He passed the gas station and saw the kids in the parking lot. He poked his head out the window and when Kayla saw him, she gave him a thumbs-up. Jasper nodded and drove back to the motel where he was staying.

The kids were safe. He had done what he had set out to do. Now all that was left was to heal and wait for the latest scar to form.

———◦———

JASPER STUMBLED BACK INTO his motel room with one hand clutching his side and the other holding a dagger that was still red with blood. He dropped the weapon on the table and then sat on his bed. *Bastards,* he thought as he lifted his torn shirt from his body. The cut was deep, and a blackened puss was clotting around it. It had been the first wound he had received in years, and that made the pain even worse. He was better than this. Over one hundred forty years fighting this one-man-war had made him better than this.

Everyone makes mistakes.

He shook his head. *An amateur warlock in the middle of Sticksville, Michigan gets the better of you and you want to make excuses?*

You're right.

I know.

Fuck off.

Jasper's duffle bag was sitting on the bed next to his small pillow. He opened it and took some bandages and a bottle of brandy that he had been saving. He wrapped his cut and then opened the bottle.

You don't deserve this. You lost.

I won.

You're wounded. That means you lost.

I killed them all and I lived. Go away.

In the last two decades the voice in his mind had grown louder, always berating him and pointing out his shortcomings. Jasper hated it, but at that point in time it was his only companion.

It had been a bad night. He had been careless. Getting the drop on a small renegade cult broken off from the Order was easy, but he had underestimated their skills. The children that the group had captured where going to return to their parents as soon as the police showed up. That meant Jasper had little time.

Though I've done nothing wrong.

He had heard reports of kidnappings in the area and so he had come. He felt that his prey was near, and as he approached the town, and the feeling grew stronger, he knew he was right. He could sense the presence of these witches and warlocks, and he could track them half-way around the world if they were not skilled enough to hide themselves.

He shook his head again as he remembered the knife. He drank his brandy and dwelled on the fight and wondered where he would go tomorrow.

He should have left that night, but he was tired and wounded. He decided to stay one more night, hoping that he would be healed enough to travel.

He laid back on his bed and kicked the duffle bag to the floor. The remote control was on the night stand. He took it and switched on the television set.

The TV was set on channel 52, which was the *Investigation Explorer Channel.* Jasper didn't bother seeing what else was on. He hadn't even intended to pay attention to the TV. Background noise was all he needed as he drank.

The show was one called *American Legends.* There was a pretty blonde on the screen wearing a black suit and sunglasses.

"Welcome back to *American Legends,*" she said. **"I'm Brenda Ellis. Today we are in Ravenwood, Michigan, learning the truth behind the century-old tale of the Monster of Ravenwood."**

Jasper looked up from his drink at the mention of Ravenwood. His eyes narrowed as he heard reference to the Monster. He knew what she was talking about. She was talking about him.

"The story goes," she said, **"that in 1870, there was a beast created by a witch that destroyed the town and killed everyone there. He was said to be ten feet tall, with the body of a man, long claws on each hand and a spiked tail. Some say he still lives in the woods around the area, though no one has gotten a clear sighting of him in the last century."**

Claws? Tail? Ten feet tall?

"There are experts on this legend that live right here in Ravenwood. This town may look a lot different from the days of the Monster, but that is because he left nothing but destruction. It was a ghost town for almost thirty years after the Monster's rampage, and then it was rebuilt in 1899. Local legends say there were many strange things that happened here in Ravenwood for the next half a century until a priest came to exorcise the spirits.

"Today we will talk to one of those experts and learn just what the Monster of Ravenwood truly was, and if there are any explanations that are based in reality."

Jasper switched off the television. *The Monster of Ravenwood.* The thought was bitter in his mind. These bastards on TV were making money off of the misery that had been brought to that town in 1870.

He slammed his bottle on the nightstand, shattering it. He didn't care though. Alcohol no longer mattered. The memories of that night back in 1870 were returning to him, and he knew his dreams would be haunted.

Sure enough, not an hour later, after falling into a deep sleep, he dreamed. He found himself in the midst of Ravenwood as it was in 1870. The buildings were burning and the people were screaming. He could see no one, but he could hear them.

"You killed us," the voices echoed in that fire-lit night.

"No," Jasper said.

"Killed us! Why couldn't you stay away! We didn't deserve this!"

"No!" Jasper screamed. "It wasn't me! It was them!"

And then he woke in a cold sweat. The black puss had seeped through his bandage, but the pain had lessened.

Jasper sat up and thought of what he had to do. He knew what he had do, actually. The bastards were spreading lies about what had happened in Ravenwood all those years ago and there was one way to get the truth out there.

He had to write it.

He had thought of doing this for a long time. The world needed to know about the Order. The damned cult still existed in the shadows even though they had been around since before recorded history. Jasper wanted to expose them in their depowered state. They were depowered because of him, and if the world knew of their existence, they could be destroyed.

But no one ever believed him when he talked about the Order. They would rather come up with outlandish tales like the Monster of Ravenwood. There were other such stories from all over the world, and they all revolved around things that had been done by him against the Order. Jasper decided while sitting in that motel room that he had had enough of the lies and myths. He would tell the truth, and he would start at the beginning.

He left the next morning, taking the bloody dagger and the duffle bag full of blood-stained bandages but leaving the shattered brandy bottle behind.

He drove out of town. He wasn't going to go far this time. If he was going to write his story he had to go where it took place and that meant that almost a century and a half later, Jasper Gunne was returning to Ravenwood.

2017

I REMEMBER MY HANGING. It has been one hundred forty-six years since it happened, but I remember that day. I remember staring out into the crowd of angry faces and feeling the rope tighten around my neck. I remember the floor opening beneath my feet and dropping to what should have been my death. Of course, I knew it would not be my death. I had survived many things before that. Hell, I was already seventeen decades old when this happened. I knew that the hanging would do nothing, but at the time I was too weak to resist the rope. I dangled for a while before the crowd grew tired of waiting. It was then that Sheriff Warson put a bullet in my head. They thought I was dead then, but I wasn't. The bullet passed out of my skull while I was in my wooden coffin where I woke with a nasty headache. Bullets couldn't kill me. Rope couldn't kill me. Age couldn't kill me. I was an immortal man hanged by an ignorant people who couldn't understand that what I had done was necessary. The massacre that had led to this was not my fault. Yes, I started it by attacking the group of cannibal witches that had been living in Ravenwood and yes, that fight had escalated and a lot of people had died. But none that I killed were innocent. The innocent were all killed by **them**. In fact, if I hadn't been there, the few survivors that were left to hang me would have likely been dead as well. But *that story is forgotten today. The legend grew in the years since the massa-cre. I am known in the stories and legends as the Monster of Ravenwood. But the legends are mostly nothing more than vampire ghost stories. I'll tell you what really happened in Ravenwood in 1870. I will tell you of the massacre that ended with my hanging. I remember it all too well.*

⸻

JASPER GUNNE STOPPED TYPING when he heard a knock at his door. "Who?" he asked himself as he got up from his desk. Another knock. "I'm coming," he said. He sighed and ran a hand through his grey-streaked hair that hung like curtains around his face. Then he walked to the door. Once it was open he saw an old woman standing there with a pie in her hands.

"Hello," she said. "My name's Carol Krane. Welcome to the building!"

Jasper began to grunt but caught himself before he was com-pletely impolite. He smiled. "Thank you. Just moved in today."

"I know," Carol said. "My husband and I were watching. Not a lot to move in though. Not much to unpack."

Jasper raised an eyebrow. *She watched me move in?* "Would you like to come inside?" he asked.

"Would I ever! I'll even cut you a piece of my apple pie. I'm told it's the best in Ravenwood."

"Sounds great," Jasper said with a fake smile. All he wanted to do was get back to work on his story.

"Do you have dishes and silverware?" Carol asked when Jasper had closed the door. She stood in the small area meant to be a kitchen.

"I have some paper plates I bought," Jasper said. "There should be knives, forks, spoons in that box on the counter."

Carol opened the box, took out the cutlery, and sliced the pie. She handed Jasper a piece on a paper plate and gave him a fork. Then she watched expectantly while he ate it.

"Thank you," Jasper said, still smiling that fake smile and wish-ing the old woman would leave.

"I like to welcome new neighbors," Carol said as Jasper took a bite. "What do you think?"

"It's good. It really is." Despite his irritation at being interrupted from his work he found himself enjoying the dessert.

"Well, I'm so glad you like it! Tell me, then. What made you decide to come to town? You're not from here, I don't think."

"You know that? Do you really know everyone in Ravenwood?" Jasper asked.

"I know most of the people, and I have never seen you before."

"I was here a long time ago, and now I'm back for a little while." Jasper glanced at his desk as he said this. The computer screen was displaying his last page of manuscript.

"Are you a writer?" Carol asked.

"Kind of," Jasper said. "I came to town to write a story. I don't think it'll be very long, and I don't think anyone will read it, but I wanted to write it anyway."

Carol's eyes narrowed as she looked around the room.

"I live modestly," Jasper said. "And I'm only here until the story is done. Then I'll be on my way."

"To where? Where is home for you?"

"That's the question, isn't it?"

"I'm sorry," Carol said. "Being nosy. But welcome to the building. Enjoy your pie."

"Thanks, again," Jasper said.

He closed the door behind Carol Krane when she left and then latched and dead-bolted it. Then he filled a glass with water from the faucet, drank it in one swallow, reflected for a moment that he wished it was whiskey, and then returned to his desk and to his work.

1750

MOST OF MY LONG YEARS on this earth have been dark. The incident in Ravenwood which led to the legends of the fabled Monster was only one stop along my shadowy path. The year in which I write this story is 2016. I am three hundred sixteen years old. I was the first of my family to be born in the New World in 1700. Jasper is my name. Jasper Gunne. Son of Richard and Sarah Gunne. Not only was I the first of my family born in the New World, but I was also the only child who survived into adulthood. I had four brothers and two sisters who had passed away before they reached their teenage years. But not me. I lived and I thrived. I outlived both of my parents and had children of my own. As I neared the age of fifty, I became a grandfather.

My daughter was named Sarah after my mother. She married at the age of twenty and had a son. And, just as I named her for my mother, the boy was named for my father. Richard Gunne II was my one and only grandson, and he was the tool used to transform me into what I am today. I will tell you my story that occurs in Ravenwood in 1870, but first we must go back to when I was changed. It was the absolute darkest and blackest event of my life.

The year was 1750, and I was living in the colony of Massachusetts. My wife, Charlotte, had died of a fever that summer, and I was living with my daughter and her family. Sarah did not mind nor did her husband, David. Their son, little Richard, had recently turned one year old. The house was outside of the village, located on a small farm that David worked. In retrospect, we were the perfect targets. A constable was too far away to reach us in time, and we would all be long dead before anyone in the village would know something was wrong.

That was my old life. It had already been set to change by then, but I did not realize it until years later. Now I see the progression of events. Now I know how things ended up the way they ended up.

———

MY STORY STARTS WITH me sitting at the pub where I had come to buy whiskey for the young doctor who had taken such good care of my daughter in the last week. At first he had resisted the invitation for the drink, but he relented after I insisted. "You're a good man who needs to unwind," I told him. "One drink. On me. As a thank you."

The doctor's name was Riden. Thomas Riden. I will never forget that name. He was a tall man with a thick accent. His shiny black hair was combed perfectly and his face was shaved clean except for a thin mustache. He always wore his best clothes and this night was no exception. He was the only man wearing a suit in the bar.

The pub was small. There were two tables with chairs encompassing them, a bar with five barstools—Thomas and I occupied two—and a cabinet full of liquor. I could see mouse droppings next to the whiskey bottles on the counter and I wondered how many of the rodents were scuttling about in the shadows. The place was nearly empty. There was just Thomas, myself, the barkeep—Sally was her name—and two other patrons.

"This is the first time I've come for a drink since arriving," he told me.

"Really?" I asked. "Been busy with the ladies then?"

"No," he laughed. "Just work. Too much work, but when it's a matter of life and death..." he shrugged.

"You're the talk of the town," I said. "They say you're working miracles."

He laughed at that. "Miracles? No. I've studied all over the world before coming here. I thought there would be less doctors in the colonies than in Europe, and I was right. Europe has enough doctors."

"Then here's to you," I said. "Doctor Riden!" I raised my glass and we drank.

"Thank you," Thomas said. "This is nice."

"Another," I told the barkeep. She smiled and poured the glasses. I passed one to Thomas.

"So I'm the first one you drank with since being here?" I asked. "Seems hard to believe."

"I've wanted to come out," Thomas said. "I just hadn't found the time."

"Any places like this over in England or wherever you come from?"

"Yes, there are. Some are nicer. Some are... not. I like this one."

As he said this his stool began to creak and suddenly it broke beneath his weight. He tumbled to the floor and cursed as he landed on his wrist.

"Doctor!" I yelled, reaching down to help him to his feet.

"Damn, doc, are you all right?" one of the other men in the pub asked.

"I don't think so," Thomas said. "I think I broke my wrist."

"Well that's not so bad!" the patron said. "You can fix anyone so you can fix yourself too. By tomorrow you'll have yourself all healed up!" The drunk fool then laughed at what must have been his feeble attempt at a joke.

"Let's get out of here," I said to Thomas. Then I turned to the woman behind the counter: "Sally, I'll settle my tab tomorrow."

"Sure thing, Jasper," she said with a wink.

I grinned at her and grabbed my cane. Then I limped as I led Thomas Riden out of the pub.

"I didn't think I'd be knocking out the town's star doctor," I said as we walked.

"Don't worry about me," he said. "I know some remedies."

"You need any help?" I asked. "Say the word."

"I'm fine," he said. "Really. You don't have to do this. I don't need repayment or anything."

"Sarah is alive thanks to you," I said. "You came all the way to the farm in the middle of a blizzard, and you saved her life. I know you saved her life."

"Maybe the Lord chose to intervene through me," Thomas said with a modest smile.

"That's not what the church says," I said. It was true. The more fanatical Christians in the town had accused Thomas Riden of witchcraft and of consorting with the devil to find his miracle cures. Back then, I just thought he was a good doctor.

"The church is not fond of me," he admitted. I was surprised to see that he was still able to carry on conversation. I knew he had to be in considerable pain.

"They are just cowards," I said.

"Perhaps," Thomas said. We arrived at the inn. He had been renting a room there for the last three weeks that he had been in the village though I thought he would soon find better accommodations.

"Goodnight," he said. "I must tend to my wound."

"Call on me if you need help," I said. I remember feeling eager to be useful again. My leg injury made working almost impossible. I could walk but I needed a cane to brace myself. Sarah and David never said anything about supporting me as I got older and feebler, but they didn't have to. I berated myself for what I was. I loved my life at the time, but I also hated myself.

———◆———

I MET THOMAS RIDEN when I summoned him to save my daughter. Sarah had been sick for two weeks. It began as a cough. That was nothing out of the ordinary for the dead of winter, but then she had lost all of her strength and was confined to her bed. I couldn't believe it was happening to her. It was just like what had happened to my wife, Charlotte. I remember kneeling at her bedside and praying to God to spare her. I couldn't lose her too. And baby Richard needed his mother.

These days, the Lord and myself are not on speaking terms, but back then I was still devout. I fasted for days while I prayed, convinced that it would make my prayers louder so God would hear them. David, my son-in-law, tended to the cows on the farm, and I tended to my daughter. She was so weak during those two weeks.

"Father," she said one night. "I don't want to die."

It was the only thing that she said, she was so weak. She lay there, drifting in and out of sleep and unable to speak anymore.

I touched my finger to her lips and said: "Don't speak. You won't die. I won't let you die." I was lying and she knew it. I saw her sad smile and I knew that I would likely have to say goodbye to it before the week was out. I was going to lose my child.

"It might snow," David said the next morning. "Wind's picking up."

"It could," I said, standing over the cradle that held my small grandchild. His eyes were the same color of blue as his mother's. Looking into them made my own eyes sting with tears.

"I think I'll head into town," David said. "Take the wagon. Bring back some food. May not be able to get out of here for a few days."

I nodded and continued looking at Richard. Then I had a thought and decided to act on it. "Wait," I said. David stopped in the doorway. He was about to wrap himself in a thick coat and face the winter weather.

"What is it?" he asked.

"This is your house. Your wife. Your family. I'll go into town."

"That's okay, Jasper," he said.

"No," I said. "I insist. You spend some time with them. I need to get my mind of off all of this for a while anyway." I smiled and shrugged.

"Sure," he said.

I left the house that day and rode on a wagon pulled by two horses into town. My leg ached in the cold, but I brought my cane with me. I hated having to use the cane, but I'd been injured a year earlier and my leg had never properly healed.

I arrived at the general store just after ten that morning. I was there for more than just food and wine. I had one desperate thought and one longing hope. I needed it to work.

THERE WAS A NEW doctor in town according to rumors at the pub. As I was looking at Richard sleeping in his small bed, I remembered the rumors and decided my course of action. And so, on that day, as I traveled into town to get what we needed for the upcoming blizzard, I also went to locate this new doctor.

The store was the sort of thing you would expect of a small colonial village. This was two hundred sixty-six years ago and the idea of a supercenter was still centuries away. I bought wine, flour, bread and some other things that I don't remember.

Peter, the grocer, tallied the bill, and I gave him the money. He was a large man with a bald head and perpetually rosy cheeks. He wore a green apron over his clothes as he worked. The general store was his business, and though it was modest, he was proud of it. "Think a storm's coming, Mr. Gunne?" he asked.

"Could be," I said. "Listen, do you know anything about a new doctor in town?"

"New doctor? You mean Tom Riden?"

"Is that his name?" I asked. "I remember hearing about him a few weeks ago."

"Started about last Sunday," Peter said. "Wasn't even open for business yet when he was called down to the Oakman Farm. I guess Mr. Oakman went to sleep and wouldn't wake up. Dr. Riden fixed him up though. Don't know what caused it, but I bet old Mr. Oakman don't want to go to sleep no more."

"I suppose not," I said. "Do you know where I can find Dr. Riden?"

"You leave here," Pete said, leaning close to me and pointing with his finger. "You walk down the road a little ways. Then, you turn at the pub. Now, don't get to drinking there. I know how you get, Mr. Gunne."

"The doctor," I snapped.

"Past the pub. Down to the end of that road. There's a small cabin. You probably know the one. Dr. Riden bought it. That's where he set up shop."

"I know the place," I said. I left a few extra coins on the counter for his help. Then I waited as his sons loaded my wagon. Then, when everything was loaded, I drove my horses forward. Down the road. Past the pub. And to the old cabin that had been empty since the last owners passed away. I rode to meet Thomas Riden. It was a meeting that changed my life.

I limped to the door and knocked. Thomas Riden answered it, greeting me with a wide smile. He held the door open and beckoned me inside. "Welcome," he said. "Come in out of this cold. It can't be good for that leg."

He shivered as the wind picked up again. I limped inside as fast as I could, and Thomas closed the door behind me. There was a fire going that warmed that small cabin well.

The office consisted of a desk and chair, a bed for a patient, a table with some chairs and the fireplace. A shelf next to the desk was full of books. Each had the look of being well-read. I understood right then that Thomas Riden was probably smarter than me and probably smarter than anyone in town.

"What's the problem?" he asked.

The wind blew around the cabin, making a whistling sound. The cracks and holes in the wall let the cold air in, and it made my wounded leg ache. I massaged it absentmindedly.

"Is it your leg?" Thomas asked.

"No," I said. "Nothing to be done about that. It's my daughter. She's very sick. I don't think she'll last much longer. I'm sorry, doctor. I need your help, and I need it as soon as possible."

"I see," Thomas said. He opened the door and looked outside. "The snow is really blowing now."

"She'll die," I said.

Coming to this doctor was a thin and stupid hope. I doubted anything that this young man could do would bring Sarah back. She was too far gone.

"Let's go then," he said.

"Truly?"

"Truly." He wrapped himself in his own coat, put out his fire, then met me on the wagon.

"What's your name?" he asked.

"Jasper Gunne," I said.

The blizzard was getting heavier by the time we reached Sarah and David's farm, and shortly after we arrived, we were snowed in.

———◈———

THE HORSES WERE COLD and tired. David tended to them as I led Dr. Riden to Sarah's room. She was sleeping, but she was still alive.

"Jasper, what's happening?" David asked when he had joined us in the house.

"This is the new doctor in town," I said. "I asked him to come and take a look at Sarah. Maybe he can help."

"Dr. Riden is my name," Thomas said with that same smile he had used when he first greeted me. "I'll do everything I can for her."

"Thank you," David said.

Dr. Riden went to work, closing the door to the room and leaving me with my son-in-law. David took a seat in the rocking chair, but I remained standing, leaning on my cane for support.

"You think he can do anything?" David asked.

"I don't know," I said. "I just hope."

David shook his head. "We can't afford a doctor right now."

"I have some money left. I'll pay everything I have if it gets her well again."

"And if it doesn't, we are broke and we have lost her. I don't see a way out of this."

"Do not give up hope," I said.

"It's too late."

He got up and began pacing around the room. I knew this side to my son-in-law. He was giving himself over to his grief, and there was nothing to say to encourage him. I just had to let the despair run its course. I had learned this in the last few days, and I accepted it as the way he dealt with the stress of losing the woman he loved. I remember how I was when Charlotte had died. After her funeral, I locked myself in my bedroom for days and refused to eat or drink. Grief affects us all so differently.

I limped to the end of the living room where Richard was crawling on the floor. I sat in a chair next to him and waved him to me. Then I picked him up and sat him on my lap.

"It'll be okay," I said to him. Tears were stinging my eyes. "It'll be okay." He touched my face and giggled. I laughed too. "No matter what, it'll be okay."

The night passed as the snow piled higher and higher. I heard Sarah scream three times during the night at different hours. Each time I wanted to barge into the room, but each time Dr. Riden heard me coming and yelled that everything was okay. That hateful night passed so slowly and yet so fast. I dreaded every tick of the clock because I was sure it would bring about the time of Sarah's death. Yet, I wanted it to be over so I could see whether or not Dr. Riden had been able to save her.

Eventually I dozed in a rocking chair. David was getting sleep for he would need to be awake and tending to the livestock in the morning. I was meant to stay awake and wait, but I was a tired old man with nothing to occupy my mind except dread. I don't know the hour that I fell into sleep. The next thing I remember was a small hand nudging me awake.

———◦———

SARAH STOOD BEFORE ME completely recovered. At first when I woke I thought I was dreaming. It took a moment for me to realize that what I was seeing was indeed real.

"Sarah?" I asked.

She nodded.

"Sarah?" I asked again.

"Yes, Father. It's me!"

I sprung to my feet and embraced her, ignoring the pain in my thigh. I hugged her tightly then let go and kissed both of her cheeks. "I can't believe it."

"Believe it," Thomas Riden said. I turned to see him standing in the doorway to the room where Sarah had been lying. He had my grandson in his arms. "It's just science. Or maybe it was the Lord. Or maybe both." Then he looked at the child in his arms. "What do you think?" he asked the boy. "You happy that your mother is all better?"

The baby coughed and looked away.

Sarah and I walked across the room. She took her son in her own arms, and I shook Dr. Riden's hand. "Thank you," I said. "Thank you."

"It was a pleasure to help you and your family, Jasper," he said.

"What do I owe you?" I asked.

"Not one cent. I won't take your money," Thomas said.

"No?" I asked.

"No," he said. "I just want a reputation for the moment. Income will flow later, I am sure."

"I will spread the word," I said. Then we turned back to Sarah. "Look at her," I said. "Look at all of her energy."

"She is back to her normal self," the young doctor said. "She had a disease that is passed from parents to their children. It would not surprise me if someone else in your family had the same sickness."

"My wife, Charlotte," I said. "She died of it."

"I've seen cases like that before, and I had the right medicines to cure it." He patted his long coat that he had wrapped himself in when we left his office.

I embraced the doctor again, fully thankful for what he had done for my family. I was blissfully unaware that I was hugging my future enemy.

———————

THOMAS RIDEN STAYED THE day with us. He did not do this because he was taking advantage of our hospitality, but because the weather was too severe for him to return to his office.

"Where do you live, doc?" I asked at dinner that night. David had killed a cow and broke out the wine in celebration of his wife's regained health. After Dr. Riden said that she should be okay to eat and drink, a feast was busily prepared. I will say this for my late son-in-law, he could cook. We ate steak and fresh bread and washed it down with the expensive wine that was only reserved for the most special of occasions. The last time it had been opened was a year earlier when baby Richard was born.

"I live at the inn for now," Riden said. "I have to get a house soon. I think I'll have one built. Have to wait for the spring though."

I nodded. "Came at a bad time then."

"Just in time for you though," Thomas said, taking a sip of wine.

"Indeed," I said. "Thank you. I just wish we could pay you."

"Don't worry," he said with a smile. "We'll work something out."

I nodded enthusiastically. I wanted to pay this man for what he had done. It was such an unbelievable blessing that it didn't feel right getting it for free. Miracles are priceless, and Thomas Riden knew that. He would be expecting payment soon enough, though he acted as though everything he did was out of generosity.

But I never should have gone to Thomas Riden. I should never had brought him to the farm. Sarah, my one remaining child, would have died that day, but I believe that would have been better.

———◦———

IT WAS A WEEK LATER when Thomas and I had our drink. I left him at his door to tend to his broken wrist. I then walked back down the road where I had come, limping with my cane. Dr. Riden had offered to take a look at my leg and perhaps find a remedy for it. I told him I would take him up on that sometime.

As I limped away I wished that he already would have looked at it. *But what could he do? No one can fix this.* But that wasn't exactly true. Sarah had been at death's door and Dr. Riden had pulled her back. Couldn't he do that with my leg?

The street was mostly empty that night as I made my way back to the pub where I had tied my horse. The blizzard of a week ago was mostly melted by the sudden warm-up that was sure to cool down for one last blast of wintery weather before spring arrived.

Reverend Jim Adamson was waiting for me at the pub. He wasn't inside of it. No. He was much too religious for that. He was the leader of the one church in the village and therefore, probably the man with the most influence.

"Good evening," he said. His black coat ended at his knees, and his brown boots were streaked with mud from the street. He had a hat on his head that he removed when he began talking to me. His black eyes were almost beady, and they stared into mine with a strange and almost fanatical intensity.

"Reverend," I said.

"How's the family?" he asked.

"Just fine, thank you." I climbed onto my horse.

"I hear that you had the new doctor up there," he said.

I groaned. "Yes," I said. "We did. He saved Sarah's life." Reverend Adamson had known all about Sarah and her illness. She had been anointed and prayed over by the church when it first appeared that she couldn't get rid of whatever she had. The prayers had continued until the Sunday she had arrived in church. There were shouts of praise to the Lord's name that day, and we didn't tell any of the church members that we had seen the new doctor in town. Our church was old-fashioned in the sense that it viewed medicine as a sin. I had wanted to avoid this conversation.

"Some might say it would have been wiser to trust in the Lord," Adamson said.

"Perhaps the Lord sent Dr. Riden to us to save Sarah," I said.

Adamson smiled. "Beware your new friend," he said. "I've asked around. He's performed a few too many miracles on people in this town. I think there's something else to him." He shrugged. "But maybe you're right. Maybe the Lord sent him."

———◉———

REVEREND ADAMSON TURNED OUT to be right. At first I tried to resist the curiosity, but I was an old man who could do little more than limp around town. *Too many miracles,* Adamson had said.

There were half a dozen people in the village that all had similar stories about Dr. Riden. All of them centered on him performing what had been a miracle. There was a child with smallpox that was cured in two days. There was a man who was paralyzed from the waist down that was now able to walk with crutches. A deaf woman was able to hear. A dog that had been run over by a cart was alive and well. All of these stories were surrounding the new doctor and they were all too good to be true. There were others, of course, but I've forgotten them. One thing I knew for sure back then: I was right. He was sent by God.

Oh, how foolish I was.

———◉———

THOMAS RIDEN HAD FRIENDS, I discovered. They were Europeans like himself and they arrived toward the end of February. They didn't go many places in the town though. They stayed in his room at the inn, and few ever saw them out and about.

Until his friends had joined him, Thomas Riden and I had become friends. We had dinner together, usually at the farm where David and Sarah both prepared excellent meals. Thomas seemed to have grown to like them both and offered to cook for them one night.

"You can cook too?" David asked.

"I can," Thomas said, taking a drink of his ale. We were drinking ale that night instead of wine, and that was what I preferred.

"And here I thought I had one up on you," David said.

"I do not doubt that you have one up on most men in this village with your abilities in the kitchen," Thomas said. "But I have cooked my own meals for most of my life. I am particular on what I eat."

"How old are you, exactly?" David asked. "Sarah and I can't tell."

"Forty-nine," Thomas said, smiling at my surprise.

"You don't look like you've hit thirty yet," I said.

"Medicine and an understanding of the human body can help with aging."

"You're not forty-nine," Sarah said.

"I am," Thomas said.

I doubt anyone at the table truly believed him. We assumed he was just trying to pull our leg though I remember wondering why someone would lie about such a thing. Later, much later, I remembered the conversation and realized that he had been telling the truth.

IT WAS A WEEK LATER when Thomas provided a meal for my family. He brought it to the farm for he was still living at the inn. "It's a nice place to sleep, but there is really no room for dining," he had said.

He did not tell us what the meat was that he had brought. "It's a special recipe that I have developed for years," he said. "I don't give away any secrets."

We ate it and found it was delicious. The taste of it still haunts my memories. A few more times during the dinner we tried to find out what type of animal we were eating, but Thomas Riden would only smile and raise his wine glass. It tasted similar to pork, but there was a slight difference.

That bastard must have been so amused.

When we finished dining that night, Thomas Riden took his leave of us, declaring that he would meet us again in seven days for our weekly dinner.

That next dinner never happened.

His friends arrived that Saturday. They stayed with him at the inn, and like I said, they were rarely seen in public. I saw the doctor in town that week a few times and waved a greeting but making sure that I was leaning against something as I did. I didn't want him to see me. There was a reason for this. The morning after that last dinner with him, I woke to find that my leg was healed.

<hr/>

I WAS AFRAID THAT something was actually wrong with me. I had not been treated by Dr. Riden or by anybody and suddenly I was walking without my cane. It wasn't right, but I was afraid that if the doctor found out what was wrong with me, my leg would go back to the way it was.

That couldn't happen.

Therefore, when I saw him, I made sure that I was not standing. If I had to, I would lean. I wanted to postpone him finding out about my lack of a limp for as long as I could.

<hr/>

WE WERE IGNORED BY Thomas Riden. At first we didn't realize this but eventually, we came to understand that since he had his companions from Europe living with him, he no longer needed us to fill the friendship void.

He missed our regular dinner night the week after we ate his mystery dish. There was no letter or anything to let us know that he was not coming, and so there was extra food left over.

"I guess he's busy," Sarah said. "Probably an emergency. Being a doctor and all."

"Lots of people calling on him," I agreed.

"Next week then," David said.

And then when next week arrived, Dr. Riden didn't show again.

"I've seen him in town," I said. "He's always in a hurry. And those strange people he is with don't seem to like to come out of the inn."

The next day I began to investigate a bit more and found that he had not been making any house calls in the last two weeks.

Ever since his friends arrived.

Reverend Adamson pulled me aside one Sunday morning as the church was being dismissed. He asked about Thomas Riden.

"You were right," I said. "There has been a lot of miracles in the village since he arrived."

"And now he seems to have abandoned doctoring," Adamson said. He was a tall thin man with a receding head of grey hair.

"Maybe he's taking a break. Maybe he's waiting for medicine to arrive."

"I don't like those people he is with either," Adamson said.

"I haven't met them," I said. "But if they're good enough for Tom then they're good enough for me."

Adamson regarded me for a moment. "Truly? After what you have learned yourself, you still believe that Riden is someone you can trust?"

"Our Lord and Savior healed the sick," I said.

"But Thomas Riden is not our Lord and Savior," Adamson said.

"I believe he has the power of the Lord with him and that's how the miracles are happening," I said.

"Then why has he not come to church?" Adamson asked.

"Maybe because he feels like the people in this church won't accept him," I said before walking away from the reverend. I had begun to dislike that man more and more in the last year, and at that moment, I considered not coming back to church. That would've been a first for me in my life. I had always been a good Christian man. You had to be back then. But on that Sunday, I was tired of Reverend Adamson.

Later I would realize to my horror that James Adamson had been right all along. If I would have listened to him, much could've been avoided. At least, that's what I tell myself. I don't know what could've been avoided. Maybe it was all meant to happen. All I know is that Thomas Riden turned out not to be a friend and because of him, I am here today, writing this tale that will likely never be read. Thomas Riden was not a man of God.

He served a devil.

———◦◉◦———

THOMAS CAME TO OUR home one last time. It was the beginning of March. A snow had just fallen on the land for what would likely be the last time for the year. David was tending to the cattle. Sarah was reading a story to Richard. I was napping.

My friend's arrival woke me, and I walked to the door to greet him. As soon as I opened the door I realized that I had forgotten to bring my cane. A cold dread crept over me. He would see I wasn't limping, and he would want to know why. Then he would find something wrong with me, fix it, and then I would be back to needing the cane.

Stupid old fool. I look back on who I was then with such loathing. I was a pathetic waste of skin who should have died with his family. In a way, I guess I did, but in another, I am cursed to live with the memories. I had no idea what evil was back then. I was worried about my damn leg. My leg!

Thomas Riden was at the door. He was with two other men who had their heads bowed.

"Thomas!" I said. "Glad you could stop by. We've been missing you these last couple weeks!" We had too. Weekly meals and regular visits with one another in town had caused Thomas to become friends with my whole family. "I am sure that being a doctor, you get called away far too often."

"Might we talk, Jasper?" Thomas said. There was pain in his voice. The men with him did not look up.

"Something interesting on the floor, lads?" I asked with a laugh. Neither responded.

"Please," Thomas said. "We need to talk."

"Okay," I nodded. "Let's go in the study. Sarah's with Richard now."

"I would rather talk to you alone," Thomas said.

"Alone?"

"It's quite important."

I nodded again. "Are they coming with us?" I asked, indicating the men he was with.

"They need to come along too," Thomas said.

"Fine," I said. "Let's walk into the yard. Edge of the field."

I led the way, walking without my limp since I decided then not to worry about it unless Thomas said something. The two men with Thomas still did not speak, and my friend would only grunt as I tried to talk about the weather. Something was on his mind, and it was serious.

"I have something to tell you," Thomas said.

"Okay," I said. "What is it?"

"You must keep an open mind, Jasper," he said.

"An open mind?"

"Indeed. There are things that you need to know about me. I am telling you this for the sake of our friendship."

I saw my friend's companions reach into their coats. I realized, to my horror, that they had guns with them.

"You know about me," Thomas said.

"For about six weeks now," I said. "We've become friends."

"That's not what I mean," Thomas said. "You know what I am."

"A doctor," I said.

"Oh, don't be a fool!" he snapped.

I was startled, and so I took a step back. "What's wrong with you?"

I don't believe that Thomas was angry when he snapped at me. He was stressed and he looked exhausted.

"How is your leg?" he asked. He looked to the men he had come with and then turned back to me, smiling as he did so.

"It's great," I said, feeling dread. This is what he had come to talk to me about. There was something wrong with me, and he was going to fix it and make me limp again. I knew that was why he was here. It could be nothing else.

Oh, how I wish that I had been right.

"When did it start to feel better?" Thomas asked.

"Some time after our last meal together, I think," I said. I didn't want him to continue this talk.

"The next day, if I am not mistaken," he said.

I didn't reply. He was right. It had been the next day.

"There was something different about the food that night," Thomas said.

"What was it?"

"It was..." he looked around. "I can't tell you now. Come to my office tonight. We'll talk."

The two men lifted their heads and looked at one another. Thomas said to them: "Trust me. This is my friend."

"What is going on with you?" I asked.

"Tonight. Please, Jasper. I need to discuss things with you. I'm not discussing them here."

Thomas walked back to his horse and carriage. "What time?" I called after him.

He turned back to me. "Sundown."

"I'll be there," I said. I no longer worried about my leg. I worried for my friend. I feared he was in some kind of trouble.

Oh, how I wish I was right.

———— ◦◦ ————

AT SUNDOWN I FOUND myself standing outside the door of Thomas Riden's office. I raised my hand to knock on the door, but then it opened before I could touch it. Thomas stood in its frame.

"Jasper," he said. "Please come in."

In the six weeks that had passed since I first met Thomas, he had made improvements to his office. There were two rocking chairs next to the fireplace and a bookshelf as big as the wall and full of books. A large clock was against the opposite wall and a desk and chair was in front of it. In the middle of this cabin that served as an office was a table where patients would sit or lie down while the doctor examined them. Thomas led me to one of the rocking chairs. I took one and he took the other.

"Brandy?" he asked.

"Please," I said.

He got up and walked to his desk where he found two glasses and a half-full bottle of the liquor. He poured two full glasses and returned to the fire. He handed me my glass.

"Thank you for coming," he said, sitting back down and sighing.

"What is it about?" I asked. "And who were those two men? They were strange."

"Yes," Thomas said with a laugh. "They are indeed. They are here to watch me, Jasper."

"Watch you?"

"My father sent them," Thomas said.

I said nothing and just sat there sipping on my drink.

"My father has plans for me," Thomas explained. "And they are watching my moves."

"I don't understand," I said.

"You will," Thomas said. "At least I hope you will."

"Just tell me," I said. "I'm sure I can handle it."

"I know you can," Thomas said. "I'm just not sure that you will."

"What?"

Thomas took a deep breath and drank the rest of his brandy in one swallow. "You've heard what the church is saying, right?"

I nodded. "You're practicing witchcraft."

"Yes," Thomas said. "Though I've never heard them say it to my face. I don't go to church. That might be why Father Adamson doesn't trust me."

"I don't think he thinks much of you," I said. "He's said things to me before, but I defended you."

"Did you now?" Thomas asked. He got up to refill his glass. "Do you want me to top off your drink?"

"No, thank you."

"You're a good friend, Jasper." Thomas returned to his chair again. "A good friend. I've only known you a little over a month, and I feel as though you and I could be brothers."

"I feel the same, actually," I said.

"That's why I am going to let you in on a secret."

I leaned forward, listening for what he had to say. It was important to him. I could tell by the way he drank his next glass of brandy and the way he was sweating and fidgeting.

"Just say it," I said.

"The church is right!" He spat out the sentence and then downed the last of his second glass of liquor.

"What did you say?" I asked.

"The church," he said. "They're right. Adamson is right."

"Are you saying that you're a witch?"

He leaned close to me and whispered as if he could be overheard. "That's exactly what I'm saying. And I'm a man. That makes me a warlock."

At that moment I thought that perhaps my friend had slipped into a drunken madness. He was on his feet and headed to pour another drink as I sat contemplating what he had just said.

"A warlock? An actual warlock?"

"I am one of many," he said. "We are a religion that has been around since before history was recorded."

"Be serious, Thomas," I said. "What is this really about?"

He looked me in the eye. "Jasper," he said, "I am being serious."

"All of your cures you've done?" I asked.

"Magic. Or... you would call it magic. We don't have a word for it. It just is."

I laughed then. "You had me going. You almost had me for a moment there. You are really convincing."

"Remember when I broke my wrist?" Thomas asked.

I nodded.

He held out his arm and twisted his hand back and forth. "I shouldn't be able to do that," he said. "But I can. I healed myself."

"Thomas..." I still did not believe him.

"I took the sickness from your daughter's body and destroyed it. I healed your injured leg without even examining you. I have cured cripples in this village and I've restored the hearing of a man who had gone deaf. I have done other things too. I'm sure you know about them, because you've been asking about them."

And there it was. The accusation was out in the open. I had been asking about Thomas Riden's miracle cures but not because I had suspected him of witchcraft. I had wanted to prove Father Adamson wrong.

"You know all that you know," Thomas said, "but you won't believe in a supernatural explanation?"

On a deep level, I began to believe him. This frightened me and made me wish I had not come to my friend's office that night. "Maybe I should leave," I said.

"I want you to understand what I'm saying," Thomas said. He was on his feet before I was on mine, and he placed his hands on my shoulder. "I am offering you something here."

I found the nerve to ask: "What are you offering?"

"A chance to be a part of it," he said. "That's why I brought you here tonight. My father would disapprove, but I want you to join my religion."

"You want me to join it?" I asked, not believing what I had just heard.

"Yes." His eyes seemed to brighten as he said this. I saw the tension of the conversation easing off of him.

"Thomas," I said, "you need some rest. And perhaps you need to stay away from these friends of yours that have come to town."

"Damn it, Jasper!" Thomas spat as he threw his glass into the fire.

"What is wrong with you?" I asked, alarmed at his sudden temper.

"I have to be honest and I am trying," he said through gritted teeth. "This is the only way. My test. If I fail…"

"Thomas!" I was growing impatient with his ravings.

He sat back in the chair and put his hands over his face. I think he may have even sobbed for a moment. I once more wished that I had not come to his office that night.

"I am tired of this," he said. "Tired of everything. I try and do good. I try to help people and do the right thing. But there's a price. No miracle is free. There is always a price that has to be paid. Is it fair? No. But then, I saved so many. I don't know, sometimes. Jasper, honest to God, I don't know."

"Thomas," I said, "are you truly believing what you're saying?"

He looked at me through bloodshot eyes. He had indeed been weeping. "I know how it sounds, but it's all true.,"

No miracle is free. I remembered those words over all the years of my long life. I had witnessed a miracle when my daughter had been healed in a night. But if I had known what the miracle would cost, I would have thrown Thomas Riden from the house and never subjected my family to the horror that awaited them.

The door opened.

I turned from the fire and saw people entering the office. Three men and three women. I recognized two of them as Thomas Riden's companions that had been at the farm.

"Hello," I said with a nod. I was much friendlier back then.

"Thomas," one of the men said, "have you reached a decision?"

"Leave us," Thomas said. "I am talking with my friend." He got up from the chair and crossed the room to where the group was standing.

"I want to know," the man said.

"I don't care what you want to know," Thomas said. He no longer seemed troubled when speaking with these people. He seemed in command. "I am the son of Christophe Riden, and I will be treated with respect by every person here. I demand it! Now, when I say to leave, Frederick, I mean that I want you to leave."

The one called Frederick was evidently not one to back down from Thomas Riden. "You do remember," he said, "that you are untested while I have been travelling the world for a decade? I am in charge of you."

"I remember that, though I am untested, I am still a Riden and therefore more powerful than any of you." Thomas said this, and I thought I saw Frederick's face twitch.

Frederick was a small man with thinning black hair. His nose had been broken before, and it was now misshapen. He had a scar across his lips that he tried to conceal by growing out his beard. Like the other five, he was clad in an oversized black coat. Beneath the coat was more black clothing. There was a sneer on his face that day. I remember thinking, years later, that Frederick had undoubtedly felt that Thomas was not worthy of the power he possessed. Indeed, I believe Frederick was angry about being required to watch over Thomas, and my friend was not making it easier by challenging him in front of his subordinates.

"Leave me," Thomas said. "I will not ask again. Send word to my father if you want. I believe that is your way, Frederick. Now, leave me."

"All that power," Frederick said, "and you waste it on pretending you are a doctor."

"I am a doctor!" Thomas yelled.

"You are a child who is playing with his father's gun," Frederick said. I saw that Thomas winced as though he had been struck.

"I am a Riden and one day I will make you wish you had never spoken to me in such a way."

"Will you?" Frederick asked. "I doubt it. I see you are already trying to get out of giving to the goddess what you owe."

"Leave!"

Frederick smiled. "As you command, my master. But remember, I am taking him no matter what."

And then they were gone. The door slammed behind them, and Thomas returned to the chair.

"Interesting companions you have," I said.

Thomas stared at the fire for a moment and then raised his left hand. The flames in the fireplace began to dance in unnatural ways as he moved his fingers. I noticed it and then noticed the glowing red in Thomas' eyes.

"My god," I said, backing away from him. "My god!"

"Jasper," he said.

"No," I said.

"Jasper!" Thomas' eyes had returned to their normal blue color, and he was now walking toward me. "Don't be afraid."

"I just saw," I said, pointing at the fire. "It's not possible."

"All things are possible," he said. "They are possible when you serve the one true goddess."

I could not understand what I had seen. I could not understand what I had been told. My brain could not take it. It just couldn't.

"This is impossible," I said again.

"Jasper," Thomas said, "please understand what I am saying. You of all people should be able to understand. Hell, this power saved your Sarah. It healed my wrist. It cured your leg. You are witness to it. Don't deny it. Join it."

I shook my head. "Witchcraft is a sin."

"So by your understanding of sin, I should have left Sarah to die?"

"No," I said. "No." I was defeated. I was not nearly intelligent enough to have a debate with him on this subject. Thomas had told me that he chose me because I was smart enough to handle it. That was not the truth. He thought I was dumb enough to brain-wash.

"Let's sit and talk for a bit and you'll understand it all the better."

"I don't know," I said. I was no longer feeling sorry for my friend's supposed insanity. I was feeling terrified over what he could do and what he wanted me to do.

"Please, my friend," he said, "let's talk."

And so it was that I had a talk with Thomas Riden that would turn out to be the first exposure I was to ever have to the group of witches that called itself the Order.

———◦———

I WAS NO LONGER friends with Thomas Riden after that day. It was morning before we had finished the conversation, but by that time I was furious and disgusted by the man I had thought was my friend.

"Jasper, you don't know what you're doing," he said. "Don't turn your back on this. It's already too late."

"No," I said, glaring at him. "Stay away from me and from my family. I will have the church here by the end of the day, and they will burn you out of this town."

I left then, aiming to rally an angry mob and return to Thomas Riden's office. The things he had told me were appalling, and there was no way I could be a friend to someone who had done something as despicable as what he had done. He had to face justice.

And what was it that Thomas Riden had done? He had marked my family as a target for his vile band of witches.

To understand the nature of the Order is to understand evil itself. They have power, and that power must come from somewhere. *No miracle is free.* Thomas Riden knew this when he first came to town, and he knew this when he was trying to bring me into the Order.

"A whole new generation of the Order living in the New World," he had said.

The Order offered their goddess a living sacrifice. That was where their power came from. Honestly, I believe that their goddess, Valayra, exists. I've seen and experienced her power for myself.

"There is power in the blood of the innocent," Thomas had told me. "There is power in all blood, really, but the most is found in young children. But they don't suffer. They are folded into the arms of our Lady Valayra."

"Power in their blood?" I couldn't believe the things he had just told me.

"Yes. And I needed to make my own offering, Jasper. That's why I wanted you on my side. I wanted you with us. Please. Allow me to introduce you to the Order. We are older than your religion, and our ways are pure and true."

I need to make my own offering. He had said that and it filled my heart with dread. I looked across the room at him. The dying fire's orange glow was the only light in the cabin, and the shadows seemed to have swallowed us during our conversation.

"What do you mean that you need to make an offering?" I asked.

"Please, Jasper. For your sake and the sake of your family, heed me."

"What do you plan to do, doctor?"

He closed his eyes and did not reply.

"What did I eat the night before my leg healed?" I asked.

He blinked at me, so sudden was the change of subject. He then realized where I was going with the conversation. "Jasper..."

"You monster, what did you feed me?"

"I think you know," Thomas said in a low voice.

"Jesus," I said. I was not swearing. I was praying, though I do not know what I was praying for.

"Jasper," Thomas said. "It's proof of what I've said. We offer the sacrifice and then eat it. The meat was blessed by me, and that carried healing powers to your body. You recovered from your limp!"

"Stay away from my family," I said.

"Jasper, you don't know what you're doing. Don't turn your back on this. It's already too late."

"No. Stay away from me and my family. I will have the church here by the end of the day, and they will burn you out of this town." And that was the end of the conversation. I never talked to Thomas Riden again. Though his actions... I felt his actions throughout the long and endless years of my immortality. The man destroyed me.

And birthed a monster.

———◦———

I MOUNTED MY HORSE and headed for the church. I cursed myself for not believing Reverend Adamson, and I felt horrified and sick that I had unknowingly gobbled down a cooked infant. I had even asked for seconds! This could not stand. These monsters had to be dealt with before they could do any more harm.

I believed Thomas Riden that day. I had to believe him. The proof was in my leg. It was healed. I would have never asked for it in such a way though. And then the bastard had wanted me to join his Order?

I need to make my own offering. That line alone was enough to inspire me to do whatever needed to be done. If Thomas Riden needed an offering, there was an infant in town that he just might set eyes upon, and I would die before I let my grandson become a meal for those maniacs.

I galloped through the town, yelling for people to get out of my way. I raced up the hill that led to the church. It was a Thursday, if I remember right, and most people should have been about their various tasks and jobs, but as I got closer to the church, I saw more and more people wandering the roadway. I was confused at first, but only at first. I soon realized why everyone was lurking on the road. There was smoke up ahead.

I made it to the church and saw a large group gathered around the charred remains of the place where we worshipped. I dismounted and pushed my way through the crowd. Sheriff Henry Collins and two of his deputies were at the edge of the burned debris, and they were standing over the corpse of the reverend.

"No," I said.

Sally, the barkeep, was next to me though I hadn't noticed her. She put her hand on my shoulder. "Horrible," she said.

I turned and looked at her and said: "You have no idea."

Could it have been an accident? A coincidence? I wanted to believe that. I wanted to believe that the Order had no power, but my healed leg was already proof of their abilities. I wanted to believe that the church had not fallen to this evil cult, but the blackened-by-fire inverted cross in the grass told me that this had been the work of Thomas Riden's Order.

"Sheriff," I said, making the three men look at me. I stepped out of the crowd and walked over to them. "I know who it is that did this," I said.

"Do you now?" the sheriff asked me. "Who then, Mr. Gunne?"

Henry Collins was an old acquaintance of mine. We had never been friends, but that was not because of dislike. We just never ran in the same circles or had the same interests. I will say this of him. He was a good man. Honest and brave and smart.

"Thomas Riden and his people," I said. "I have much to tell you. You'll need to move fast if you're going to catch them though."

"Calm down, sir," he said. I realized then that I had been talking frantically.

"Sorry, sheriff, but might we talk? I can tell you what I know and why I think that this is the work of the doctor."

Collins looked at his two men and then shrugged. "Very well," he said. "Let's talk." Then to his men: "Finish up here, boys. I'm heading back to the office."

I mounted my horse and Collins mounted his. Then we rode back to town as I talked. Collins listened as I spoke of things that I knew made me sound insane. He nodded along as if he were understanding what I was saying and agreeing with me. I told him about the cannibalism and the witchcraft. Collins humored me the whole time.

"Jasper," he said, after I was finished, "you need some rest."

"What?" I asked in disbelief. "No! I don't need rest. You need to get Thomas Riden and his band of lunatics!"

"I'll check on this. I will. But please, go home and get some rest."

"You don't believe me?" I asked.

"No," Collins said. "But it's my one lead. I doubt they have these stupid powers like you say, but they might think they do. I'm going to look into it."

———————

THERE WAS HOPE THEN. Collins would look into it and he would find that I was right. That day, I confess, I was terrified. The church being burned was an audacious act that told me that this group did not care about repercussions.

I need to make my own offering.

No miracle is free.

I hurried home.

I berated myself during the time it took to ride home. Why had I not gone straight back to the farm after I finished my conversation with Thomas? I could have gotten them out. I could've made sure that they were safe.

A dark feeling crept into my stomach. I think I knew what had happened before I had even arrived. *It's too late, Jasper,* Thomas had said.

———◆———

I WAS RIGHT. I wish that I could write that I had been blessedly wrong and that my family was safe from harm and that everything turned out okay in the end. I cannot write that. The truth was that I arrived at the home I shared with my daughter and her family, and I found the door open.

I dismounted and ran inside on the leg that was now able to take my weight thanks to the dark witchery of Thomas Riden.

"Sarah!" I called. "David!" I made it to the living room and saw David lying dead on the floor. There was a hole in his head, and a musket in his hands. "No," I said.

I saw Sarah lying facedown on the couch. I approached her and noticed the pool of blood that had formed under the couch. I lifted her head and saw that her throat had been cut.

"My god," I said as I looked over my daughter's lifeless body. "No," I said. "No." I shook my head. "No!"

Through the pain of the loss that I now felt, I realized that the baby was nowhere to be seen.

"Richard!" I called, knowing that he would not answer me. "Richard!"

I sat on the floor, full of remorse for not riding home in time and angry at myself for allowing that evil bastard Thomas Riden into our lives.

I stopped feeling sorry for myself as I thought of my young grandson in the hands of those maniacs. I had to get him back. I had to save him. I was the only one who could.

THOMAS RIDEN'S CABIN WAS most likely where they had taken my grandson. I mounted my horse again and rode back across the village. I thought of stopping and requesting the help of the sheriff, but then I decided against it. Every second counted that day, and I could not waste time talking with Collins and trying to make him believe the things that were happening.

Before I left home again I made sure I was armed. I was never good with weapons, but I found a pistol and made sure it was loaded and ready to fire. That was in a holster at my side. The gun had been bought for protection years earlier. I had never needed to fire it, and I wondered if I had it in me to kill today. *Yes. I will kill if I must.* The other weapon with me was a tomahawk that David had owned.

I arrived at the cabin, and I thought at first that it was empty. I opened the door and looked around and saw no living person. *Where the devil could they be?* I closed the door, thinking I would look for something that could point me in the right direction. That was when I happened to glance behind me. To my horror, I saw Sheriff Collins nailed to the wall. The poor man had been crucified. His arms were outstretched and nails had been driven into his wrists. His feet were nailed together.

The terror that this would have brought to my heart was driven away by my resolve to protect Richard. The evil I was witnessing was beyond anything I ever imagined possible. It was like being in a story told to frighten children. I looked at Collins more closely and I saw a rolled piece of paper stuck in his mouth. I pulled it out and unrolled it. It was a message meant for me.

For your defiance you must pay.
Come home to your farm.
We are waiting.

The bastards were at my farm? Was it possible? They knew I was still alive. They had murdered my daughter and my son-in-law, but I was not present at the time. I understood then that they were probably wanting me to suffer because I turned down Thomas Riden's offer to join his Order.

But they had my grandson.

I returned to the farm with haste, and when I dismounted, I drew my gun. They were in the barn. I could hear voices. One was Thomas Riden's. It sounded almost as if he was pleading. The other voice was unmistakably that of the man named Frederick.

"You don't understand me, boy," he was saying. "You think you have control here and you don't. You're father is half a world away and even if he wasn't, I'm not following his rules no more!"

"Frederick, this is madness." The voice of Thomas Riden.

"Madness when I burned the church and killed that old reverend? Or when I crucified that sheriff bastard who came nosing around? That's survival, boy. Something you know nothing of. You lived in London too long. Too many years of not having to worry about surviving. You're father always watching your back. No more. This is the real world. This is our world."

I confess that as I stood at the door to my own barn I was terrified. I had nearly been frozen by fear. I knew my grandson was behind that door with a group of maniacs, but I was afraid of doing the wrong things. It was not for my life that I feared. I worried that anything I might do would endanger Richard's life.

"Are you all against me?" Thomas asked. "Has the name of Riden fallen from honor in your eyes?"

"Spare us your dramatics, boy," Frederick said.

"Stop calling me boy," Thomas said.

"I'll stop when you stop acting like a boy. A spoiled boy who thinks himself an heir to the Order because he's a Riden. You're not half the man your grandfather was and not a quarter of the man your father is, and still, I am walking away from his rule."

"And what?" Thomas asked. "Start your own order? You're not clever enough. You're just a brute."

And then Frederick screamed and I heard a scuffle on the other side of the door. Frederick then said: "Hold him. Don't kill him though. I don't want his father after me."

"No," Thomas said. "This isn't how it's supposed to happen!"

"He can bloody well watch what I'm going to do," Frederick said.

I summoned all of my courage at that moment, and I kicked at the door with my recently-healed leg. The force of the kick flung it open and I charged inside.

"He's here," Frederick said. "I knew he'd come."

I raised the pistol in my hand and I fired. I still remember the look of horrified surprise on Frederick's face. He must have thought that his arrogance had gotten the better of him and that he was going to die.

But I missed.

The others in the barn—there were ten besides Frederick and Thomas—attacked me. I was not able to tell if I fought men or women, but in my years fighting the Order, I have come to realize that there is no difference between the two. If they are part of this cult, they are evil and they are killers. The only way to deal with them is to kill them.

The tomahawk in my hand was not enough to fight my enemies. I hit one before I was overtaken. They were all young, and I was fifty. When I was overpowered they began to beat me. I was struck across the face again and again. Then one of them had the tomahawk, and I screamed as it bit into my shoulder. I believe that they had meant to kill me at that moment.

"Stop!" Frederick ordered. "I want him to watch what's going to happen. I want him to see."

They stopped hurting me and dragged me over to stand next to Thomas Riden. "I tried to warn you," my former friend said to me.

I was dazed from the pain but coherent enough to understand him. I spat blood in his face.

"Bastard," I said.

"I can get us out of here," Thomas said. "I can make them all pay. Soon."

I had nothing to say to Thomas Riden. I just wanted to be free and to rescue my grandson, who was nowhere to be seen.

The group chanted in a strange language. It was almost like a song. They spoke in unison and their voices soared and then fell together. The evil that they were worshipping could be felt throughout that barn. It seemed to wrap itself around me.

"Bring forth the offering!" Frederick said.

The chant ceased, and the hooded figures bowed and stepped away from the circle. I heard the cry of a child, and I watched as Richard was brought out of a chest that had been brought toward the circle of black cloaks. "No," I said.

Richard was bound and placed on a table in the middle of the circle. I couldn't believe what I was seeing. My scared and weeping grandchild was a victim to these maniacs who I had known nothing of until less than eight hours ago. Everything had happened so fast. There was just no time. No time.

As I watched, appalled, I thought of what Thomas had said. *It's already too late.* My family had been marked for death from the moment that Thomas Riden had entered our home.

"Please," I said to Frederick, "please kill me instead. Take me. You don't need to kill the child."

"But we do," Frederick said. "That's what the lady demands of us. Our goddess, Valayra, needs the souls of the innocent. She rewards us for our offerings. We would receive no such reward from you though. You are not innocent."

"Don't," I said again. "Please don't."

Frederick laughed. That was the difference between him and Thomas Riden. I am far enough removed from the evil of that day to be able to look back on the monsters that these men were. I believe Thomas did what he did out of duty though he took no pleasure in it. Frederick, on the other hand, was cruel and vile. He did what he did because he enjoyed it. Hell, even if there were no promises of rewards of power, he might still have done it to exercise his own cruelty.

I remember hearing my grandchild cry out for me. I remember hearing his scream when Frederick approached him. I remember the dripping of his blood after Frederick had cut his throat.

I said nothing. I watched in horror as my grandchild's life was taken from him by a cruel and evil man. The pain in my shoulder where the tomahawk had struck was far away. The dizziness I had felt after being struck in the face and head again and again was gone. Everything was clear at that moment. I had failed, and my family had died.

All because of Thomas Riden.

"This is your fault," I said to Thomas, tears stinging my eyes.

"Now, Mr. Gunne," Frederick said, "would you like a taste of your grandson?"

I looked at him and spat. He was too far away for me to hit him, but I spat just the same. He laughed.

"There's an order to things," Frederick said. "You don't understand this yet, Mr. Gunne. You chose wrong when you turned down Mr. Riden's offer. You chose wrong! Though it won't happen in our lifetime, there will be a day when we rule the world. We already run so much of it from the shadows. You could have been a part of that. Instead, you chose to defy us. No one defies the Order. This is your punishment."

I shook my head. "We were already marked," I said. "Already marked."

"You're not so stupid after all," Frederick said. "You're right. You and your family were marked, but Thomas offered you a way out. You should have seen sense. Ours is the true faith. The true goddess. Valayra."

I spat again to show what I thought of what he was saying. Thomas was silent, but he was watching me.

"Fine," Frederick said. "Let's all have a taste."

He took a wine goblet and approached the bleeding corpse of Richard. After a moment he turned to me and began crossing the floor. There was blood running down the side of the goblet in his hand.

"No," I said, understanding what was about to happen. "No!"

It didn't take much to hold me. I was wounded and weak from the beating I had taken when I had first arrived. My arms were pinned behind my back, and I screamed at the sudden increase of pain in my shoulder.

"We'll all have a taste," Frederick said. He tipped the cup to my mouth, but I kept my lips closed. He then squeezed my cheeks together and forced my mouth open. He tipped the cup and poured the blood all over my lips and down my throat. "The blood of the innocent," he said.

They let me go then, and I collapsed on the floor, spiting and heaving, trying to make myself vomit the blood. "Just kill me," I said between heaves.

"I will," Frederick said. "I'm bored now, anyway."

He approached me, and as he did, I began to stand. I would not die on my knees to this monster. The knife was in his hand. I saw it was red with blood, and I knew it was the same one he had used to kill Richard. I braced myself for my own murder.

"No!" Thomas said. "Frederick! Not that knife! Don't do it!"

But Frederick was paying no attention to Thomas Riden. He drove the blade into my stomach. I gasped as I was stabbed and then again as Frederick pulled the blade back out. He stabbed me again and again. The world went black.

And I was gone.

2017

A S SOON AS JASPER GUNNE had finished the beginning piece of his story, he printed it, turned off his computer, poured a tall glass of whiskey and downed half of it at once. The death of his family had been the part he had dreaded the most when he had decided to tell his story. The memories, long buried, came back to him as fresh as if they had just occurred. Two hundred sixty-six years was not enough time for him to get over what had happened.

He finished his glass and poured another. The bottle was almost empty then, but he had planned for that and had three more ready to open. It took a lot to get him drunk, but he was intent on getting it done.

He sat on his couch and drank the second glass, making this one last longer. The unearthed memories stayed with him. He could taste the blood. He could feel the blade. He could see that maniacal grin on Frederick's face. He could feel the ghost of his own terror that he felt on that day so long ago. The hopelessness. The anguish. The pain. It had all returned, and it was lingering.

I wish I had died that day, he thought, finishing his second glass of whiskey.

He was halfway through his second bottle before he felt the buzz. It wasn't enough. He drank in silence, brooding in the darkness over the injustice of his life.

———————

HE WAS AWOKEN SUDDENLY by a knock at the door at seven thirty the next morning. Jasper shook his head and got to his feet. One of the perks of having his abilities was his inability to be hung over. He had finished three bottles of whiskey and made no attempt to hide them before he answered the door and found Carol Krane on the other side. She was carrying a pan with oven mitts.

"Hello," he said, blinking rapidly. "Just woke up."

"Well, you young people do like to sleep the day away," Carol said. "I just wanted to give you this. It's a breakfast casserole. Eggs, cheese, sausage, onion, bacon, potatoes, ham."

"All the healthy stuff," Jasper said. He took the pan from her. "Thank you."

"Careful! That's hot." Carol's eyes widened as she saw Jasper having no problem holding it.

"I'm okay," he said. "Thank you again."

"How is your book going?" Carol asked, walking into Jasper's apartment behind him. "Getting lots of ideas?"

"It's going," Jasper said. He took a fork sitting on his counter and started digging into the casserole. He took one big bite. "That is good."

"I'm glad you like it," Carol said. Her voice seemed a bit distant. Jasper looked up from his food and realized she was staring at his empty whiskey bottles.

"Medicine," he said.

"I see," Carol replied. Jasper saw in her eyes the same sort of judgmental look he had seen time and again in the eyes of people he had known over his long life. *Let her think what she will. If she had seen what I had seen, and been through what I had been through, she'd tip a bottle or two herself.*

"So, the book," Carol said.

"What about it?"

"How is it really going? I may be able to help you out if you're interested."

"What?"

"I have a friend who has a daughter who has written a book."

"Oh yeah?" Jasper asked.

"Yeah," Carol said. "And I talked to her last night, and she said she's going to talk to her about helping you publish yours."

Jasper took another bite of the casserole then filled a glass with water from the sink. "That's kind of you," he said, sipping on the water, "but I really only just started. I won't be ready to think about publishing anything until weeks from now, I think."

"Well, when you finish your story, let me know, and I'll see if my friend's daughter can help you."

"I will," Jasper said.

Carol Krane left and Jasper locked the door behind her. He shook his head as he walked to his desk. Carol was a nice lady and a damned good cook, but he found her a bit annoying. He knew she meant well, but he had not come back to Ravenwood to make friends. He had come to tell a story.

He turned on his computer and printer, clicked the "Word" icon, found the place he had stopped and began to type.

1750

I DON'T KNOW HOW to tell you what happened next. Over two centuries later, I still don't understand it. I slipped into darkness as I was stabbed again and again. I remember feeling my throat being cut, and then there was nothing.

Only that's not quite true.

There was something. I was no longer in the barn. I was no longer in my own body. I found myself standing on a plain of black with dazzling blue light flashing through the darkness.

The last thing that I remembered was of course being run through by Frederick's blade. I did not know how I had managed to escape, and I did not know how I had gotten to that bizarre place.

It is strange to think of how my mind had not arrived at the obvious conclusion. You reading this may be thinking: *you were dead.* It is so obvious, but I was unable to see that at first. Then, when I realized that I was beyond the doors of death, I began to tremble.

This was not the heaven that the church had always told us about. This was nothing but emptiness and blue light.

"Sarah!" I called out, thinking I might be able to find my daughter. "Sarah! Are you here? Sarah! Richard! David!" Then I called for my dead wife. "Charlotte!"

I moved forward though I was without form. I drifted through the blackness toward the blue light that at times surrounded me and at other times was gone far off in the distance. There was no one but me in this place though I could hear what sounded like singing.

"Sarah!"

It could have been this way for a minute or a day or even a decade. Time seemed nonexistent in that place. When I called out my daughter's name yet again I finally came across another person.

"Will you please stop that?" he said.

I stopped where I was and then peered in every direction for the source of that voice.

"It's a bit annoying," he said.

I looked around again. "I can't see you," I said.

"Then look harder."

"What?"

"Very well," the voice said. Suddenly the speaker appeared before me. He was made up of green light, but he had the shape of a man. "You are not like the others," he told me.

"What are you?" I asked.

"You're in control of yourself. You're different. You can think. You can ask questions. So many of them can't."

"What are you talking about?"

"You," the green man said. He waved a hand and suddenly my own body was visible. I was made of orange light.

"What is this?" I asked in surprise.

"The color is different too," he said. "You not like the normal ones."

"What I am is lost," I said.

The man laughed. "Of course you are! Dead and nowhere to go! Heaven is not ready. Hell is in ruins. The only place that's left is the earth where you come from. And here."

"And what is here?" I asked.

The green man held out his hands. "It's here. You were murdered, I would suspect."

The memory of my last day on Earth came back to me. It had been buried in my mind because of the strangeness of where I was, but it had been just below the surface. If my soul could have wept, I would have been bawling.

"Valayra," the green man said. I was crouched and my hands were over my face. It was odd that I could feel my body though I was only made of light. "Am I right?" he asked. "Of course, I'm right."

"That's what he called it," I said. "Valayra."

"Who?" the green man asked.

"The one who did this. Frederick was his name."

"Did they call themselves the Order?"

I nodded.

"Been around for a while. Gonna be around for a while more."

I stopped talking for a time. I sat and waited in silence, watching the ribbons of blue light swirl all around me. I could not understand what this place was. It was unlike anything I had ever heard about in church or from reading the Bible. My thoughts turned to the possibility that my own religion had been false. Maybe I was in the afterlife of some other god that I had never worshipped. And that made sense to me. Why would the God I worshipped let my family be murdered the way they were?

And then I realized I must be in Valayra's hell.

"You're not," the green man said. He must have known what I was about to ask. I had lifted my head and spun quickly to ask the question.

"Then where am I?" I asked.

"It's complicated, but everything is to a human."

"Where?"

"Heaven is not ready to open and Hell is long ago conquered."

"You said this," I said.

"You're dead. In a way. But you're a special kind of dead. I haven't seen many like you."

"What do you mean?"

"Usually when people die they sleep."

"Sleep?"

"Until the end. People wake up at the end of the world and they are judged. By God. Your religion was close."

I nodded.

"There is a demon. Many demons. Back when Lucifer fell and took his followers with him, some stuck with him and others rebelled themselves and went their own ways."

"But Lucifer was an angel?"

"Indeed."

"So Valayra is an angel?"

"Once," the green man nodded. "Now she is a demon."

"And they worship her?"

The green man turned around and stared into the shifting blue energy. "She is a demon that has figured out how to grant power to her followers."

"So when they kill..."

"Her followers take power from her through the sacrifice of the innocent."

"Then this is where they go?" I asked.

"No," the green man said. "Well, yes. But no. They come but they don't stay as you did. They can wander back and forth actually. And they don't look like you. You're orange. They're purple."

"Purple?"

"The victims of the sacrifice. The victims of the ritual."

"I still don't understand."

The green man shrugged.

"If they can leave, can I leave?" I asked.

"Maybe," the green man said. "Or maybe you're trapped here like me."

"Like you?"

"I've been here for eight thousand of your years. Just watching."

"Okay, stop," I said. "Stop talking like this and tell me what the hell is going on!"

"Humans," the green man said with a shake of his head. "After the Lord banished Lucifer and his people from his sight, they came to Earth. I was one of the warriors sent to follow them. Valayra was my mission and I failed. She trapped me here though I still do not understand how. I am only free if she perishes."

I nodded. What else could I do? This entire experience was beyond my grasp of normality.

"Those that can enter and leave are the ones that were sacrificed. I think she is creating an army for herself. Not just those on Earth but those in the spirit world. I think. I could be wrong though."

"And because they were given to her they can come and go as they please?"

"I think that's the reason."

"But what if you die for another reason?"

"Then I would assume that you would simply sleep in your grave until the end of the world."

I considered this for a moment and then said: "That brings me to another question. How am I here if I was not an offering? How is any of this possible?"

"Of course you don't understand, human," the green man said. "I barely grasp it. You're not meant to understand."

———◦———

AND SO IT WAS that I was indeed trapped in that place. The green man was my only companion. Now and then I saw the purple beings wander into our realm and then wander back out. I envied them their freedom.

Arthan, that was the name of the angel who I have been referring to as the green man. There was nothing but time in that place and yet time did not exist. We talked, for there was nothing else to do. Arthan had been a warrior angel who hunted what he called "renegade fallen." Valayra had been cleverer than Arthan and had trapped him in this place outside of the realms of Earth or Heaven or Hell.

And now I was there.

"I feel odd," I said after what could have been years in that place. I don't understand how time worked there. I wasn't there for more than a few days, but I felt as if I had been imprisoned for an eternity. The memory of my dead family was far away, and the anger I had felt at Thomas Riden and his order was unimportant. My mind was locked into eternity, and that makes you see things differently.

"You *feel*?"

"I do," I said. "I'm changing. It's different."

"Yes," Arthan said. The green man's face was full of delight. "I hoped for as much."

"What do you mean?"

What was I feeling? At that moment, I didn't know. It was like I was being pulled. But pulled where?

When I realized what was happening, I felt like a fool. But I had spent so long in this strange purgatory that I did not think that I could be actually leaving. Once I determined what it was, I knew it could be nothing else.

And then I felt an increase in the pull.

"Arthan!" I yelled. "I'm going back!"

Arthan, who had been watching me, merely nodded. "Yes, you are," he said.

And then I was hurtling through waves of light and energy. Dazzling colors danced in my vision. I passed into the realm of the Earth and saw the town where I had lived a life that seemed so long ago. I saw the home I shared with my daughter's family. I saw the barn.

And I woke in darkness.

WHEN I OPENED MY eyes I forgot everything that I had just experienced. Perhaps you reading this might be wondering how I could have written about it if I had indeed forgotten. The trials of my existence have led me back to that place time and again and my mind has developed an ability to retain those memories. But back then, in 1750, at that moment upon waking under the floorboards of the barn, as far as I was concerned the murders had just happened.

I thought I had been buried alive. It was pitch black, and when I reached forward I felt wood. I was in a coffin or a crate. Of course I was. What other explanation could there be? I didn't feel a pain in my stomach nor in my shoulder where I had taken the blow from the tomahawk. Somehow it was better. Somehow I was alive.

And in a grave.

Then get out of here, I said to myself. *Right now.*

But how?

I reached my hand forward again, and I remembered all of the pain of the moments before what I thought would have been my death. Rage coursed through me as I made a fist and drove it upward into the wood.

And it cracked.

I had meant to cause myself pain. Perhaps I thought that I deserved it for failing my family. I don't remember the reason of my intentions. But when I heard the wood crack, I knew I had a way out.

Maybe it's rotted, I thought with controlled excitement. I couldn't afford to get my hopes up yet. I had a possibility of getting out, but if it failed, I needed to keep myself collected. The air would run out soon. I was surprised it hadn't already. I focused all of my concentration on escaping that grave. If I could get out, I could bring these monsters to justice. That was my hope.

I punched again. And then my hand went through the wood. I flexed my fingers and then brought my hand back through the hole. No dirt. I laughed in astonishment and realized that I was not in a coffin at all. I was under the floorboards. I was probably still in the same damn barn!

I punched my way out of what was meant to be my grave and then stood in the barn where my grandson had been murdered before my eyes.

I stepped outside into the dazzling morning light. The remains of the snow had mostly melted, and the day was warmer than it had been when my family was killed. I had indeed been under that floor for a while. I didn't understand, but soon all questions of myself were forgotten as I gazed at the trees in what had been our front yard. I almost fell over in surprise, for one of the trees was full of hanging corpses.

"My god," I whispered as I approached the tree. These were the dead bodies of those who had killed my family. I recognized Frederick hanging from a higher branch than the others.

Their eyes were gone.

Of all the corpses on that tree not one of them was Thomas Riden. I closed my eyes, felt the tears form and run down my cheeks, then looked at the corpses again. There was a strange sort of aura in the air that was strong near that tree where dead bodies hung like macabre Christmas decorations. I cannot tell you what the feeling was like. I doubt you reading this could imagine it. I can only say that it felt like *darkness.*

I looked up at the killers of my family again. My eyes narrowed in loathing as I watched the corpses sway in the wind. I could still see Frederick in my memory. I could see him killing Richard. I could see him approaching me with his knife. I could feel the blade...

The blade!

I felt the shirt I was wearing. It had been stained with dried blood and dirt and torn by the weapons used on me, but there were no holes in my skin.

Instead I felt scars that were completely healed. *That's impossible.* I remembered my throat being cut.

The scars were there so I had not imagined it. Somehow I was completely healed.

And then I fell to my knees and wept. I remember rain falling on me as I cried though that could just be my memories making the event more dramatic. I hated myself then. I wished that I had died. Why was I allowed to live? Why was I healed? I had been stabbed and cut. Why would God heal me?

It had to be God, right? Who else could have healed me? And why did He do it?

And then I got an idea. It was a dangerous idea for it only set me up for a shattering disappointment later on but once it occurred to me, I had to know.

I will not recount the search through the house. I will not tell you of how I was devastated once again after I found that the house was just as I had left it. The dead bodies of Sarah and David were still in the living room.

They had remained dead and I was still alive. I knew that baby Richard was dead too. Everyone was dead except me. I touched the scars that had been my wounds.

I'll change that.

And so I walked away from the farm that day. I walked on and on until I thought I should be tired and still I kept on walking.

I walked into the wilderness to die.

2017

J ASPER WALKED THE TOWN, taking a brief break from his story and the flood of memories it had brought to his mind. It was a chilly autumn day, and the cool air felt refreshing after spending nearly a week in his small apartment writing and rewriting his experiences.

The feeling was still part of Ravenwood. It was the feeling of *darkness*. He described it as such to himself and to the few allies that he had acquired over the years. Over a century later and the *darkness* was still there. Of course it was, though. Truly dark happenings spawned the legends that kept the tiny little town of Ravenwood alive. Tourists come from all over to have a paranormal experience. Kids tell stories of the Monster of Ravenwood to try to scare each other. Movies had been made. Books had been written. Jasper's was the only real nonfiction account, and judging by what he had seen and read of the other versions, his was the strangest of all.

This whole endeavor was foolish. He had known about the legends of the Monster of Ravenwood for decades, and it had never bothered him as much as that damn documentary did the other night. What was it that was compelling him to suddenly tell his story? He didn't know, but he reasoned with himself that he had nothing else to do until he happened upon the Order once more.

So why not write a damn book?

He had other problems though. The police were onto him.

Jasper did not bother much with television, and so he did not watch the news. He had been buying coffee when he overheard the reporter on the television talking about the murders in Stetson, Michigan a week and a half earlier.

Jasper watched the reporter on the TV screen—a pretty young brunette by the name of Alison—talk about the kidnapped children that had been rescued, the slain men and women in the factory parking lot, and also the suspicion that this was the work of a vigilante that had been doing similar things all over the country.

Damn, Jasper thought. *They're noticing.*

And it wasn't just all over the country. It was all over the world. Jasper liked to think of himself as the devil. *Going to and fro on the earth and walking up and down upon it.*

And every now and then someone took notice. There were dozens, perhaps hundreds of urban legends and folk stories all over the world that began with Jasper Gunne, and many had lost all resemblance to what had actually happened.

The cops are looking for me yet again.

They'd found him a couple of times and he had spent more than a couple nights behind the bars of a jail cell. They would always find that Jasper was not exactly easy to keep in a cage.

Even so, he should be on the move. It was better that way. Settling in one place too long could create friends, and friends were a hindrance to his life. He had buried enough of them.

Ravenwood was a small town that had been built upon the ashes of the original Ravenwood that was destroyed in 1870. This town had no chain restaurants. There was only one small grocery store and only one gas station. A couple of mom and pop shops lined the main road. There were two diners and a place that sold liquor. If you wanted anything more than that, you had to drive at least twenty minutes.

Jasper walked into a small store that was located on the street corner across from the one gas station. It was remarkable to him how Ravenwood was famous across the nation and even in various other places in the world, but it was still a small little town where few would even bother stopping or noticing if not for the old legend.

The store was not much. There were groceries, beer, a few random household items and a toy section. The toys were what caught his eye as he passed the store and they were the reason he went inside. There was an exclusive toy being sold. It was made by someone in town. It was a toy version of the so-called Monster of Ravenwood. Jasper picked up the small action figure and studied it for a moment. It was grotesque. The Monster's head was misshapen, and he seemed to be too big for his clothes which had been torn across his bulging blue body. He had claws for fingers and large fangs that covered his chin. Jasper laughed at it when he saw it. Yes. That was the depiction of the Monster of Ravenwood.

But Jasper's truth was far stranger.

Jasper decided to buy the toy and use it as decoration for his writing desk. As he walked to the front of the store he passed a magazine rack. Glancing at it he saw there were a few slots devoted to paperback novels. He saw a name on one of those books that made him stop where he was.

The name was Valen. Calista Valen. *Haunted Earth* was the title of the novel. Jasper took it and flipped the book over to look at the author's picture. Calista Valen stared back at him. "The resemblance," he said to himself. "Could it be?"

He bought the toy and the novel that day and then returned to his apartment where he resumed work on his story. He knew what he would tell next.

He had been a drifter for a while after his family's death, but he had not remained that way. In fact, he had found a new life for himself years later. He had not always been as he was now. For a time, he had friends and a surrogate family. The Valen family.

He began thinking about his friendship with Melvin Valen in the year 1800. This led him to his memories of being a security man of sorts for the traveling sideshow *Amazing Wonders*. It all led to the Massacre and it was all vital to his story.

He placed the monster figure on his desk along with his copy of *Haunted Earth.* Then he switched on his cheap laptop, read over the last few lines he had written.

And he began to work.

1750–1800

OVER THE NEXT FEW WEEKS I was determined to die. I did not understand my own immortality at that point. I tried to hurt myself again and again, and I found that I couldn't even break my skin. Slitting my own throat was out of the question. The best option that I could see then was to drown.

It was the end of March of that year, if I am not mistaken, as such, the river must have been freezing, even if the winter's ice had melted. I was able to tolerate the cold, though I did not yet realize why I was able to do this. I merely assumed that the water was not as cold as I had imagined it would be. I slipped under the water and inhaled.

Nothing.

I waited to blackout from the lack of air, but soon enough I realized that I was not drowning. I returned to the river bank, spitting out the water I had ingested.

I remember touching my scars again. That was when I began to understand what had truly happened to me.

Please no.

I couldn't believe it. I wouldn't.

I could have returned to the village. I could have found a gun perhaps. David had one that I could've loaded and then used to shoot myself. But I didn't want to die in the same place as my family, and even if I had decided to do that, I had a feeling that a bullet wouldn't do the job.

I took a sharp rock from the edge of the river. I knew what would happen before I even attempted what was in my head, but I needed to see for myself. I placed my left hand against the ground that was now muddy from the melting snow. I slammed the rock into the top of my hand and winced in pain.

Yes! There was pain. But it was not nearly the amount of pain that should have come with that blow. My slow brain was piecing these things together, and I finally understood.

I could not die.

Those monsters had done something to me. Something far worse than killing me. They had left me alive. That was the only explanation. I had seen firsthand the magic that they could use, though none like what had been used on me. Not only could they take life, they seemed to be able to give it.

But why? Why do this to me?

These people had murdered my family and then tried to kill me. Frederick had driven his knife into my stomach and had then cut my throat. He had wanted me dead.

But Frederick's the one who's dead.

And then I knew why I was alive. It was so obvious. Thomas Riden. He had done this to me. What other reason could there be? Thomas was not among those dead in the tree. No. He had done that to them because of what was done to me. He had brought me back as a way of saying he was sorry. That had to be it. It had to be.

Bastard! I'll kill him!

Suicide had been banished from my mind at that moment and I returned to my village to find the man who had ruined my life. If I could not die, I could at least get some satisfaction. I wanted to end my former friend's life with my own hands.

I had never taken a life in anger. I had tried to kill to save Richard from the cult, but that was in defense of my family. This was premeditated vengeance. But I was angry, and I was in pain. At that moment I knew I was capable of murder, and I was okay with that.

I BEGAN IN THE PUB where I had spent so many lonely nights drinking. It was the same place I had bought Thomas Riden a glass of whiskey for the care he had given my Sarah. I had spent all day walking and now it was after dark. The streets were mostly empty, and that prevented any unwanted encounters with those who were once my neighbors. Just a few hours ago I was trying to kill myself and now I was on my way to commit murder. I knew that I would be leaving as soon as I had done what I needed to do.

Sally, the trusted barkeep, was there as I had expected.

"Jasper!" she said when she looked up and saw that it was me. I had walked through the door, up to my favorite stool and then set my hands on the bar. There was no one else there but me and Sally. When she saw me I thought she was going to drop the tray that was in her hands, but she steadied it in time. "Where have you been?"

I smiled at her and nodded. "Can you answer something for me?" I asked in response to her question. "It's going to sound strange."

"What is it?"

"How long has it been since I've been in here?"

She seemed a bit taken aback by the question, but then she shrugged and said: "Three weeks now."

It had been two weeks from my last bar visit to the time of my family's murder. I was under that barn for seven days!

I nodded. "Thank you."

"So where were you?"

"Have people been talking?"

"Everyone's been talking! Your family was found dead and we hear that there is a tree full of dead people on your property."

I nodded again. "Things have been bad," I said. I didn't exactly know how to tell her what had happened.

"I don't believe it," she said, looking hurt.

"What?" I asked.

"Tell me you didn't kill them," she said.

"Who?" I asked, my eyes narrowing to slits.

She leaned close to whisper though there was no one in the bar to hear her. "Your family."

"Is that what people are saying?"

"That's what they've been saying, but I haven't been believing it," Sally said.

"Go on believing that I haven't done it," I said. "Because I haven't!"

Sally poured a glass of whiskey and passed it to me. "What happened then?" she asked. "You have to admit that it looks awfully suspicious."

"The ones in the tree are the ones that killed my family," I said. "But I didn't kill the ones in the tree. It was someone else." I downed the whiskey.

Sally poured me another one. "I suppose that makes some sense. How could you have done all of that yourself?" I knew she was implying that I was old and crippled. I didn't care. It was the truth. "And I hear that they were the friends of Dr. Riden."

I nodded. "Have you seen the *good* doctor?" I asked.

She shook her head. "He hasn't been seen for a while."

"When did they discover my family?" I asked.

"I hear it was today. They say you were seen leaving town, disturbed, ignoring everyone and muttering to yourself. Someone overheard you mention death or killing. I don't know which. They went to your farm. Found what they found." Sally had another glass ready when I threw back my second shot. "What really happened then? Where have you been? Three weeks is a long time for you. And no one has seen you since you were talking to the sheriff."

"He's dead too," I said.

"I know. But you didn't do it?"

I shook my head.

"I'd like to know why I shouldn't call for help right now."

"Because you don't think I'm a killer. That's why."

"True. But you are not giving me any answers."

"I just want to find Thomas Riden," I said. "That's all."

She stared at me for a moment. I could tell she was trying to work out what she knew in accordance with what I was telling her. I remember her right eyebrow lifting as she stared into my eyes. It was such a cold stare, but then, that was Sally. She was a cold person who did not think with her emotions. She thought with her mind, and because of that, she knew that I was telling the truth.

"I'd leave soon if I were you," she said. "Dr. Riden hasn't been seen in days, and I think he left town. If they find you, they'll kill you."

"They *can't* kill me," I said.

Sally laughed. She must have thought I was being a cocky fool. I considered showing her what I meant but then thought better of it. Sally was always nice to me and I didn't want to burden her with the knowledge of the dark magic that created me.

"Thanks for the drinks," I said. I stood up and dropped some coins on the counter.

"It's on the house," Sally said sharply.

"Take it," I said. "Thanks, Sally. Thanks for everything you've ever done for me."

I knew I would never see her again. I had not even planned on seeing her that day. Suicide had been my one and only priority, and when I discovered that I could not kill myself, I determined that I would leave my home.

I buttoned my tattered dirty coat and stepped out of the bar. The sun was now beyond the horizon and the moonlight had washed over the world.

I left the village that day, knowing I would probably never come across Thomas Riden again. He was gone. He had to be. And even if he wasn't, what could I do? I found that I had had my fill of murder, and I wanted to leave before my fellow villagers could arrest me and accuse me of committing the horrors against my own family.

———◦———

I WAS ALONE IN the world, and I was starving. At least that's what I thought. It turned out that I could not starve, though I could still feel hunger. After weeks of walking from town to town and having no money for food or drink I was still alive, and I was still strong. It was all a part of the transformation.

How miserable that I could not die.

The transformation itself was something that was on my mind constantly. I kept having nightmares about it. That was to be expected, but there were things in my dreams that I did not remember happening to me. I would feel the pain and misery of that night all over again, and then I would be in a room filled with blue light. I would hear a gentle voice, and then I would wake. I know now what it was, but back then my mind had blocked out my memories of that place beyond death. I was remembering.

When I first began walking the world, I had given up hope and decided to live in the forest, avoiding people and living out my days among the beasts. I just wanted to fall out of existence. The best way to do that, I thought, was to leave any type of society behind. In that way, I died in the year 1750.

But years passed, and though I was getting older, I was feeling younger. My body did not need so much rest as a normal person. I could walk for days and not feel fatigued. I traveled from place to place, wandering aimlessly through the forests of the New World and dreaming of the revenge that was robbed from me by Thomas Riden. I cursed myself for not seeking him out while I was still in my old village, but I knew that I had little choice in the matter. I couldn't have dealt with the anger of my neighbors. I couldn't have dealt with the accusations. My mind had seemed on the verge of breaking apart, and I needed to leave it all behind to heal.

After a time, I returned to the world of people. I had overgrown hair and a beard that was down to my chest. I was filthy. I wore deerskins, and I was barefoot. The kindness of strangers allowed me to purchase adequate clothing for myself, but I still felt less than human. I had spent years with no companions except animals.

But there were also the dreams.

I saw them each night, and each night I remembered a little more. It was something that I was supposed to remember, but the meaning would escape me.

Why had I returned to the world of people? I had been tired of the forest. I think I spent six years there, but I cannot be certain. It could have been as many as ten. Those decades have blurred in my memory. You would think I could pick out the major historical points. 1776 with the Declaration. 1783 with the end of the Revolutionary War. All of the struggle in between. The French and Indian War. The beginning of a whole damn nation. Truthfully though, I didn't pay much attention. I looked upon the world as something separate from myself. I was not interested in what happened in it. I was a cracked shell of a man with nothing left inside.

Rejoining society was a challenge. I was homeless and people who knew of me thought me crazed. My mind was not gone though. I could even be pleasant to other people if I were ever approached, but most stayed away from me. I was a vagabond and no one had anything to say to a vagabond.

I even traveled a bit to the Old World. I took a few ships to Europe in those years. The cost was labor. I worked for my passage. I never knew from one day to the next where I would go and there could have come a time when I decided not to return to the New World. That never happened. Despite the painful memories and the lonely life I led, the country that would become the United States was my home.

Fifty years I spent traveling. Fifty years I spent in poverty and hunger as I tried to cope with what had come of my life. To be hungry but unable to starve. It was an agonized existence.

The day everything changed was the day I was in need of some entertainment. There had been a traveling sideshow that went all over the states. It stuck mostly to the bigger towns and seldom stopped in the villages. *Amazing Wonders* was its name, and in 1800 – not to belittle my friends who ran the show – it was far from amazing, and it sure as hell wasn't wonderful.

But that was where I met Melvin Valen and began a friendship that would last for generations. I had never had friends like the Valen Family, and don't I think I'll ever have friends like them again. They were truly special people. They have done so much for me and they have been my most loyal allies in this fight against the Order. I haven't spoken to a Valen in over a century, but not a day goes by when I don't think of them.

2017

I T WAS CALISTA VALEN. That was who Carol Krane knew who had published her book. When she told the name to Jasper he couldn't help but think of how coincidental that was. But then, he knew that it was not a coincidence. It had been over a hundred years since he had spoken to a Valen, and that last time was not a pleasant experience. Of course he would find a Valen in Ravenwood, and of course it would happen as he approached the point in his story when he began his association and eventual friendship with that family.

Calista Valen was a short and thin young woman of about thirty. Her eyes were the same color blue as her ancestor Calvin, whom Jasper had thought of as a brother. Black hair framed her unmistakably Valen face.. Jasper felt almost unnerved by how much she looked like her family from a previous century.

Carol Krane had introduced them and then, one night later, Calista knocked on Jasper's door.

"I want to help," she told him when they had sat down on the couch to pour over the manuscript pages.

"Why?" Jasper asked.

"Because I know who you are," Calista said. "Or at least who you're claiming to be. And I didn't want Mrs. Krane hearing us talk. That's why I came by tonight."

"And who am I?" Jasper asked.

"You claim to be Jasper Gunne. There's a Jasper Gunne mentioned in my family's history again and again. You're here writing a story about Ravenwood, and your name is Jasper Gunne. That tells me you are either really into the history of the town and dug up the obscure name, or you might just be who you say you are."

"Could be the first one," Jasper said.

"I don't think so," Calista said. "If you were just here to cash in, you would have sought me out or someone from my family. You didn't even know who I was until we shook hands yesterday."

Jasper nodded.

"I'm known for being a believer in the shit in my family history," Calista said. "It's probably not true, but I like to believe in it."

Jasper nodded. "I lost contact with the Valens after... after what happened with Calvin."

"Calvin Valen is my ancestor," Calista said. "He chronicled a lot of what you and he did in journals. My great aunt has them, though she keeps them hidden in a safe. I have only read them one time."

"He did keep a journal," Jasper said with a nod.

"According to the journals, there was a man who was immortal named Jasper Gunne. He led Calvin on many dangerous adventures hunting an evil cult of witches." Calista took a sip of the coffee that Jasper had given her. "That's how we talk about it in the family."

"And that is pretty much how it happened," Jasper said.

Calista nodded.

"I'm sorry," Jasper said, "but how is it you believe me?"

"I meditated on it last night," Calista said with a shrug. "Kind of like meditating, I guess. It's what I do. Usually for my books. It reveals where stories need to go and which character should do what. I used it for you and figured out you're not lying. There is no reason to lie and you look a lot like Calvin described in the journals."

"Really?"

"Have you finished it yet?" Calista asked with excitement in her eyes.

"I only have the beginning done," Jasper said. "My beginning."

"You mean when you became what you are?"

"Yes. It was a long time before we got to Ravenwood. It was a long time before I even met up with *Amazing Wonders*. That wasn't until 1800. I had already been the way I am for fifty years by then."

Calista took another sip of her coffee and nodded. "Calvin wrote that you were unnaturally old."

Jasper leaned back with his arms outstretched. "Three hundred sixteen years old and only my mind feels the age."

"You stopped at fifty."

"Yes."

"I can't imagine what it's like to be you."

"It sucks," Jasper said.

"So can I read what you've written?" Calista asked.

Jasper waved a hand. "It's on the desk."

Calista walked to the desk and picked up the small pile of papers. "We can get this published," she said as she thumbed through the pages. "I can make it readable. We'll get this story out there. People can know what really happened."

"No," Jasper said.

Calista looked up at him with puzzlement. "What did you just say?"

"I said no. I'm not letting you get involved in this."

"Involved in what? This is my family you dragged into this. It's my family's story."

"You silly fool," Jasper said. "The story is not over. I just dealt with these same monsters not long ago. If I drag you into it, you could be hurt. I got Calvin killed all those years ago. I was the one who sent him back to your family. I'm not doing that with you."

She stopped arguing then. Sitting in his desk chair she drank the rest of her coffee. "They're still around?" she asked after a few moments of silence.

"I haven't even made a dent," Jasper said. "I've been fighting for years, and all I've done is save lives. That might sound worthwhile, and it is. But I want to do more than that. I want to take down their order. But I can't. They keep coming back. Again and again and again."

Calista shook her head. "No. They can't be. We would know. The world would know if these monsters were around. It's impossible."

"The world doesn't know because the world is blind," Jasper said.

"But someone would have seen it by now. I understand back then no one knowing, but this is 2017. We have technology and the internet and all sorts of things that track everything. Someone has seen them. Someone knows. Someone would have to know. Right?"

"Wrong. Check the news. Stetson, Michigan. That was me. I fought a group broken off from the Order. Fought and killed them all. Saved a bunch of kids. No one knows what really happened there because the Order is able to cover itself somehow. That's why I don't want you involved. They know about me, and I'm sure they know all about the Valen family. Do you really want them targeting you?"

Calista said nothing for a while. She paced back and forth in the small apartment and didn't seem to know how to respond.

"Are you okay?" Jasper asked. "Why are you so bothered? They've been around forever. Nothing's changed."

"It's just…"

"What?"

"I remember being afraid of them when I was a child. Afraid of the Order. Calvin's stories are told constantly in the family. My older brother would tell them to me before bed, and I would have nightmares."

Jasper nodded. "It's always worse when the monsters are real."

"And as I grew up I was able to convince myself that it was all in the past. I'm one of the only ones who ever believed in Calvin's journals as being true, but I convinced myself it was all finished."

"And I just told you that your childhood fears are alive and well," Jasper said.

"It's a bit unnerving," Calista said.

"So that settles it then!" Jasper said, clapping his hands together. "You won't be getting involved."

"It settles nothing," Calista said. "Of course I'll be involved. How about I act as a ghost writer? I read over what you've written and I redraft it. My name doesn't need to be on the book. I want to help. I really want to help."

"For God's sake, why?" Jasper asked.

"So we can expose these monsters."

"But if they are able to hide themselves with their powers, they might come after whoever wrote it. There is a lot of trouble coming for me just by writing this book."

"So I stay anonymous. And they don't mess with me after it's done. They won't know."

"Fine," Jasper said. "We'll leave your name off. But I don't want you getting involved in any of the things I might need to do afterward. I am not burying another Valen. Ever."

"That's fair enough. I don't want them to kill me anyway." She laughed at this.

"It's not funny," Jasper said. "Your ancestor was killed by them. It hasn't stopped haunting me."

Calista nodded. Jasper would accept her help as long as she remained anonymous. That had to be the deal. He would be gone from Ravenwood as soon as he was finished anyway.

He figured he should get back to work. The beginning was over, and it was time to write about Calista's family. The Valens.

In all of Jasper Gunne's long life, he had never again had friends like the Valens. They were his second family. They had come into his life almost fifty years to the day of his first family's demise.

Jasper sat at his desk after Calista was gone, and he typed well into the night.

His mind was lost in the year 1800.

1800–1819

FIFTY YEARS OF PAIN. Fifty years of being alone and wandering the world. Fifty years of regret and longing for the death that would forever elude me.

I was alone because that was what I chose in the year of my transformation. With my family dead, my neighbors against me and my one friend the monster who caused my pain, I thought there was no better alternative than to be alone. I drifted from town to town and saw the world, yet I spoke to few people.

Begging was what I did mostly. Sometimes I would work if someone would hire me. Mostly, I just wanted drink. The one merciful thing about what I became was that I was still able to be drunk. And I got drunk a lot during those fifty years.

On a chilly night sometime in the early part of the year 1800 I was in a town not too far from Philadelphia. I had a coat wrapped around me, and I was trying to sleep under a tree. There was no snow on the ground, but it was already freezing. If I were a normal man, I might not have been able to stand it.

I remember an empty bottle at my side. I had finished it before trying to go to sleep, and I remember being annoyed that I was not nearly as drunk as I wanted to be. The place I had come to find quiet so I could sleep was an open field with a few trees. It was an ideal place for a campsite if you travelled in a caravan.

And a caravan stopped there.

I must have dozed off for a bit, for when I woke, there were wagons being unloaded all around me. They obviously hadn't noticed me sleeping there. That was nothing new for me. No one ever noticed a homeless vagabond.

I stirred and then got to my feet. I knew that with all of this noise, sleep was out of the question. I would need to go elsewhere.

"You!" I heard a voice call. I turned and saw that someone was talking to me. This man was crossing the field from the wagons to me and pointing a finger. "Kindly clear out! We need this here place!"

"Don't have to yell," I said. "I'm going."

"Hold your horses there," another voice said. "This is public land. Anyone can be here, so they can!"

I looked at the new speaker and saw the opposite of the first man. The first was thin and tall and stuck with a scowl across his face that made him seem even less friendly than he already was. He rolled his eyes at the second man then threw his hands in the air as if to suggest that he had nothing to say on the matter.

The second man was short and fat. He had a thick mustache and a bald head that he kept under a top hat. He laughed as the other man left the area.

"Poor Will," he said. "Always thinks he has to control everything."

"It's fine though," I said. "I need to get going. I'm tired."

"I've seen you before," the fat man said.

"You have?"

"Yes sir! I recognize your hair. Black and silver. My name's Valen. Melvin Valen."

"Jasper," I said. "Gunne."

"Nice to meet you, Jasper Gunne. What's the matter?"

I must have been looking uncomfortable, but no wonder. I hadn't had much of a conversation with anyone in years. "Nothing," I said. I began to walk away.

"Hold up," Melvin Valen said.

I stopped and turned, hoping that maybe he would throw me some money so I could get something to eat or maybe another bottle. "You need a friend?" he asked.

"Do I need a friend?"

"Something about you. I don't know. I want to help you out."

I shook my head. I didn't know what to say to this. The cold air blew through the holes in my coat and chilled me.

"Come with me," Melvin said. "I have whiskey."

Against what I thought was my better judgment, I followed Melvin Valen to his wagon. Most of the people in the caravan were sleeping in the wagons to escape the cold, but Melvin had one almost entirely to himself. The one called Will saw me and narrowed his eyes, but he said nothing as Melvin led me through their makeshift camp.

We sat across from one another in the wagon and passed a whiskey bottle back and forth. That was the unlikely way that I met Melvin Valen.

———

IT WAS NOT A chance meeting. I know this now, looking back over the many years that I have spent in friendship with the Valen Family. Something drew us together. There are patterns in my past that were not visible until long after the events had happened. I see the Valens as being the most significant part of my story apart from the events of the year 1750. Melvin and I talked for hours. He told me much later that he didn't understand why he was so determined to help me when he had seen me. Something in his mind just commanded him to do it.

I didn't open up to him that night. I didn't tell him my story and what had happened to me. We simply talked. By the end of the night, we were friends and I was given a place to live among these people. They were actors in a sideshow called *Amazing Wonders*.

The show travelled the country in a caravan, stopping and putting on shows for a low price and then moving on to the next stop. They had no home to call their own and they were, in a sense, wanderers just as I was.

We had jugglers, and we had dancers. We had poets, and we had musicians. We had storytellers, and we had magicians. I knew that my abilities might draw a crowd, but I dared not tell Melvin Valen what I could really do. The idea danced in my head for the first month that I travelled with the band of entertainers. The act I had in mind involved me being gunned down before a crowd. I saw myself fall from being shot and then standing and showing that I survived the bullet. I knew it would bounce off of me and leave a welt, but I also knew that it could potentially bring in more people to watch the show. I could use that, or my speed, or my strength. If people could be accepting of it, I could help make *Amazing Wonders* into a profitable business instead of a group of talented homeless people literally singing for their supper.

But of course, the problem was that people would not be accepting. I didn't tell Melvin Valen what I could do. I didn't tell him how old I was. I merely accepted his charity and helped work around the campsites. It was food in my belly, but there was no drink unless one of the others in *Amazing Wonders* decided to share with me. I feared rejection from Melvin Valen and the group of new friends I had made. I feared the people watching the show would run us out of town or worse if I were to perform with my abilities on display. There was something else too. I didn't feel right about making money off of what I could do. It wasn't a talent I had. It was a curse that came with the death of my family and the end of my life. What I'd had since 1750 wasn't life. It was living death.

It was charity that kept me connected to *Amazing Wonders*. Melvin gave me a place to sleep and food to eat. In return, I helped set up and take down the camp. It was a simple job, and I gladly did it. It was good to feel productive again. Useful. But to tell the truth, I wanted to do something to actually earn money like the performers did. That way I could afford more than just food. I could drink.

You reading this may be thinking that I was using alcohol as a crutch. And you are right. The memories were always with me. The nightmares came almost every night. The alcohol kept them away. I'm not proud that I'm an alcoholic, dependent on my next drink to get through the day. I merely did what I had to do. Things are somewhat different now, but not much. There are times when I feel I will go out of my mind without a drink. And so I keep a bottle with me to drive out the memories of things that I have seen, and things I have heard, and things I have done.

Back then though, I was mostly sober. Apart from what Melvin Valen gave me to drink, I was on water. I didn't have many other friends around the camp, for most kept to themselves. The one called Will who had tried to chase me away from the campsite the night I met Melvin had not grown to like me at all. In fact, I overheard him telling Melvin it wasn't fair that I got food and shelter for nothing. Melvin told him that he had an arrangement with me and that was final. I did not know why Melvin was so kind to me. He would just tell me that something urged him to be. He called it God. And maybe it was, but I know God is probably about as fond of me as I am of Him. For some reason, Melvin was compelled to this kindness. And in a way, it set up my life for what it became.

It was not long before I was able to get a job among the actors and performers of *Amazing Wonders*. It was a different sort of job than I expected to get, but it was one I was perfect for. It all began when we were at one of our many stops.

THE PEOPLE STARTED COMING soon after the stage was set. I could hear the murmur of excited voices from where I stood behind the stage.

The stage was lit by candles and torches. The first person to step to the front of it was Melvin Valen. He beamed at the crowd with his rosy fat cheeks and his bushy mustache. He laughed and then bowed.

"Welcome, welcome," he said, raising his voice for all to hear. "Ladies and gentlemen and boys and girls, we have something truly astounding to show you!" He seemed to be excited although he had done this very performance a dozen times in the past month. "We have things that will amaze you. We have things that will thrill you! Magical things. Wondrous things. After all, this is *Amazing Wonders!*"

He bowed again and left the stage. The performance was about to begin. The curtain was swept to the side and a pretty young blonde girl—Penelope was her name— who was no more than twenty, stood before the audience in a dress. It was low-cut and tight and it made the men in the audience whistle as their wives narrowed their eyes in annoyance. The dress on the attractive girl may have been to grab the attention of the audience, but when she began to sing, she held that attention and had everyone cheering and clapping by the time her song was over.

"Penelope, the Angelic," a voice announced as Penelope bowed to the audience. "She will return for another song, so wait around!"

The next part of the show featured jugglers who moved back and forth across the stage, never dropping the balls that they kept in the air. It was definitely a lesser performance than what I had seen from Penelope, and the rest of the crowd seemed to share my view.

The jugglers were just a filler act though. The next act was truly amazing. It was the act of our magician, Hector. It a typical magic show for Hector. It always was. The difference is how he made all the magic seem real. I know it was all for amusement, and I know they were merely tricks and not real magic, but I still wonder how he seemed to levitate on the stage and how he was able to breathe fire, and most of all, I wonder how he was able to cram a dead rabbit into his top hat, put it on his head, tap it with his wand and then stand there as the rabbit came to life and hopped off with his hat. We all laughed at that. It looked at first as if his hat had jumped from his head and was trying to get away from him. Then the rabbit showed himself to be very much alive. I don't understand how he did that, and I never got it out of him in all the years that I traveled with this sideshow.

But I am getting ahead of myself.

There were other acts. New jugglers took the stage and instead of balls they juggled knives. That made it more interesting. There was an act where an apple was shot off of a man's head. Simple stuff to today's crowds, I have no doubt, but back then in 1800 it was extraordinary. At least to me. I still hadn't gotten used to the talent of the group. The highlight though was the return of Penelope, the Angelic. She sang one more time and melted the hearts of all who heard her voice. It was a soft, sweet song about love and loss and tragedy and it resonated with me.

The show ended and the crowd left.

The actors all pitched in to tear down the stage and pack up the seating. It was the normal routine. The cast of *Amazing Wonders* went about their business with perfect efficiency.

I saw Melvin speak to Penelope, hand her a bucket, and point to a row of trees a hundred yards away. Without hesitation Penelope walked in that direction, swinging the bucket in her hands as she went.

Others were standing there watching the actors tear down their stage. Many of the spectators were rude and made derogatory comments about the show and mocked the group for even bothering to put it on in the first place. I had begun to assist in the work. First I decided I needed to piss. I had to pass by the remaining crowd to get back to the section of trees close by, and that was when I heard someone mention the girl.

"They let that bitch go get water," one man said.

"I know. She was the best damn thing about the whole show. I'd like to get her alone for a private performance."

"I have an idea," the first man said.

I had stopped walking and pretended to be watching the actors work as I listened to what the two men were saying.

"Are you serious?" the second man asked after a long pause.

"Right now. Let's go."

I saw them head for the woods and I knew what they were planning. I also knew that I had to stop it. I followed the two men who had followed Penelope, the Angelic.

Penelope had gone to the river, filled the bucket, and began carrying it back when her two attackers stepped into her view.

"What do you want?" I heard her say.

"Nice show up there," one of the men said.

"Thank you. Come see us tomorrow night if you liked it so much."

"We liked you the best. How about you come home with us and we have our own show?"

"How about you get out of my way so I can go back to work?"

That was when the bucket was knocked out of her hands. I was walking toward them, trying to be silent so I could get the drop on the two men. Neither of them saw me nor did Penelope.

Penelope picked up the bucket by the handle as the man moved to grab her. She dodged his grasp and swung the bucket, hitting him across the forehead.

He cried out in surprise. "BITCH!"

She swung the bucket again, this time at the other man. He caught it, but then Penelope turned and elbowed him in the face before spinning around and kicking him in the groin. He fell to the ground, clutching himself. I stopped just a few yards away from the fight and watched it unfold.

The first man got up and pulled a knife on the girl. That was the end of my watching. I charged the bastard.

"Hey!" I called, running head on toward him. Penelope saw me, backed away and I tackled the man with the knife. It took a moment of struggling, but when I stood the man was dead, his own knife imbedded in his throat.

The other man latched onto my shoulders and managed to throw me to the ground. It was not because he was skilled or strong. He had merely taken me by surprise. I looked up at him as he bent over me to deliver a punch. It must have been a hard hit for he cried out in pain and clutched his hand.

Then the gun was fired and the next second I had a corpse on top of me.

I moved him off of me and stood. Penelope was holding a pistol in her hand. She had it pointed at me now. "What are you doing?" she asked.

"I heard these two talking." I gestured at the two corpses.

"And you thought you'd join in? Maybe take me for yourself?"

"No," I said, appalled. I knew that some in *Amazing Wonders* weren't fond of me, but I didn't think they thought I could be a rapist. "I came to stop them. I came to help you."

"Did it look like I needed help?"

"The man had a knife."

"And I have a gun," she said.

"I didn't know that. I came to stop them. I didn't want them hurting you."

"Kind of you," she said. "But don't assume I need your help because I'm a woman. These were two dumb drunks with the brains of a goat. Easy enough to handle and even a bit fun." She put her gun in a holster on her belt that I had not noticed in the dark.

The gunshot had been heard, and during our conversation, Melvin had made his way from the stage area. "What happened?" he asked.

"Dead men wanted a piece of me," Penelope said, taking her bucket and walked back to the river to refill it. I was stunned at how she was able to remain so calm and practical when she and I had just killed two men.

"And what are you doing, Jasper?" Melvin asked.

"I came to help," I said. "I heard these two talking." I waved a hand at the corpses. "So I came to stop them. Turns out I didn't need to do anything."

"No," he said with a laugh. "Penelope looks after herself."

"That's why you sent her down here?"

"No," he said. "I mentioned wanting water and she took the bucket and told me she would go get it. I argued with her, but she told me she was armed, and I know she knows how to use that gun. I told her where the stream was and pitied anyone who would try anything with her in the dark."

"I see," I said.

Penelope returned, swinging the bucket slightly, letting a bit of water spill. "I think I found an answer to your problem, actually," she said to Melvin.

"What?"

"Jasper can be your new security man."

"I can what?" I asked.

"There's an idea," Melvin said.

"Jasper killed one of these men himself when he pulled the knife," Penelope said. "He tackled him, took the knife and killed him. I shot the other one."

"What say you, Mr. Gunne," Melvin said. "Do you want the job? I hadn't thought of it before, but damn if you're not perfect for the job. And you'll even be paid."

"Paid?"

"We've been talking about it for a while. The actors will all pitch in for a security man for the group. No one's wanted the job. Do you want it?"

It was so obvious a choice that I ended up nodding and smiling within seconds.

"Then it's settled," Melvin said.

———◦———

FOR FIFTY YEARS I was little more than a ghost walking upon the earth. I was a man of the wilderness and a man of the sea. I was a wandering vagabond and a roamer of the streets. No one noticed me. No one cared. I was nobody. No friends to call my own and my family long in the ground. I kept to myself and never let anyone get close. I liked it that way. Long after I had given up ever finding Thomas Riden, I found myself content to simply be a ghost.

I witnessed the birth of a nation, but I did not participate. I had considered it a few times during the Revolutionary War. I knew that my abilities would ensure that I could win any battle I fought. But I couldn't bring myself to care about the politics of the world back then. I still didn't care in the year 1800. But it had been fifty years and I was happy to have friends again.

There is a long history of my time with the sideshow. I stayed with it for seventy years. I could write entire books on my time with *Amazing Wonders*. I could write more on the adventures I had at the various towns and cities where we stopped. *Amazing Wonders* became my life.

<hr />

AMAZING WONDERS DID NOT get to be amazing at all until long after Melvin Valen was gone, and his nephew, Richard, took over the show. That was in 1819. I remember the day Melvin died. It was a sad day for all of us and a frightening one for Richard because he had been willed control of the show. That's when things changed for the better though. Richard was a hell of a businessman.

But don't get me wrong. Those nineteen years with Melvin running things weren't bad times. In fact, it was the first time in my life (since the incident that stole my family and made me what I was) that I had a place where I belonged and friends to call my own. Melvin was a good man and he treated us all well and paid as much as he could afford. We may not have been rich but we never wanted for food or drink.

And slowly I began to move on.

Melvin was such a loudmouth. I remember a time we were in some tiny little town that no longer exists. There was a tavern, and we were both there drinking. Melvin was one of those people who seemed to have an opinion on everything. I can't remember what the subject was, but Melvin was arguing with everyone who would bother paying attention to him. Brandy had caused his state of temper, but he probably would have been almost as bad if he were sober.

"Friend, I think you've had enough," the barkeep said.

"I think not!" Melvin declared. "Another round for me and Jasper here!"

"No sir," the barkeep replied.

"Tell you what," Melvin said, "let me get another round and I'll give you a free show at *Amazing Wonders* tomorrow night."

"That stupid show that travels around?" one of the patrons asked. He was the one who had been debating with Melvin.

"The same," Melvin said. "And I'll thank you not to call my livelihood stupid."

"But it is stupid," the man said. "No wonder you're so full of shit! You *run* that thing?"

Melvin got to his feet, staggered for a moment, then spat at the man. "That's what I think of your opinion!"

The man and two of his friends were on their feet and approaching my boss. I leapt into action. The fight was quick, and when it was over, the show was forced to move on to the next town to avoid any angry people that might come looking for their version of justice.

It hadn't been that bad. I had only broken one of their arms. I left them all bloodied and unconscious though. Everyone in the tavern was afraid of me, and they should have been. It still amuses me when I think on it. Melvin was a loud and obnoxious man. God, I miss him.

"You know, I don't really know what to make of you, Mr. Gunne." Melvin slurred this sentence at me as I helped him back to the camp after our brief bar fight.

"There's nothing to me, sir," I said.

"There is. You move. Move faster than a man. Not natural."

"Just quick, sir," I said.

He didn't say much more to me then, and I soon was able to put him to sleep in his tent. I made my way back to mine, wondering if I could ever tell him what had happened to me. I decided not to worry myself over it because he surely would have forgotten everything by morning.

I was wrong.

Melvin was not feeling well at all in the morning, as you could imagine. When I found him dunking his head in a bucket of water I had to laugh.

"Something funny, Gunne?" he asked.

"You're pretty funny, actually," I replied. "When you're drunk. Not so much now."

"Yeah, and you don't seem to be sick at all though you drank as much as me, if not more." His hair was not tied behind his head, so it hung on either side of his face like wet curtains. His cheeks were red, and that was something he told me he had always dealt with. He had the look of being perpetually jolly. It was comical to see the rosy cheeks and the scowling eyes on the same face. "I mean what I said last night. Not natural."

So he remembers.

I had travelled with *Amazing Wonders* for less than a year when this conversation took place. I think it was about seven or eight months into my career as a security man. I hadn't wanted this to happen. I hadn't wanted to explain myself, but Melvin Valen was smarter than he looked.

"I am willing to talk about it," I said, "when you're feeling better. How about tonight after supper?"

"Fine, sure. We need to be leaving town soon anyway."

TO MY SURPRISE, and to Melvin's credit, he did not seem disgusted by what I was. He seemed disturbed when I told him my tale, and he even seemed sympathetic. I told him that I had not been honest with him and that he had a monster working for him. I apologized again and again.

"Stop it," he said.

"What?"

"Apologizing. It's getting annoying. I'm not mad."

"After what I just told you?"

"Especially after what you just told me. Does Penelope know?"
I nodded.

"And she didn't run screaming, did she?"

"No," I said.

"Then don't worry about it, Jasper. I am not much for magic and spirits, but I saw the things you can do. Quicker than a man. Stronger too. I saw you fall through the stage a while back and it didn't even cut you. I've seen you carry things that would take two or three men to carry. I've been watching since I met you because I knew something wasn't normal. I'm glad I wasn't crazy."

"No," I said. "Not crazy."

"Damn shame though. And this was all fifty years ago?"

"About that. 1750."

Melvin shook his head. "You don't even look old. Apart from the hair, that is." My hair, which was streaked with gray and white was tied in a ponytail beneath my hat.

"I thought you would be afraid of me," I said.

"No, I'm not afraid of you. I'm paying you! I'm just glad I hired you now. No one will be able to rob our show again."

"It's been robbed before?" I asked then. The subject was changing slightly and I was glad of it.

"A few times. One really bad time when my brother was killed. Cal was his name. Damn fool wouldn't part with his money. It was a shame."

"Hard thing to part with," I said.

"Harder to part with your life though," Melvin said. "That was three years ago now. Wish you'd been there then. Cal would still be alive, *and* we would've kept our money."

"Well, you have my word," I said. "That I will not let anyone kill or rob anyone in this camp."

"And I believe you," Melvin said. "You might want to keep what you are quiet though." His voice dropped to a low murmur as he said this. "Some people like me will think it's great that you're part of the show and part of our security. Others—the more religious types—will be terrified."

MELVIN TURNED OUT TO be right. There were many over my seventy years with the show that were terrified of me when they learned what I was. Some called me heretic. Some called me the devil. Some said I had the devil in me. That might all be true.

The part that made some of the more devoutly religious members of our group turn on me was the time they all went to church on Christmas Eve. The snow had settled on the world and the moon and stars were shining down. It was a blessedly peaceful night, and one that is marked in my memory by conflict.

"If you're not the devil, come with us to church," one of them demanded of me. I cannot remember the name of this man though I try and I try.

"I can't come to church," I said.

"Because you're possessed," he said.

The bastard. This was after I had saved the camp from a group of would-be robbers. They had descended onto our caravan, circling around on all sides. They were all armed and they were wanting every cent that we had.

"I'll handle this," I had said. I knew they couldn't kill me. As soon as they started to fight, they would turn and run when they saw me take the bullets and stay standing. That was my hope, at least.

The robbers—there were about six—wound up unhorsed and broken. Two were dead, if I remember right, and the rest were all running away on foot. We kept the horses. It was a swift victory that saved lives and our hard-earned money, but I had been seen taking bullets. The rumors began flying in the camp.

"The devil's in you!" they had told me. Melvin had been right.

They confronted me on that Christmas Eve and tried to get me to come to church.

"I can't come," I told them, "because I don't want to."

That was true enough. I didn't want to be in church. I still believed in God, but I was not on speaking terms with Him. There was another reason for avoiding church though. I literally couldn't stand being in one. It burned. That is one way I think I can commit suicide if I want to die badly enough. I just need to deal with the pain.

I had tried to go to churches a few times since the year 1750. Each time I couldn't make it through the front door. I could feel heat coming from the building when I was at the door, and when I tried to enter, it was like stepping into fire. Whatever was done to me to give me my abilities also seemed to bar me from holy ground. I can't have communion. I can't wear a cross. I can't even hold a copy of the Bible. I can have nothing to do with God.

And that's just fine with me.

But it made things more than awkward that Christmas Eve. If not for having confided in both Penelope and in Melvin Valen, I might have been left at that stop as *Amazing Wonders* moved onto the next town.

"I saved your skins," I reminded him. "I didn't hear you complaining that I was possessed then."

He said nothing.

"Maybe next time I should stand aside. Let them take what they want."

"No," he said, shaking his head.

"Now you listen to me," I told him. "There are things about me that you will never understand. I don't even understand them. So don't tell me I'm possessed. If there is one thing I know, it's that I'm not possessed."

———

I DIDN'T WANT TO fight with anyone from the show. That's why I was glad of Melvin vouching for me in front of the whole cast and crew. The group of actors and workers associated with *Amazing Wonders* were more than just friends to me. They were like a surrogate family. I loved them all, and I would have done anything for any of them.

I had an affair with Penelope that turned into a relationship that lasted for five years. We never married. Indeed, I have not married since my Charlotte died. I cared for Penelope. I even loved her and she loved me, but it all ended when she succumbed to a fever in 1805.

When Penelope died, I buried her myself. When that was done, and a slab of rock with her name carved into it was laid across the fresh dirt of the grave, I wanted nothing from anyone except to be left alone.

I got past my sadness eventually, though it was many years until I found myself loving anyone again. It was just too painful especially when I knew I would outlive everyone.

My friends started dying of one thing or another. Sickness was common. A drunken brawl with locals could leave a man dead. Some got old and worn out and were found in the morning, passed away.

The Valen family was close, and when it came time for old Melvin Valen to pass on, his son was ready to take his place. The year was 1819. We had known that Melvin was dying for the past month. He coughed day and night and seemed to get weaker by the hour. The doctors we saw at our stops could do nothing for him, and the fat, jolly, mustached leader of *Amazing Wonders* accepted his fate with grace and dignity.

He too has a slab of rock with his name carved into it serving as a tombstone. If you ever wander the woodlands of Tennessee you might stumble onto his grave. It's not too far from Penelope's final resting place as they both died at the same stop in different years. I wonder if they are still there or if the woods are all gone and a highway now sits on top of their bodies. I guess I could look for myself one day. I have the time.

I remember the day he died so clearly. *Amazing Wonders* had survived many hardships, and we had always gotten through them because of Melvin's leadership. We survived winters. We made it through the War of 1812. We encountered bandits on the road who wanted whatever they could get from us, and I always made them wish they had passed us by. Melvin had always vouched for me. When legends began to grow about me, he would deny all of the rumors that I had special abilities. He always respected my wishes and never made me part of the acts. He was a good man and a good friend.

I was standing at his bedside the day he died. That was when he told me the truth about the day that we met.

"There are things I have kept to myself," he said. "And it's not fair. I think you've told me everything."

"Mostly," I said.

He broke into a coughing fit that only stopped when he began heaving as if he was going to vomit. Then he regained his composure and sat up on his bed. "Laying down too long makes me cough. But sitting hurts. Pick your pain, I guess."

"I guess," I said, taking a drink from my flask.

"There's something I need to say," Melvin said.

"Go ahead then. It can't be anything too bad. I lived through hell already."

"I knew that," Melvin said. "I knew that when we met. I knew it."

"What did you know?" I asked.

"I knew about you. Kind of. Not exactly."

I smiled at the old man, assuming he was growing delirious in his final days. It was in fact, his final hours. He would be dead before morning's light.

"I saw you in a dream," Melvin said. "A dream that you were wandering and alone and needed help. Saw you. Had to come get you."

"You're telling me you saw me in a dream?"

"I did. I have this thing. Sometimes I can see things I need to do. I can see people. Places. I see what I need to see. Don't know. I think it's the good Lord talking to me."

"The Lord and I are not talking at the moment," I said.

"That's what you say. But I think He has something in mind for you. Something different than what you expect."

"He can keep His plans," I said. "I want no part of them."

Melvin laughed. "I figured you'd say that. I just needed to tell you. Never felt like the right time. I don't like talking about it."

"Your power?"

"I don't think it's a power. I just don't like bringing it up. People will think I'm crazy or something."

"I understand that."

We said nothing more for a while. I sat at the edge of the tent, looking out to the camp that was operating under Melvin's son, Richard. Things were different now that Melvin was dying, but they would be all right. The show would carry on, and Melvin's vision would outlive him. There was comfort in that.

"Thanks for finding me," I told him when I turned back to Melvin's deathbed. "You saved my life."

Melvin chuckled feebly then stopped before it could turn into a cough. "How can anyone save your life? You can't die."

"You saved me from what I was. You gave me a life. Thank you."

Then Melvin Valen, the first friend I'd made since Thomas Riden, died. I wept when he passed, though I knew he was no longer in pain. I wasn't one to pray in those days, but I offered up a prayer, asking the Lord to accept Melvin Valen into paradise. If any soul ever deserved it, it was Melvin Valen.

<hr />

IT IS STRANGE HOW things become so chaotic so quickly. It had been known that Melvin was sick. His son, Richard, was in charge of *Amazing Wonders*. When Melvin died though, it was like the structure that we had built the show upon was gone. Nothing significant had changed. Melvin had already removed himself from the show, and Richard had been doing a proper job of running it. Hell, when Melvin died, it made our lives a bit easier because we didn't need to worry about sitting with him and helping to feed him. I don't want to sound as though taking care of my best friend was a bother and a chore. I just mean that once he was gone, that was something we no longer had to worry about.

And everything fell to chaos.

We were setting up our stage in a town in Ohio when we realized our two lead acts were nowhere to be found. The show was cancelled that night, and Richard and I went to find our magician and our singing girl.

"I DON'T LIKE THIS at all, Richard," I said after we had questioned a few people in the local tavern.

"Me neither," Richard said. "I hate having to lose money on a show."

"Not that," I said. "I don't like this feeling I'm having."

"A feeling, Jasper."

"It's a bad one," I said, but I would say no more. Richard wasn't fully aware of the things that had happened to me, and he did not know the full extent of my abilities. The feeling I was having then was one I hadn't had for decades. It was the *darkness.* Upon arriving in that town I began to feel it, and its essence was like a hated memory recalled in the early morning hours when sleep is elusive and the shadows play with your mind.

And I didn't like how I was feeling it at the same time two of our own were missing.

The rainclouds had gathered overhead and blocked out the moonlight. We had nothing by which to see except for the lanterns we carried.

"I think I'm heading back to camp," Richard said after a time. "We have been searching for hours now. Who knows where they are? Maybe they ran off together."

"No," I said. "I think something bad has happened."

"Something bad?"

"Trust me on this," I said. "In fact, it may be better if you get back to the camp quickly. I don't want you getting hurt."

"I'll be fine," Richard said, oblivious to the warning I was giving him. He did not know the danger as I did.

"Get back to the camp. There are dangerous people out here that I need to find."

"Sure. Fine," he said. He then patted his pistol that sat snug in his holster. "I'll be okay."

We arrived at the sheriff's office finally and knocked on the door. This was the last stop we wanted to make since we always tried to leave the law out of the affairs of *Amazing Wonders*. But we had been through every option that day and still the *darkness* was there and growing worse.

"Good evening," the sheriff said when he answered the door. He wore a ten gallon hat and a badge on his vest. His guns were at his side where he could easily reach them, and though he looked old and relaxed, I was sure he was quick with those weapons if he had to be.

"Forgive us," Richard said. "We're from the show that's in town this week."

"*Amazing Wonders*," the sheriff said with a nod. "We've been expecting you folks for a couple months now."

"We had a couple of our own come up missing tonight, actually," Richard said. "We thought maybe you'd seen a couple strangers around. Anything?"

"Can't say I have," the sheriff said. "You think they quit on you?"

"I'm not sure," Richard said. "I feel responsible for them though. If you see or hear anything, please, let us know."

"Will do, son," the sheriff said.

———✦———

"I'M THINKING THEY QUIT," Richard said to me as we walked back to the camp. "Had a lot of quitters in the last few weeks. Only right that some of our stars start quitting."

"Maybe," I said. "But I still don't like this. That feeling is only getting worse."

"Okay. What is that? What feeling are you talking about?"

I looked at him, and he looked back at me. For a moment I said nothing. The essence of the *darkness* was thick in the air, engulfing us and everyone in the town, though I was the only one who could feel it. "Do you trust me?" I asked.

"Of course I do," he said without hesitation. I had been a part of the show and his life for so long that he trusted me as he would have trusted his own father.

"You know me and my power. You know the things I can do."

"Yes," he said. "We all do."

"Then trust me now. Something bad is out there. I can feel it. *Feel* it. It's one of my talents. I think we should move the camp tonight. Make for the next town on the list."

He began shaking his head before I finished talking. "There is no way that I am doing that. We've already rented space in this town for a week. We need to make good on it."

"It's dangerous," I said.

"Then you had better prove that you are worth what we pay."

That was something I had seen more frequently in the last few weeks. Richard Valen was able to turn instantly from friend to boss. He did it that day, and he would say no more to me.

———◦———

THAT NIGHT, DREAMS CAME to me in a different form than their usual horror. Instead of dreaming of my dead family talking to me and accusing me of killing them, I saw my one time friend, Thomas Riden.

"Jasper, my friend," he said, "how are you keeping?"

"Get out," I said. We were standing in the house I had shared with my daughter's family. It was full of dust and spider webs. No one had lived there for some time.

"Jasper, Jasper. I warned you not to say no to me. Look at us now. Enemies. And why? Your family is gone now. It's time to come home to us. To the Order. Come, Jasper." He extended a hand. "Come with me."

"Get out!" I ran forward and grabbed Thomas by his throat. I began squeezing the life out of him and all the while he laughed at me.

I woke drenched in sweat.

I left my tent and headed straight for the wagon where we kept the alcohol. Soon I found a whiskey bottle, opened it, and began trying to drink the memory of the dream away. But it was more than a dream. It was a vision. The Order was near. They were in that town, and I was sure they had our people. I thought for a moment about waking Richard but then decided against it. Instead, I left him a note.

If I don't make it back, get everyone away from this town as fast as you can.

I didn't think he would listen to me, but I had no other option. At three o'clock that morning, I began seeking out the Order. The first priority was to find our people and make sure they were safe. The second priority was revenge.

————◎————

THE *DARKNESS* WORKED ALMOST like a scent. When you smell a foul odor in your house, you seek it out. The smell gets stronger as you get closer to the source. Finally, when the stench is almost overpowering you find the dead animal in your basement. That is what the *darkness* is like. I felt it and I moved in the direction where it seemed "thicker."

Why now? Why after all these years? And so suddenly? It made no sense to me. I had thought in my deluded ignorance that the Order may have been finished after what had happened with the group that had mutinied against Thomas Riden. After searching the world for a time and finding no sign of them, I thought they were gone. Ever since feeling the *darkness* I had begun to fantasize about the possibility of revenge. It was true that those I was seeking now had nothing to do with what had happened to me, but they had destroyed many lives and would destroy many more.

But not if I found them first.

The feeling drew me miles out of town. The sky was still shrouded in clouds, and that made seeing nearly impossible. I did spot, in the distance, a cabin with candlelight in the windows.

I climbed down the hill I was on and began running to the small lights. A few times I tripped, but I managed to get back to my feet without losing a second step. The *darkness* was thicker, and I was closer than ever. I should have known they would be away from the town. There was no one to hear them out here and few to bother them.

When I was within a dozen feet of the cabin, I looked up and stopped where I was running. "No," I said.

Clara, our young singing girl who had been fifteen, was dead. Not only was she dead, she had endured hell before death. Her body had been whipped bloody and then nailed to the side of the cabin. The horror she had endured was frozen on her face. I stepped forward and looked at what those monsters had done. They would pay for this. They would die screaming.

I looked inside the window and saw the magician, Malcolm, tied to a chair. The group of black-clad people were all around him and they were taking turns whipping him.

"Her blood is still on it," I heard one say. "Will you scream as loud as she did?"

Malcolm. That poor kid. He was sixteen and a master of sleight-of-hand. Richard had taken him and Clara on three weeks ago. They'd had bright futures with the show.

It was all happening again, and I was too late to stop it. Too late to save them both. I could save Malcolm though. And I could make them pay for what was done to Clara.

This was different than last time. They were more vicious. More sadistic. Before, they had seemed to view it as a necessary evil for their power. Only that bastard, Frederick, had taken delight in causing pain. This was a whole group of Fredericks.

I got a running start and kicked the door off its hinges. The cloaks turned and stared at me with wide-eyed astonishment.

"No," a man said. "Not possible."

"It's him," another said.

"Lord Riden was right."

I started toward the group. "Untie that boy, now!" I demanded.

They hesitated at first and then one of them moved behind Malcolm and held a knife at his throat. "Don't make any stupid choices here, Mr. Gunne."

"You know me?" I asked, my eyes narrowed as I stared down my enemies.

"Please," the one said. "Don't kill us. We are only here to give you a message."

"A message?"

"Yes. Our lord sent us with a message to give to you and only you. We didn't think you would be here. We didn't think you were real."

One of them began walking across the room. I took a step toward him, but he held up his hands and continued toward the table where there were piles of paper and a box with black wrapping. He selected that box and walked it over to me.

"My message?" I asked.

He nodded.

"Untie the boy," I said.

With one quick slash of the knife, Malcolm was free. He fell on the floor, too weak to stand. I stared at him for a moment. I thought of Clara, whipped and crucified. These monsters had taken these two young people in an effort to get my attention. The cloaks even begged me not to kill them. No. They would pay.

I moved across the room at such a speed that none of them were able to defend themselves. With my bare hands I killed them all. Malcolm was lying on his stomach watching me as I killed one after the other. I choked. I smashed. I broke bones. The screams of my enemies filled the night air.

And when it was done, and my rage was quenched by their spilled blood, only then did I feel the pain in my back. I fell to my knees and reached around to find a knife in my back. One of the bastards had actually wounded me.

"Could you pull it out?" I asked Malcolm. I had a hard time believing I was actually feeling pain. Malcolm took hold of the blade and he pulled. Once it was free, my blood started to flow. I stood, staggered, then fell again. The world went black before my eyes.

And I was gone.

2017

"THAT TAKES AN UNEXPECTED turn," Calista said as she poured over Jasper's manuscript. She was sitting on a stool at his counter, manuscript in front of her and a coffee mug in her hand.

"Where I met the Order again?" Jasper asked.

She nodded.

"Took me by surprise too. Didn't think I'd ever come across them again and suddenly there they were."

"Sixty-nine years later. It took them *that* long to come back?"

"There were things going on with the Order that I wasn't aware of at the time. They were locked into a place in England and kept there because of what had happened in the New World. 1819 was about the time they started creeping out into the world again. You see, the Order is something that grows and shrinks depending on the leader and what has happened among its members. That's how they've survived for eight thousand years."

Calista nodded. She had kept her promise of help though Jasper had wanted her to forget about it. It was dangerous work and he was worried she would attract the Order's attention. There were splinter groups in the world now, the remains of the shattered potential empire that Jasper had ended, but the true Order was still out there, quietly and patiently waiting for the right moment to return.

Jasper opened a bottle of vodka and mixed it with his orange juice. This earned him a reproving glance from Calista. "Must you?"

"What?"

"You know what."

Jasper shrugged. "I drink. It's the one thing in my life I like."

"I'm a recovering alcoholic."

"If it bothers you then don't come over," Jasper said. "I was doing just fine without you."

"You really are an ass," she said, talking to him as if they were old friends. There was a strange comfort between Jasper and Calista. It came from the bond he had shared with Calvin so long ago. That bond was evidently still there.

"That's what Calvin called me," Jasper said with a faint smile. "An ass."

"So you died a second time?" she asked, changing the subject.

"I don't die," Jasper said. "I just go away for a bit while my body heals.

"To that place? With the angel?"

"Between the realms," Jasper said. "When my body is healed I am drawn back. It's only for wounds that would kill me. My body will recover but my soul is gone while this happens."

"What's it like? I know what you wrote, but what is it really like to be away from your body? To be a ghost?"

"Pretty much like being alive," Jasper said, "Except I was always trapped in that place. It's a nice break at first, but it gets tiring. It's always such a relief when I return to my body."

"And the angel is stuck there forever?" Calista asked.

"Arthan is trapped there. He's still there now, and he'll still be there a thousand years from now. Poor fool is stuck."

Jasper sat at his computer again and read over the last lines of manuscript on his page. Then he swallowed his orange juice and vodka all at once and began working.

1819

"YOU'RE BACK, ALREADY?" Arthan asked. I opened my eyes and saw that I was once again in that strange place between the realms. Blue energy circled all around continuously, and the green-glowing angelic ghost was my only companion.

"I remember this," I said. "I remember being here."

"That's because you *were* here, Jasper Gunne."

"That's the thing though," I said. "I didn't remember until now."

Somehow my mind had erased the experience of being in this place. As soon as I had returned, the memory had returned.

"Valayra's people again?" he asked.

I nodded. "Sixty-nine years. It was sixty-nine years since the last time."

"That long? I suppose that happens. The passage of time isn't quite the same here. To me you were only gone for a bit."

"I'm sure years seem like seconds to you," I said. "The years sort of blur for me now, and you've been around a lot longer than me."

Arthan shrugged. "It gets so dull here. I wish I could leave like you did. You were healed, right?"

I nodded. "My body recovered in its grave. Then I woke up. I forgot everything though. Until now."

My body was made once again of orange energy. It indicated I was different from Arthan and from the purple souls that wandered in and out of this literally god-forsaken place. My body was healing. I knew it was. And when I was healed, I would return and probably find that all my friends had left me buried. Good. They didn't need me. I had brought this on them, and I swore then that I would never bring pain to anyone else again.

One of the purple souls wandered over to where I was standing. Arthan tilted his head in curiosity. I looked at the ghost and saw the face of Clara, our singing girl.

"No," I said. "Clara. I'm so sorry. I am."

She said nothing in reply. Then she returned to the group of souls who were wandering aimlessly.

"I did that to her," I told Arthan.

"*You* killed her?"

"May as well have. The Order. Valayra's followers. They were trying to get my attention. Kidnapped two friends. Killed her. The other might be dead now. I don't know. He was alive before I came here, but who knows?"

"Then you didn't kill her. The Order did. Valayra did."

"She died because of me."

"She died because of them," Arthan grasped me by my ghostly shoulders, and I was amazed that I could feel this. "Listen to me," he said. "The Order is out there and Valayra is getting stronger. Always. I can't leave here, but you can. I need you to do this for me. I need you to fight them. We can still win this war."

"Win what war?" I asked. "Why am I the one to do this? Why are you? Why can't God come down from His cloud and kill them all?"

"Jasper," Arthan said, "please do not question the Almighty."

I didn't know how long I had been talking with Arthan, but suddenly I felt the familiar pull. "I'm going back," I said.

"Fight them Jasper," he said. "Fight them!"

And then I was gone.

I WOKE IN A SACK. At first I didn't realize where I was or what was happening, but then I felt dirt fall on me and realized I had returned just in time for my burial. Another load of dirt fell onto the sack, and that was when I began to move.

I could hear screaming above me as I began to rip the sack apart with my hands. I emerged from the grave with dirt on my hand and my back covered in dried blood.

"Good god, Jasper," Richard said. He was staring at me with the Bible in his hand. He had performed my funeral and was presiding over my burial.

"Stop screaming, I'm fine!" I growled. My memory was foggy that time. I remembered being in the cabin. I remember being stabbed. There was something else between then and when I woke in my latest grave. I remembered something... blue. I'd had a conversation, though I did not remember what was discussed or who I talked with.

They were all frightened of me. Some had fled and others were watching me with fear in their eyes. Some had knives drawn. One man had a gun pulled on me. They had known before then that I was different than a normal man, but they were discovering just how different I was.

"Damned unnatural," I heard one of them say.

"It's the devil, it is," another said.

"Don't come no closer now!" another said. His gun was pointed at me.

I shook my head and stepped out of the shallow hole that was meant to be my grave. "Do you really think your bullets will put a dead man back in the grave?" I asked him. "Are you *that* stupid?"

Richard put the Bible away and then offered me a hand. I shook it. "I'm glad you're not dead," he said. "We all thought you were."

"He was!" the man with the gun said.

"I say he wasn't," Richard said. "You have a problem with that, you can walk away from the show right now."

"This is shit," he said. "I'll have the law here. There's something not right."

With that, the frightened man with the gun left our group. He would never be part of *Amazing Wonders* again, but he was about to make a lot of trouble for us.

———————

I WANTED TO LEAVE right away, but Richard insisted I have a drink with him and get something to eat. I agreed out of friendship, but I intended to be on my way as soon as possible. I was done with this life. It had only brought pain to those that were my friends.

"So this is one of your powers?" Richard asked over a steak one of the camp cooks had prepared for us. We split the meat down the middle and had more than enough. I was more focused on my whiskey.

"One of them," I said. "It happened before. Long ago."

"Hell of a thing," Richard said. "You died, Jasper. I mean you were gone."

"And this afternoon I came back," I said. "I don't understand it any more than you do. I really don't. But tell me, is Malcolm okay?"

"He's shaken up," Richard said. "Couldn't even get him out of this tent for the funeral today. Whole town was pretty shaken."

"Did you bury Clara?"

"Yes," Richard said. "Two days ago. That was a bad day."

"It's my fault," I said. "They came to look for me. They came to draw me out. I'm the reason she died. If I had been any later, Malcolm would have joined her."

"Why though?" Richard asked. "Why are they looking for you? Why do they want you?"

"I don't even know how they can know about me after all of this time," I said.

My mind was somewhat distracted as I tried to remember the place I had been before waking in my latest grave. I remembered the color blue. That was all. Yet there was time spent there. I knew there was. I just couldn't remember what occurred. I could see blurred images in my memory and even remember my feelings while in that place, but I could not remember the place itself. It didn't matter though. I hadn't been put in a grave for nearly seventy years, and I would likely go decades before returning to one.

"Richard," I said, "I think I need to leave."

He sighed. "Jasper, I need you with the show."

I shook my head. "It's too dangerous."

———⋙◎⋘———

DURING OUR MEAL AND conversation, those in *Amazing Wonders* that had witnessed my resurrection and who were frightened of it ran to the law and to the church. I had finished my last sip of whiskey and had shaken Richard's hand when I heard the horses. I poked my head out of the tent and saw that the camp was being surrounded. A mob had formed and they had torches.

"The devil's caravan!" I heard a woman shriek. "Bring the demon out!"

I stood.

"Don't," Richard said.

"I'll be fine, Rich," I said. "Good luck with the show."

I stepped out of the tent and walked slowly through the camp. My hands were over my head since I was surrendering. My intent was that they would take me alive, let *Amazing Wonders* leave town, and then I would escape and go about my life. I could sense the *darkness*, but it was so faint that I could not pinpoint the direction I would have to go to find my enemies.

The torches blazed in the night, and the church leaders were all gathered in front of the crowd. This was their battle. One of our stage hands was next to them. After all these years, I cannot remember his name. He had been the one so frightened when I had stepped out of my grave.

"I want no trouble for my friends," I said.

"Your friends have plenty of trouble, son," the deacon said. The pious bastard's eyes were narrowed to slits, and in the torchlight he looked more like a messenger from Hell than a servant of Heaven. "Those in that camp have allowed you to go on. Thou shall not suffer a witch to live. Says so in the Bible, it does."

"I am turning myself over to you," I said. "I can make trouble for you all. A lot of trouble. But I won't if you let my friends leave in peace."

I could tell the deacon was considering his options. He had prepared himself for a big battle between good and evil here in this clearing where the camp had been made. I wondered if it was more because we were a travelling sideshow and less because I had supposedly risen from the dead. Hell, the deacon may not have actually believed it, but he could use it to do what he wanted. The church didn't particularly like our brand of entertainment.

"Sounds like a good deal to me," the sheriff said.

I looked at the tall man with a bushy beard sitting on his horse next to the deacon. His badge reflected the torchlight. With that one sentence he had taken away the deacon's authority. The holy man nodded.

———◦———

THE NEXT MORNING I woke in my jail cell. The show had moved on the previous night, and I was once again alone in the world. I would break out when I was ready, but until then I just wanted to sit and think.

I had killed all of the cultists when I had saved Malcolm. The bloodlust was somewhat assuaged, but I wanted to find more of them. I wanted to kill and kill until I had removed their stain from the world.

How many victims did they have? How many had died just as horribly as Clara? How many families had been torn apart by their sadism and cruelty?

And what had I been doing? Travelling with a circus act and pretending to have a normal life while my enemies were still out there. Still killing. Still destroying lives. Still living without consequences. Doing as they pleased. No more.

I heard the door open, and the deacon of the local church walked into the sheriff's office.

"The heathen is awake," he said. "You think you can threaten the will of God, boy?"

I stood and approached the bars. "Don't call me boy," I said. "I'm much older than you."

"Sure you are, boy," he said. "You think you're safe in there? Well, we'll see about that. The sheriff don't want to hang you, but I do. I do the will of God and His will is mightier than the law's."

"Why do you want to hang me?" I asked. "I've done nothing wrong."

"Consorted with the devil, you have! And we are not to suffer a witch to live!"

"I'm not a witch," I said.

"You're friend from that evil show you were part of told me all about you. Sounds like a witch to me. Good thing you got them all out of town. I was fixing to burn that whole camp to the ground. Kill you and all your witch-loving friends."

He was out of his mind. For so long he had been a power in this town. The head minister of one of the only churches in miles. It had gone to his head, and he was wanting to abuse it.

"You'll be rid of me soon," I said. I was tired of sitting in my jail cell, and by midnight, I would be gone. I just had to give *Amazing Wonders* more time to get away.

"You'll hang," the deacon said. "We're coming tonight."

And then he left me alone to sit in the cell and brood on his death threat. I was never concerned with his threat though. I doubted he could even hurt me.

———◈———

The day slipped into night, and the only other visitor I had that day was the sheriff. He didn't say much to me, since he was planning on handing me over to the fanatics in that town.

I didn't care. Midnight was when I would make my escape. If the deacon and his followers came for me first, then so be it.

No killing. Just get away.

And go where? I would be wandering again. Alone. Friendless.

The night went on, and the sheriff left. He said not a word to me before he was gone. I knew what was coming as much as he did. It didn't matter. In fact, it would give me a sort of twisted pleasure to terrify this deacon and his followers.

The deacon came at half past eleven that night. With him was a man with a lantern. It was the only light in the room. I thought about beating them down and escaping as soon as my cell was opened, but then I wondered if *Amazing Wonders* was far enough away yet.

"You've come to kill me?" I asked pleasantly.

"We've come to do the Lord's work," the deacon said.

"Then get on with it," I said. "I'm really bored."

The deacon snapped his fingers, and then the man with the lantern used the sheriff's keys to unlock the cell. I noticed the lantern light reflecting from the barrel of the pistol the deacon was holding.

"If I die, won't I just come back?" I asked. "If the devil and I are good friends, as you say, maybe he'll let me come back again."

"Be silent, heathen," the deacon said.

"It was an honest question," I said, before I was escorted from the jail.

The street was mostly empty. A small crowd had gathered to watch my execution. I was to be hanged. That was expected. There was a platform set up with a noose. They had been busy today. Beneath the platform they had crammed firewood and brush. It was evident that they were going to burn me as I swung from the rope.

"I hope you understand that I'm not going to get in that rope," I said. "It's too much of a hassle especially with the fire you're going to start. I don't want to have to clean the ash off of me when I get away."

He struck me across the face, and I braced for the blow. The deacon backed away, cradling his hand and weeping in pain.

I rolled my eyes in annoyance.

"Kill him!" the deacon shrieked. "Do it now!"

"Father?" one of the followers asked.

It was then that the deacon composed himself. He stood and clutched his hand against his chest. I guessed it might have been broken, and I chuckled.

"I, Isaac Harrison, deacon of the Holy Messengers Church, hereby condemn you to die, demon. In the name of the Father and of the Son and of the Holy Ghost, I banish your filthy soul from this world."

"I'm done with this," I replied.

"Hang him and start the fire," Deacon Harrison said. "I want him in Hell an hour ago."

A rope was thrown around my neck, and I felt the slipknot tighten. As I was pulled, I reached for the rope and broke it with one hand. I never did make it to that platform.

"No!" the deacon yelled. "Shoot him! Kill him!"

The guns were fired. The bullets hit me. They didn't slow me down though. I was out of the town before my pursuers were on their horses. I heard them chase after me, but I hid in the woods. They all passed me by, and there, in my dark seclusion, I remained silent.

———◦———

THE DEACON LIKELY RAGED against me the next day and many days after as he preached his sermons from the pulpit of his church. He had nearly been salivating at the thought of killing me. It doesn't seem all that Christian of him. Old Testament, yes. But I can't imagine the Jesus described in the Gospels leading an angry mob and trying to hang a man. Perhaps the deacon didn't understand what he believed. Perhaps he thought he knew better than God. I spent most of the night thinking on that and thinking about my friends in *Amazing Wonders*. I already missed them, and I felt wounded. It was a wound that I knew would likely never heal. They had been my second family. They had been my friends when I had none. Melvin Valen had taken me in, and in return, two innocent people had been taken. They had been little more than children, and they had suffered because of me.

Just to get my attention.

I could never let that happen again.

I stayed in my hiding place all the next day. When the sun set I knew I was probably safe to travel. I climbed out of the trees, set foot on the ground, and began walking. The latest haze of violence and madness was behind me, and I was intent on finding the next one.

But where was the Order? Europe? That was likely. I would need to find a way over there, and I would need to stay there until the job was done. The one thing in the world that I had was time.

2017

"I THOUGHT YOU STAYED with the show until the massacre," Calista said when she arrived at Jasper's apartment that day. She had finished reading over his latest piece of manuscript and had come with her notes suggesting changes.

"Hello to you, too," Jasper said as he waved her inside. "Coffee?"

"Coffee? Really? No whiskey in it?"

"Just a bit," Jasper said, ignoring the disapproving tone in her voice. "I'll save most of it for later."

Calista threw her purse on the couch, then sat next to it. The manuscript was clutched in her hand. She propped her feet on the coffee table and began thumbing through the pages.

"I left the show for a time," Jasper said. "I thought it was too dangerous for them. I thought I should leave and not endanger anyone else."

"What happened was horrible," she said.

"I know it was. That's why I let them leave without me. I couldn't take it."

"And the deacon? What happened with him?"

Jasper shrugged. "That was his one and only appearance in my life. I learned later that he died of pneumonia the next winter."

"So how long were you away from the show?"

"Not long," Jasper said.

"And when you were in Ohio, that was your first encounter with the Order in decades? Truly?"

"First," Jasper said. "I had never forgotten them, and I always had the feeling I would see them again. I was right."

Calista sipped her coffee and nodded as Jasper talked. She still had a difficult time believing that she was helping an old family legend write his book. Occasionally, she would get the feeling that he was undoubtedly a fraud. This feeling would not come from any observation. Indeed, logic was the only thing that was keeping her tied to this project. This man with the long silver-streaked hair could be no one other than Jasper Gunne, yet that was still hard to fathom.

"I wrote some notes," she said. "You may want to use them for your rewrite."

"I will," Jasper said.

"You don't have any more done though?"

"Not yet," Jasper said. "Sometimes I just have to stop. This story. My story. It takes a lot for me to remember and to write down."

"And you need your bottle for that," Calista said with her usual tone of disapproval.

"Yes," Jasper said. "When you live three centuries and deal with all the death and madness I've dealt with, then you can judge whether or not I should drink. Until then, keep it to yourself."

Calista stiffened and looked as if she were about to respond. She thought better of it though and simply nodded. "You're right. I don't know what that must be like. I just don't like alcohol. I have my reasons for that, but it's none of my business if you drink."

"Thank you," Jasper said.

She nodded. "I'll be back tomorrow. Will you have more then?"

"I'll have more done," Jasper said.

"Great," she said. "See you then."

As soon as she was gone, Jasper poured himself a drink out of spite. Then he sat down at his computer and resigned himself to another afternoon of exploring the pain of his immortality.

1819

A MONTH PASSED, AND I was a drifter again. I stayed mostly in the woods. My beard and hair grew. I wore a thick coat made from bear fur. I looked wild and dangerous, and most people avoided me. I was just as I had been before I was found by Melvin Valen and given a new life and a new set of people to call friends and even family.

I was alone.

It was somehow worse than the last time. I had purposely exiled myself to protect the ones I loved from the retribution of my enemies that hid in the shadows all over the world.

I spent most of the time trying to gather the money necessary to voyage across the ocean. It was difficult, but I finally managed to get work on one of the boats. It would have been back-breaking work for a normal man, but I did it with ease, taking care to look as though I were strained so as not to frighten any of my fellow voyagers. Superstitions could get me tossed overboard. While I know that I would survive whatever was in the ocean and eventually make it to land, I did not want the hassle.

I sought the Order when I arrived in Europe. The *darkness* was thicker in London than it had been in the States. Of course it was though. I remembered that Thomas Riden had been English. Therefore, if he had been part of the most notable family in the Order, it only made sense that their presence would be strongest in England.

The voyage had not helped my appearance, and I was left alone by everyone on the streets. I was an unfortunate beggar who looked so imposing the police would go out of their way to watch me. I never gave them reason to arrest me though. I could have. There were many run-ins with drunkards who thought they could take out their liquor-induced aggressiveness on an old homeless beggar. I rolled with all the punches and stayed on my ass until they were gone. If I had begun fighting back, that would have made trouble. So I took the abuse and the random beatings. They didn't hurt me. They just annoyed me. I didn't want the Order to know I was in London.

THE *DARKNESS* WAS GUIDING ME. I used it like a compass from the depths of Hell. I wandered the streets, lost and grasping for direction. The *darkness* is not a thread that I follow like the myth of the labyrinth. It's just there. I step toward it and feel it grow or lessen in strength. Sometimes it's so subtle that I cannot tell the difference from one mile to the next.

Over time, as I searched for my enemies, a few good people had stopped me and put coins in my hand. One day, when I was tired of looking for the Order, I went to a pub for a drink.

Sitting there, I began to throw back shots of whiskey. It was cheap and tasted awful, but it seemed like nectar to me, it had been so long since I'd had a drink. Even crossing the ocean, there had been no rum on board for the captain was deeply religious and he had thought that it would bring a curse from God to have alcohol on our ship.

"Haven't seen you before," the barkeep said.

"Not from here," I said. "American."

He nodded.

"Here on personal business," I explained.

He had nothing else to say to me. Another customer came in and the barkeep began a conversation with him. I was glad. Small talk is not easy when you're alone for so long.

The *darkness* seemed to "glow" all around me. I wondered if I was indeed getting close. I had an idea, and so I closed my eyes to test it. I felt for the *darkness*. It was indeed close. I was closer than I realized at first. The *darkness* was with me in that very room. I opened my eyes again and set them on the patron who had come in for a quick drink. He'd swallowed his shot, and paid. I dropped my coins on the bar and followed him. Here he was. My first prey.

He wore an expensive-looking black suit and top hat, and he carried a cane in his hand. As I followed I felt more and more sure that this man was part of the cult that I was hunting.

I grasped him by his neck and pulled him into a side alley. He yelped in surprise so I punched him once in the stomach. He doubled over, dangling by his neck from my hand.

"What?" he whispered. "Why?"

"I want information," I told him as I dropped him. I rolled him over and put my boot on his neck. I was hoping that no one had seen me take this man into the alley. The street had been empty, but I was still afraid of being interrupted. The Order could not know that I was coming.

He looked up at me with fear in his eyes. I might have pitied him and stayed my cruelty if I could not feel the *darkness* within him. That alone was evidence that he had done horrific things to people, to children, to families.

His sin had found him out.

"Are you him?" he asked me.

"What?"

"Are you him?" he asked again. His voice was little more than a whisper.

"Who do you think I am?" I asked.

"The man from America. The one that was left behind years ago. He said you'd come."

"Who said?"

"Our Dark Master said so. He said you would come. No one thought you were still alive. He did though. He said."

I gripped his collar and raised him to his feet. "Start over," I said. "My name is Jasper Gunne. I *am* from America. I'm here for you and your people. You will take me to the Order, and you will do it now."

"They'll kill me if I do," he said.

I stooped to whisper in his ear. "I'll kill you anyway, only I'll make it much slower and much more painful."

He swallowed and looked from side to side. No one was there to help him. And I could be wrong about this, but I swear that there were tears in his eyes.

"So, you'll take me to them?" I asked.

He nodded.

"Good."

I followed him out of the alley and into the street. He knew better than to try and run from me. I followed at a leisurely pace, no longer acting like an aged and worn-out vagabond. I was a hunter who had found my prey.

We went down another alley. And then another. The twists and turns in these strange passages through the old time-worn streets were enough to confuse anyone. I would probably not have made it to the lone house in the center of it all. Concealed by an illusion, I didn't see the house until I was standing before it. That was the magic of the Order though. That was what had kept them hidden in London for so long.

"Open it," I ordered the man who had brought me there. He obeyed and then led me inside.

And my hopes of revenge were dashed.

———— ◆ ————

THE HOUSE WAS EMPTY. Completely empty. The only thing left was a layer of dust on the mantle. No furniture remained. Indeed, the place had long been abandoned.

"What is this?" I asked, rounding on the man who had brought me this far. The surprised terror in his eyes told me what I needed to know. He did not realize that this house was empty.

"It was here. It was all here!" His voice was shaky as he began to weep.

"When was the last time that you were here?" I asked.

He thought for a moment and then said: "Six weeks ago."

I nodded. "Where else would they be? Where would the Order be?"

"I don't know," he said.

"Liar."

"I don't know!"

I put my hands on his head and started to squeeze his face. "Tell me," I said.

"I don't know!"

I snapped his neck then, immediately regretting it once he was dead. He had been my one and only lead. As his body dropped to the floor, landing with a soft thud on the wood, I wondered if I would find anyone else to interrogate. Someone had to know where the Order was hiding. Someone had to know.

I searched the house. The feeling of *darkness* was thick like smoke. Many bad things had happened in this house. Each room was as empty as the next. Each except one. I found a note pinned to the floor with a knife in one of the upstairs bedrooms. I removed the knife and took the note in my hands. After all these years, I still have this note. It is on my desk as I write this book. This is what it says:

> *Well, look who it is! I am sorry I cannot be there to greet you, Jasper. I understand that you are likely confused and also very angry. You were so angry the last time we saw one another. I want you to know that I am well, and I am traveling! We will meet soon. Count on it.*

But not in London. No. I have other plans for my people. I am across the ocean now. Back on the old task assigned by my dear old father. I look forward to meeting you. Don't bother searching for me. You'll never find me. We will only meet when I decide that we will meet.

Your eternal friend,
Thomas Riden

I remember my hands shaking as I read the words. I refused to believe them. It couldn't be Thomas Riden. It was 1819. Sixty-nine years after my family was dead. That would mean that Thomas was well over a hundred years old. Could he possibly still be alive? Could he be healthy enough to travel? It didn't make sense to me. No. It was a trick. A deception of the Order. They figured out who I was, and they were trying to frighten me.

And damn them, it almost worked.

The Order was sure to have records that anyone could have used to figure out who I was. The records would likely have talked of Thomas Riden's friendship with me. I was a sort of abomination in their eyes, and they wanted to be rid of me. They had left a note to tell me they knew who I was, and they had written the deception to frighten me. It was the only explanation that made sense.

But they would not succeed in frightening me.

I would not stop. I read over the note again and then folded it and put it in my pocket. They would not meet me until they were ready? We would see about that. I wondered if they were trying to make me leave London. Perhaps they had not gone to America at all. I thought that was false though. I was drawn back to the United States. I could feel it. They were in the New World.

I'd come all this way for nothing.

2017

"THAT WAS ANTICLIMACTIC," Calista Valen said when she had finished reading what Jasper had written.

"Sometimes that's how life is," Jasper said. "You plan for things. You dream of them. You want them so badly you can almost taste them. Then, nothing happens."

"It seemed a bit soon for you to take them on," she replied. "The massacre happened in 1870, right? There's still fifty-one years to go."

Jasper nodded. "I encountered this cult a few times in the decades leading up to the massacre, but I never had a major confrontation with them again after the night I killed so many in Ohio. Not until Ravenwood in 1870, that is."

"But somehow you ended up back with *Amazing Wonders*?"

"I did," Jasper said.

"How?"

"Wait until I get to that part," he said.

Calista sighed and stood up. She paced around the room as she went over the manuscript again. She had fallen into the story and now she would not be able to get out until it was done. She hadn't wanted to be drawn in this way. It was supposed to be a side-project that she could work on out of curiosity more than anything else. Now she was nearly obsessed. Her other projects were neglected, including the third volume in her *Vagabond* trilogy. Her agent was filling her voicemail box with messages asking about the progress on what was sure to be her biggest seller, and all Calista Valen could do was read and reread the pages of the story of Jasper Gunne.

She happened to glance up from the pages, and when she did, she saw into his bedroom. The headboard was broken in half and the nightstand was in pieces.

"Jasper," she said, "are you okay?" When he looked up, she indicated the half-destroyed bedroom.

"Bad dreams," he said. "They're coming more and more frequently. Digging up old ghosts and all of that."

"This book has been really bad for you," she said.

"I know," Jasper said. "It gets a whole lot worse too. Then there's another I think I want to write."

"Another?"

"There's more to the story than just the massacre," Jasper said. "Calvin Valen and I had many more encounters with the cult leading up to the turn of the century. There were more encounters even after that. I just had my latest encounter with them a few days before I started writing this story. The massacre isn't really the end of the tale. It's almost like it's the beginning."

"I remember you saying they were still around."

"They're everywhere and nowhere," Jasper said. "Even now I can feel them. The *darkness*. I can't find the real ones though. The splinter groups. I take them on and kill them with ease. The real cult though. The real Order. No. They know how to hide from me. And no one believes me when I try to talk about it either. If the governments of the world would understand the danger that everyone is in while the Order exists, they would put all their resources into hunting them down. But they're deceived. That's the real trick of Valayra. I fear once the Order shows itself to the world, it will be too late."

"So that's the real reason you are writing," Calista said.

Jasper nodded. "At first it was because I saw some bullshit on TV about the Monster of Ravenwood and I wanted to set the record straight, even if no one believed me. Then I decided to try to write it all down. At least as much as I could. There is an evil out there, and it's getting stronger. Someday it will make itself known, and then the world will need all the prayers it wastes on lottery tickets and football games."

Soon Calista was gone, and Jasper was able to once again sit down and work on the story that he had been trying to tell. The nightmares were getting worse, it was true, and he assumed sleep might cease altogether before he was finished telling about the massacre.

How strange it was. He hadn't even gotten to the massacre yet. It was still decades away. The time that he regarded as the first half of his immortal life was spent in wandering confusion. The second half wasn't much better, but at least he had purpose and direction.

The computer screen was glowing. Jasper sat staring at the last words he had typed the night before. He swallowed the shot of whiskey he had in his hand and then poured another one. His fingers began to press the keys, and soon he was back in the nineteenth century, returning to the United States from his failed crusade in Europe.

1820

B Y THE TIME I returned to the States a year had passed, and the leaders of the Order could have been anywhere in the world. I had believed that they had come back to this country though. I cannot tell you why. Perhaps I had been wrong. Maybe they had fled to India or to Africa or Russia. They might have scattered and been in all of those places. It didn't really matter if they did. I had all the time in the world to find and kill them. It would be a slow process. I was resigned to this. But in the end, the cult would be extinct, and I would still be standing. I had to recognize the horrific fact that many innocent people would be killed before I could get rid of the Order. That was life though. No life in history has ever been saved. Death has only been postponed. Even I have the hope of one day dying. If what the Christians say is correct, the earth will one day be destroyed and new one created. Perhaps the Lord will allow me to stay on the doomed earth and so be blessed with the one thing I truly desire: oblivion.

I travelled the country like I did before, as a homeless vaga- bond. I talked with few people and did nothing but beg for money to buy alcohol. I hunted my food in the woods and wrapped myself in deerskins for warmth. I was alone, and that was how I liked it.

The words of Melvin Valen came to me time and again. I remember him saying he had known I would be in that clearing before he had arrived. It was as if someone had told him to come and get me and give me a home and family. It was all so ridiculous, of course. Where was that guiding voice when it came time to save my family? Where was that guiding voice when the show's people were kidnapped and Clara was murdered? No. There was no guiding voice. Back then, I thought that Melvin Valen simply had twisted his own memories into fiction and then believed them.

Even though I was content to be by myself again, I still tried to keep tabs on the show. I would look through newspapers and hope to see advertisements for *Amazing Wonders*. I remembered the scheduled stops and knew that they would not be in the northern states until the summer. I wanted to see my friends again, but I did not dare put them in danger. It was far better for them if I was not around. It was far better for everyone.

I was alone.

But then something happened that made me question my own conclusions regarding the guiding voice. I had thought that *Amazing Wonders* was somewhere in the south. I happened to be in Indiana in the fall of 1820, and I saw a poster on the door of the local saloon. *Amazing Wonders* would arrive within a week.

The show was coming to that small town in the middle of Indiana. I couldn't believe it. This was the time of year when they toured the southern states. It had been that way since I joined them. Would Richard Valen have made such a drastic change? It didn't seem like him. Maybe I was wrong. Of course I was wrong! They were coming. My friends would be there within a week.

It seemed like a lifetime since I had seen them, though it had only been just over a year. As I read the poster again and again I began to feel my own deep loneliness. I had been able to keep it buried, but now I longed to see the entire cast and crew of the show once again. I wanted to see my friends.

I returned to my small shelter in the woods that night and sat in silence as I felt for the *darkness*. It did not feel as if it were nearby. If I stayed here for a week I wouldn't endanger any of my friends. My enemies were far away.

And so it was decided. I would stay and wait for *Amazing Wonders*. I would have my reunion.

SLEEP DID NOT COME easily for me that night. I remember having the worst headache I had ever had. I tossed and turned until I slipped into sleep.

And then I wished I hadn't.

The dream that came to me woke me as soon as it was over, and I found myself drenched in sweat on that cold winter night. The images of the dream were vivid in my memory. All these years later I can still recall them.

Amazing Wonders was burning. Black cloaks were walking among the torched wagons demanding to know where I was. My friends were begging and pleading, but they were murdered anyway.

"Where is he?" I heard the soft yet menacing voice of Thomas Riden asked. "Where is my old friend?"

And then there were screams.

The screams were coming from me. I woke soaked in sweat. *What was that? What happened?* The dream was nothing but a fragmented mess for a few moments, but then, slowly, the entire vision I'd had pieced itself together.

The Order would always be looking for me. They knew of me because of what I had done with *Amazing Wonders*. Of course, some of the stories would have spread across the country and even across the world. I was an unnatural creature. I had done unnatural things in the name of protecting my friends. The Order had realized that I was with the show. I had confirmed that by brutally killing those they had sent to find me. I would have gladly killed any of them that I came across. That was another problem though. I hadn't come across any others since the one in London.

They were going to come after my friends. They were in even more danger since I was no longer there to protect them. They would be vulnerable. They would be helpless.

I am an idiot!

Clarity is a strange thing. When you finally see the stupidity of the things you've been doing and you see the correct course of action, you can't help but wonder at how blind you had been before that moment.

I stayed awake the rest of the night thinking about the dream. It was more than a dream. It was a vision. I believed it to have been similar to the one Melvin Valen had had before finding me. There were forces at work that I did not understand. I didn't want to believe in them, but I knew they existed. They were arranging the things that were about to happen like one arranges pieces on a chessboard.

The moves were ready to be made.

———◆———

IT WAS WITH GREAT relief that I met Richard Valen the next week. I watched as the caravan made its way along the trail nearing the town. I watched as the performers and helpers went to work putting up the camp and setting the stage.

It seemed like it had been so long. Much longer than the year and a half that I had been away. I'd been such a fool. How could I have left them behind? How could I have thought they'd be safer without me? They were marked now. Marked because of me. That made them my responsibility. I had to protect them.

I walked into the camp with my coat wrapped around me and my hat shadowing my face. Few bothered to even notice me. There were always curious people who came around the camp as it was being set up.

"I see not much has changed," I said when I saw Richard Valen. My old friend had been facing the other way with a sheet of paper in his hand. If I knew Richard the paper was the plan for the show that would be put on either that night or the next. Always working, Richard Valen was. He had been talking to a man and a woman when I had spoken, and as soon as the words had left my mouth, Richard stopped, turned and smiled.

I removed my hat and spread my arms. We walked toward one another and embraced.

"What are you doing?" Richard asked. "I thought you had to leave us. I thought it was too dangerous."

"Let's have a drink and I'll explain it all," I said.

Richard nodded. He didn't need to be there supervising his people. They all knew how to set up camp and how to set up the stage. I knew that Richard would have some good whiskey tucked away. He led me to his personal supply at the back of the main wagon. We each had a wooden cup that we drank from. Together, we shared the whole bottle, talking, laughing and reminiscing. I told him all about my travels to Europe and about the dream vision I'd had. He listened to every word I said. He didn't blame me for the show being a target. He never did. None of the Valens ever blamed me. I was at fault though. Richard didn't see it that way. Neither did Calvin years later.

"It's good you're back," Richard drunkenly slurred. "We can use you. Those things try to get us, you'll kill them. That's your job." He belched.

"And I'll enjoy it too," I said. I felt guilty because I was not there just to protect them. It wasn't the prospect of having my surrogate family back or being around friends again either. I was hoping the Order would try something. I was hoping I would get to kill. I felt as if I were using my friends as bait. There was no way around it though. They were in danger whether I was with them or not.

I just had to wait for the Order to make its move.

———◦———

LOOKING BACK, I THINK of the time when Richard was in charge as the "golden age" of *Amazing Wonders*. We all had our pockets full of money, though we all had to work harder at what we did to get that money.

I locked back into the job I was doing before I'd left the show. There had been others hired as security to replace me. Two men. I came back and suddenly they were both worried for their jobs. They'd heard of me and the stories of the things I was supposedly able to do.

They needn't have worried. Tasks were reassigned, but their money stayed the same. I was paid less than when I had left, but the only thing I asked for was a place to sleep and some money for food and whiskey. Richard gave it, and later, when the show was doing better than ever, I was making more than ever. Richard Valen was not a greedy businessman. He was just ambitious. He would drive his people to excellence, and he would make great profits. Then he would share the profit equally. He was a good man.

As we travelled the country, I kept feeling for the *darkness*. Sometimes I could sense it drawing closer. Other times, it was far away. I can always feel it. Even now, as I write this book, I feel the *darkness* out there. It's how I know my work is not yet done.

And still, as we travelled, I did not come across anyone from the Order. The weeks became months, and then they became years. Nothing. I didn't know how to find them. I didn't know where to look.

And then the years became decades.

2017

THE OLD POSTER OF *Amazing Wonders* was in Jasper Gunne's hand after he'd finished with the last bit of writing for the day. So many memories. No one knew about *Amazing Wonders* anymore. Not since the show was stopped once and for all after the massacre in Ravenwood.

It was my life, Jasper thought as he traced the letters with his finger. He remembered more often than not, the show not going well. In fact, one could say that it sucked. There were always problems. And most problems were never resolved. The actors would forget their lines. The juggler would drunkenly drop whatever he was juggling. The musicians would play the wrong music to the wrong lyrics. Many nights they were booed off the stage. But they had always done the best that they could. Jasper probably could have filled the seats if they had showcased his abilities. He had never been comfortable with that idea though, and none of the Valens ever pushed for it.

Jasper decided to clear his head by going for a cup of coffee that morning. He walked through Ravenwood on that chilly morning, looking once more upon the streets and buildings that had been built over the ruined ghost town of the first Ravenwood.

There was a diner/grocery store two miles from Jasper's apartment building. He went inside and found a stool by the counter. The waitress – a big woman with a head full of curly black hair – poured his coffee without even asking if he wanted it.

"What'll you have, dear?" she asked.

Jasper blinked at her and then picked up the menu. He scanned the items available for a moment and decided. "Spinach and feta cheese omelet."

"Sounds good," she said. "Anything else?"

"Some hash browns and a cup of sausage gravy."

"Coming up," she said.

Jasper sipped his coffee black and stared at the mirror in front of him. The corner television was reflected in it, and as Jasper watched he realized from the backward letters of the news story that the events of that night in Stetson, Michigan were being discussed.

Jasper turned and looked at the television set with eyes narrowed. "Could we turn that up?" he asked the waitress behind the counter.

"Sure, hun," she said. She took the remote from a drawer on her side of the counter and turned up the volume.

Jasper stared at the television and took in the words that were being spoken. The corpses left behind after he had broken up the ring of ritualistic sacrifice were being described as victims. Not one time did anyone mention the children that he had saved. Why should it bother him as much as it did? This had been the way of the world since he started attracting attention. It was as if the world didn't want to know about Valayra and her followers. He had been fighting this war on his own for a century and a half, and aside from those he had directly influenced, no one except for the Order knew that Jasper Gunne existed.

Which made things difficult when the law would catch up with him. That happened sometimes. Jasper was reluctant to injure any normal person. He would play along so as not to endanger the lives of the police officers who were doing their job. Then, when he knew he could get away without hurting anyone, he would escape.

The law might come nosing around soon enough if what the report said was true. A manhunt was underway for someone described in a way that resembled Jasper Gunne.

Jasper finished his breakfast and paid his check. He then returned to his apartment and began writing once again. There was a sense of urgency now. Time was short.

1857–1867

R ICHARD VALEN PASSED AWAY at the age of fifty-nine. It was not because of bad health. He sometimes seemed even stronger than me. It was because of his damned horse. He was thrown by the animal, and his head smashed against the rocks on the road. It was a sudden and cruel fate. No one could have helped my friend. I remember turning him over and knowing immediately that he was dead. The year was 1857.

Unlike his father, Richard was not buried on the road. The Valen family that was not part of *Amazing Wonders* had set up a home in Ravenwood, Michigan. Richard's body was sent there. I, along with a few others in the show accompanied the body. It was my first time in Ravenwood.

The town was small then. Smaller than it is now and smaller than it was in 1870. We didn't stay long. I listened to the local reverend perform the funeral ceremony, then I and the other workers from the show headed to Chicago where we met up with our colleagues.

The show must go on.

RICHARD'S SON, EDGAR, took control for a while, though he left after a year of running *Amazing Wonders*. Back then I said good riddance and even today I look back and say good riddance. It was not that the boy was a bad kid or anything. He didn't know the business, and he was running it into the ground. His cousin, who was the same age as he, convinced him to step aside. Edgar did so without much of an argument. He went home.

The cousin was named Calvin. He was twenty-two years old when he took over in 1858. Calvin was the man who I think of as my truest friend throughout time. He might not have been the best at running the attractions, but he was better than his cousin Edgar. I remembered him as a small child, Melvin's grandson, who wanted to see what it was like on the road. His mother had reluctantly agreed to let us take him for a summer when he was five. Then it happened a few more times as he was growing, and it wasn't until he was sixteen that he professed his desire to carry on in his grandfather's footsteps, much to the dismay of his parents. The boy had been a son of John Valen, brother to Richard and uncle to Edgar.

I told few people about what had happened to me in 1750. I had told Penelope. I had told Melvin and Richard. I kept it from others though. It wasn't a matter of keeping a secret. I just didn't want to talk about it, and I found myself not getting close enough to anyone to talk about my darkest days. Calvin had become my friend though, and so I told him what had happened to me, and over the next few years he got to know me as I really am. A quiet, powerful, vengeful, possibly evil drunk.

The drinking had increased again in those days. For a time I had been sober and that had actually led to me enjoying things more. But the addiction was too strong and the memories I was trying to escape were too horrible. For all of my strength that I received as a result of the black magic I was exposed to in that barn, I have never had the willpower for self control. What I truly needed was to take my aggression out on something or someone. The drinking merely buried my anger, but I longed to release it.

An opportunity presented itself.

IT WAS 1863 AND the Civil War was raging across the states. We were still traveling the country, stopping wherever we were scheduled and offering a show for anyone who would come to see us. Security had increased because of the war. There were not only bands of soldiers who could make trouble for us, there were also outlaws who had become bolder since the war's outbreak.

There was one gang that tried to steal from us that year. Ever since I had joined *Amazing Wonders* there had been criminals who tried to harm someone in the group or steal our money. I dealt with them much like Penelope and I had dealt with the would-be rapists in Philadelphia so long ago. I wouldn't kill them all. Some I would break or maim and leave on the side of the road. They were to tell the story that *Amazing Wonders* was protected. A sort of legend began to grow around our show. People eventually stopped harassing us. The few stupid enough to try learned why the stories existed in the first place. I always enjoyed myself, but the encounters were all quick and separated by years. In 1863 it had been six years since the last thief tried to rob our earnings from a night's show. That had been fun for me. The thief wore a handkerchief around his mouth and a large black hat on his head. His hand was firmly gripped on a pistol, and he was snarling his demand that all the cash from the drawer be put into a sack and handed to him.

"Problem, sir?" I asked, stepping behind him so quietly that he did not know I was there until I spoke. He spun and fired his gun. The shot hit me in the stomach and left a nasty welt. I took the gun from him, slammed it across his skull, then handed it to our ticket seller. "For protection," I said. We threw the unconscious man in the woods and never heard from him again.

1863 was the year of the Draven Gang. That would be an encounter that would get me ever closer to the massacre. Looking back I see all the correlations throughout my life and the eventuality of what had happened in Ravenwood.

The outlaws were not sloppy. They waited until we were away from the populated cities and alone with nothing but fields on either side of the road. It had been a way we had traveled before and each time I had always paid extra attention to all the sounds I heard for I knew we were vulnerable there. We had crossed into Indiana and were tired from the long journey. There was a plan to stop and make camp that I protested.

"We need to stop, Jasper," Calvin said. "We are all tired."

"No," I said. "This is a bad idea. It's a bad place."

"So you want to travel for another day?" he asked. "That's how far we are from anything. At our speed we are a day away."

"Damn," I said. I knew he was right. We couldn't keep going like this without rest. I sometimes forgot that others were still bound to the normality of being human. I don't say that out of arrogance. I wish I was still human. I wish I was a skeleton in the ground next to my family. I wish I had never lived past that night in the barn in 1750.

Tents were put up. They were not the show tents. Those stayed in the wagons. These were simple sleeping tents. Three people to each. When they were all set up we seemed to have a small village made up of nothing but tents, and we were in a most vulnerable position for any band of outlaws who might want to try and take what we had.

Calvin wasn't concerned, and that was undoubtedly the foolishness of youth. No one had bothered us in years. He had confidence in the legend of the show's protector and that it would keep anyone from trying anything against us. I was not so sure, and so while everyone slept, I kept watch.

And it is a good thing that I did.

The eyes of the outlaws were on us as we made camp. They could've attacked then, but they waited for the cover of darkness. As soon as night fell our enemies advanced, but I was the only one who noticed.

While my colleagues and companions and friends dozed, resting from their long day of travelling, a band of robbers emerged from the woods. I heard them and looked in their direction to see a line of torches racing towards us, and I knew right then that trouble had come. The outlaws galloped toward us, pushing their horses faster and faster and waving their torches. They whooped and yelled as they drew nearer, and the commotion woke the sleepers.

"Outlaws!" I yelled. Then, as the panicking members of *Amazing Wonders* stirred themselves from their tents, I prepared to deal with our foes head-on.

There were twelve, and they all followed one small man with a hat that seemed almost too big for his head. His silhouette stood out prominently in the dark, shaped by the torchlight. He was not whooping like the others. He was bellowing orders.

"Take what you can! Kill anyone who gets in the goddamn way!"

He saw me, dropped his torch and he drew his pistol. I stood my ground, but I braced myself for the pain that always came from being shot. The bullets exploded out of his gun, and I felt the hot metal bounce off of my body. There would be welts. I was already moving, and when he saw that his shots hadn't dropped me, he hurriedly tried to turn his horse away.

I leapt and drove my fist into his chest. The force of the punch was so strong that I felt his ribs break under my knuckles. He fell from his horse and landed on his back. I stomped his head once, and he was dead.

One down. Eleven to go.

Killing the leader turned out to be the best strategy for me to use because it enraged the other outlaws. "He killed Randal!" one of them yelled.

"And now I'll kill the rest of you!" I shouted back. "These people are protected! Leave now!"

"Told you," one of the outlaws said.

"Shut up, Bill." Some still had torches in their hands, but some had dropped their torches in favor of drawing their guns.

"Yeah, Bill. Don't buy into this shit. Asshole just got lucky."

"I don't think so. I heard about them. They have a guy who can do things normal people can't and he protects them."

I spoke then. "Bill seems to be the only one smart enough to survive this night. That is, of course, if he runs away like you all should do."

"Run?" one of them asked, cocking his gun. "Why would any of us run?" He then fired his gun. As the shots hit me, I acted as though I was being gunned down, though the pain I felt was not really any more than that of a bee sting. As he emptied his six-shooter into me, I fell to my knees and then on my back, pretending I was dead. It was all part of the deception. All part of the legend that I wanted to grow so that no one would try this again.

I heard the outlaws laugh. Then, as they advanced their horses beyond where I lay, I stood. "Going somewhere?" I asked.

They turned and looked at me.

I smiled.

The fight was quick and bloody. They kept their guns focused on me, perhaps believing that if they shot me enough times I would fall over dead. I charged at one of them, leapt, grabbed him by the throat and brought him down. I choked him to death as the bullets rained down on me. By the time I turned around to find my next victim, Calvin Valen and others from the caravan had joined the fight and were trying to pick off the outlaws without much success.

I loved Calvin like a brother and a son all at once, and I do not like to speak ill of him, but that man was not much of a marksman in those days. The shots went high and wide for the most part, but a few found their marks. A horse fell dead in front of me, and the rider screamed when I lifted him by the collar.

"Jasper Gunne," I said. "That's my name. I am going to let you live."

The other outlaws were scrambling to meet the defenders of the caravan. A few other bullets hit their mark and soon there were only six standing. They began to retreat, trying to make it to the safety of the woods.

"Tell people about me," I told the man who hung in my grasp. "*Amazing Wonders* is protected. Tell them that." I then set him on his feet. He looked relieved for an instant but only for an instant. The next thing I did made him scream.

I grabbed his arm, twisted it, and heard a snapping sound. Then I punched his hip as hard as I could, shattering it. He fell to the ground, crying in pain and unable to move from where he lay. I guessed he would be lying there until he either healed or someone happened to pass by and give him help.

The six remaining outlaws were racing back to the woods, and I followed them. I caught up with the two who were the furthest behind. I leapt onto the back of one of the horses, pulled the rider off with me, snapped his neck once we had landed, then took a knife from his belt and threw it toward the other rider who had been stupid enough to stop and watch me kill his friend. He must have thought he could've done something to stop it, but by the time he realized he could do nothing it was too late.

The knife handle was what hit him instead of the blade, and that annoyed me. I have since become better with weapons, but back then I wasn't much good with them. He did fall off of his horse and slam his head on a rock, so I killed him after all, just not in the way I intended.

Out of the twelve outlaws who had attacked us, seven were dead, one was moaning in pain, and four had escaped. No one from *Amazing Wonders* had been hurt though. It was a victory. It was the last real victory that I ever had with that group because seven years later, our darkest moments came.

But on that night in 1863, I was a hero, and it felt damn good.

———◦———

THE TALE TOLD BY the outlaws preceded us wherever we went after that night in 1863. I had wanted outlaws and bandits to fear attacking us, but I had made everyone else afraid to come to the show at all. It was said that *Amazing Wonders* was guarded by some unholy creature that delighted in making people suffer. We would be in towns and no one would come. Later, I would sit in the taverns and pubs with Calvin, and we would overhear people talking about the show and how they wouldn't go to it because they were afraid that the demon who guards it would hurt someone just for fun. I had wanted a story to spread to protect my friends in the show, but I had probably cost them their livelihood.

The problem was getting worse. Some larger cities would give us a bigger turnout, but most of the stops had less than half our seats filled. Sometimes no one came at all. No customers, no tickets purchased, no income, no payment for anyone.

And it was all my fault.

Calvin, friend that he was, would not hear of me saying that I felt guilty. He told me what I did was necessary and that this was just a slump. I thought of leaving a few times, but Calvin convinced me that the rumors were the rumors, and they would continue to spread whether I was there or not. And he didn't want to leave the show unprotected.

But our luck changed one day in 1866. A horrible thing had happened to the small town of Hamlin, Tennessee. Horrible as it was, what happened next brought us back into the good graces of the public.

We had set up camp for the week, not knowing how we were going to provide for all of the workers. Our food was low, and our alcohol was nothing but a memory. I hadn't had a drink in over a month, and I was beginning to feel my memories creeping back into my mind. But then, when all seemed lost, we found ourselves in the right place at the right time.

It was four years before the massacre in Ravenwood.

IT IS AN AWFUL THING to kidnap a child and an even more heinous thing to kill that child when the ransom demand is paid as agreed. That is exactly what happened to the son of Henry L. Whinton. He was a prominent landowner who had discovered his seven-year-old son's bed empty with a note left stuck in the mattress with a knife.

The note demanded ten thousand dollars cash for the return of Mr. Whinton's son, Caleb. The instructions for dropping off the money were attached to the note, and Whinton obeyed. Three days later he was delivered the corpse of his son. The kidnappers had killed him the night he was abducted.

The shock settled over the town. Hamlin had never known violence of that kind. I remember a sense of innocence among the locals. Most couldn't understand how it happened because they didn't realize that anything like that could happen. Sure, there were stories of such horrible things that happened all over the country and all over the world, but they had never happened in Hamlin.

That was before Joseph Conrad and his brothers, James and Jeremiah. They were not from Hamlin. We learned that from Sheriff Truman after the ordeal was over. They had lived out west for some time and had become outlaws. They had cut a bloody path along the states, murdering anyone in their way and killing if there was even a chance for profit.

The investigation into the death of Henry L. Whinton's son was as thorough as one might expect. He was the wealthiest man in the town, and it seemed to the locals that if someone as untouchable as him could be a victim then anyone could be a victim. I never really thought of it that way though. I thought his wealth and prominence had made him a target for the Conrad Brothers. They had seen the town as a simple little place where everyone knew everyone. Neighbors were friendly and welcoming of outsiders. It had seemed that everyone there was ignorant to the dangers of the world. Hamlin was the perfect hunting ground and Whinton was the perfect prey.

I had a little money on me the day we arrived in Hamlin so I invited Calvin for a drink. "We need it," I said. "So let's go."

He didn't argue with me as I spent the last of my savings on two glasses of whiskey. There were other patrons in the bar, but they were quiet and kept to themselves. A hush had fallen over the community since the murder of the Whinton boy. The barmaid told us the whole story.

"Not to sound like an ass," Calvin said after the barmaid had moved to the other end of the bar, "but we picked a horrible time to come to this town. No one will buy a ticket to our show after what we just heard." He looked around the bar then. Three men were playing cards, but they weren't gambling. An older gentlemen was sipping on a drink in the corner. Two women were sitting in chairs next to the small fire that was keeping the tavern warm. Few words were spoken by any of them, and I got the feeling that the mood of the bar was reflective of the mood of the town. "Fun is the last thing on these folks' minds."

"Maybe," I said as I tipped the glass up and finished what I thought would be my last drink for a long time.

"Sheriff Truman arrested one of the killers," the barmaid said. She was a big middle-aged woman with streaks of grey in her thick black hair.

"Only one?" Calvin asked.

"Got the only one who lived. He's having his court date today. He had two brothers who were in on it too, so they say. Sheriff and his deputies gunned them down but took the last one alive. Guess he had no more fight left in him, not that turning himself in will do much good. I think we'll see him swinging from one of these trees before the end of the week. We'd better."

People are bloodthirsty by nature. That is a truth I have learned in my long life. When a crime is committed, people are eager to watch the criminal suffer for it. It's almost as if they are glad the crime happened, for they are able to indulge in their dark bloodthirsty side without guilt weighing down their conscience.

Calvin finished his drink, and we left the tavern. I sit here trying to remember the name of that place, but I am afraid it will forever elude me. Not that it matters. I've been to that area a few times since 1866 and everything that had once been standing in Hamlin is long gone and replaced. Hell, most of what they replaced it with has itself been replaced. Immortality. You see changes you would never have believed possible if you live long enough.

We walked back to the campsite, careful to avoid the puddles on the ground wet from the rain the night before. The chill in the air made me wish I had brought a coat with me. If the temperature was bothering me, Calvin must have been freezing. The morning had seemed warm enough, but by the time we left the tavern the clouds had gathered and grown dark, the temperature had dropped and the wind had begun to blow.

"We should get back soon," I said. "Storm's coming."

"Really?" Calvin asked with a sarcastic tone of voice. "I never would have known."

It was midday when the lightning bolt cracked across the sky. A rumble of thunder followed. By the time we had left Hamlin our clothes were soaked, and we were lightly running back to the camp which was still a hundred yards away.

A gunshot.

Our heads spun in the direction of the sound as we heard two more. There was a cry of frightened horses and another gunshot. And then we saw the horse and the rider. He was fleeing a mob of angry people, some of whom were on horses themselves.

"Jasper," Calvin said.

"Let's get out of here," I said. By that, I had meant getting back to the campsite and letting whatever local disruption this was play out without getting involved. I had an idea that the fleeing man was the killer that the law had caught.

It turned out I was right. Joseph Conrad, outlaw and child murderer, had escaped custody.

We ran faster. I could have been back to the camp by then, but I was running slower to stay with Calvin. I remember the feeling of the mud beneath my boots as Calvin and I got closer and closer to our people. The footfalls of the horse behind us grew louder so I turned and saw that the bastard was headed straight for us. I grabbed Calvin by the shoulders and pulled him out of the way as the man's horse ran past us. I don't think he had been trying to run us down. We were just in his way.

The other horsemen stopped beside us. One of them helped me to my feet while another one helped Calvin. We stood there drenched and cold, our clothes stained by the wet grass. Calvin was breathing heavily, but I was unaffected by the running.

"Who was that?" Calvin asked of no one in particular.

"I think it was the killer," I said. I looked at one of the horsemen. He was a tall man who sat soundly upon his horse with a pistol on each hip and a star badge on his chest. "Am I right?"

"Joseph Conrad," Sheriff Truman said in a gruff voice that one would associate with a man who had spent a lifetime smoking. "He was to be in court today. We were gonna hang him too."

"He's the one who killed the boy?"

"One of them. There were three killers, and he was the one who survived when we went to arrest them."

"Jasper," Calvin said.

"What?"

"He went to our camp. He stopped there."

"I see that," I said.

"He's a dangerous man," the sheriff said. "You have a lot of people in there?"

"Yes," I said. Then I shook my head. "I'm going to get him now."

"Where do you think you're going?" the sheriff asked.

"Sorry," I said. "Truman, is it? I am going to protect my people."

"Son, this is a dangerous thing you're thinking of doing. He's armed and dangerous. Killed one of my deputies back by the courthouse when he escaped. Still don't know how the bastard managed that, but he has a gun. Five shots left too if the gun was fully loaded when he took it."

"I am going to stop him before he can hurt any of my people," I said, speaking slowly as if I were talking to a simpleton.

He trotted his horse a few steps and then glared down at me. The lightning struck in the sky behind him, giving him an ominous and imposing appearance. I have seen western movies over the years, and I tell you now that Sheriff Truman looked like a true hero of the west by the way he was sitting on that horse. All he was missing was the hat which had probably blown away when he had gone after Conrad. "You go in there," he said, "and you endanger your life and everyone else's. Let me and my men handle him."

"You've done a great fucking job so far," I said. Then I ran. This time I wasn't jogging like I had been as Calvin and I made our way back to the camp. I was running at what may have been my full speed. I heard the sheriff shout and Calvin called my name, but I was not going to bother listening to what they had to say. Some murdering bastard was among my friends, my family, and I was going to protect them.

As I ran I started to get careless and stepped on a rock that would have twisted my ankle had I been a normal man. All it did was make me slip and fall on my backside. I admit that it was embarrassing, but I had to ignore it, get up, and, without looking back, continue into the camp.

It was not a large site. There were a few wagons and a bunch of tents set up. The show's workers were each in their tents, trying to stay warm and dry which was difficult considering the material the tents were made of.

I looked down the road from where we had made our camp and saw Joseph Conrad's stolen horse walking without a rider. He was in the camp then, and he either meant to stay, or he meant to steal a different horse.

I searched the tents, opening them and speaking with the workers. No one seemed to have seen the man though they had heard someone come and had thought it was either Calvin or me. I kept looking and found the killer lying in the back of a wagon. He was not doing much to conceal himself. Actually he was moaning in pain. I looked in and saw him lying down with his hand on his leg. A gun was in his other hand.

"Get out," I said.

He looked at me and stopped groaning. "What did you say?" he spat. "You don't order me to do nothing." He waved his gun at me. "I need someone to wrap this," he said, indicating his leg. "Got shot while getting away. Hurts real bad."

"It's about to hurt a lot worse," I said.

I grabbed his ankle and dragged him out of the wagon. He screamed in pain and that brought every worker out of their tents. I dropped him on the muddy ground where he landed with a grunt and a plop. He then raised his pistol and unloaded his last five shots into me.

Bastard.

I hate being shot. I know that I have nothing to complain about since bullets can't kill me. It still hurts, and it leaves welts that sometimes bleed. When his bullets were spent I grabbed him by the neck and carried him back to Sheriff Truman who was now sitting just a few yards from our tents and wagons.

"Lose something?" I asked.

"I'll be damned," the sheriff said. "I saw that. I saw that whole thing from here. He shot you. Five times."

"It's complicated," I said.

"I'll say," the sheriff said. He called to one of his deputies then. "Tie this shit stain to the back of my horse. I'm going to pull him back to town."

"I think he was shot in the leg," I said. "Probably won't be able to walk for long."

"He don't need to walk," Sheriff Truman said.

I dropped Joseph Conrad in the mud for the second time that day. The sheriff then bent over him. "Do you have no remorse, boy?" he asked.

Conrad spit in his face. "That's what I think of you," he said through gritted teeth. I could tell he was in excruciating pain, but he was trying to keep his calm in the face of his enemy. He spat again, that one missed the sheriff though. "That's what I think of Henry L. Whinton and his stupid boy. Screamed like a girl when he died." Conrad nodded, evidently enjoying his recollection of the event. "Screamed just like a little girl until I stuck him with my knife. So you and your law can fuck off! You killed my brothers!"

"Screamed like a girl?" I asked. He looked up at me. Though Sheriff Truman meant to hang him he didn't have the same fear of him as he had of me. Seeing me take five bullets made me seem more dangerous, I do not doubt. He was shaking as I put a foot on his gunshot wound in his right leg. I pushed down, and he lost his control and started screaming and crying. "Did he sound like that?" I asked in a conversational tone.

"Tie him to my horse," Sheriff Truman said. "Tie him by the neck. He's not going to make it back to his cell alive."

Joseph Conrad, thief and child killer was stood up though he hobbled on the spot. A noose was put around his neck and then tied to Sheriff Truman's saddle. Then the sheriff began urging his horse forward. The animal trotted slow enough, but Conrad could not keep up with his injured leg. He would fall, then the sheriff would stop, order him stood up again, then repeat it. This went on, the lawmen of Hamlin enjoying the humiliation of the man who had snuffed out the life of a young boy for no reason other than cruelty for the sake of cruelty. They were repaying that cruelty, and it did not bother any of us who watched the whole thing play out.

"Now!" Sheriff Truman called. "Back to the jail with this trash!" He kicked at his horse and the beast started running. The noose tightened around Joseph Conrad's neck as he was dragged through Hamlin. His execution was revolting, but I will honestly say to this day that I do not feel sorry for him. He was a cruel man who deserved to be treated just as cruelly. I was glad to see him dead.

That was a remarkable day for us. We had heard the story, encountered the killer by chance, helped apprehend him and sent him to his humiliating execution, and that had all occurred within the span of three hours. And it was only day one in Hamlin.

———◦———

THE STORM RAGED ON all day long so the stage wasn't set until the next day. When that day arrived we saw the largest crowd gathered for *Amazing Wonders* that we had seen in years. People were there to see us because word had traveled around that we had had a hand in catching the Whinton boy's killer. Sheriff Truman and his deputies even managed to make it to the show that week. Money was once again pouring in, and our viewers were too many for our seats.

The success we were having in Hamlin made Calvin decide to stay in town an extra week. Things started to slow down by the end of that second week, and when that last show was over, we feasted and drank until sunrise.

Sheriff Andy Truman and I became sort of friends during that time. He apologized for trying to stop me from taking on Conrad on my own and thanked me for my help. He also asked about my ability to take bullets like I did, but I did not tell him then. We met years later and that was when I confided in him, but back in 1866 the only one who knew what had created me was Calvin.

When we left Hamlin, we had friends who would love to see our show again if we could ever get back out that way. But what lay ahead of us was even better. The story of Conrad sneaking into the camp and then being taken down and turned over to the authorities was growing and evolving in a way that we couldn't have foreseen. By the time we had gotten to our next stop the story was that he had taken the camp hostage and owner Calvin Valen and his bodyguard Jasper Gunne had taken Conrad out and delivered the body to poor old Henry L. Whinton who had wept and thanked them for bringing his son's killer to justice. Strange how stories grow. I know the absurdity of how they change over time. The stories I hear about the Monster of Ravenwood are so far from the truth that I cannot even guess as to how they came to be.

For a time, I felt pride. For a time, I was happy with all the attention the show was getting. People were lining up to buy tickets and filling our seats. It was good to be successful again.

But there were others who noticed us, and they were watching. My enemies were still around. They were still waiting in the shadows. After all this time, their silence was about to break.

1867

I T WAS A YEAR after the incident in Hamlin when I began to notice the *darkness* was growing. We were holding a show in Philadelphia when I first noticed it. That night was the first time we had been in that city in over a decade, and we were enjoying the sold-out audience and the high profits that had become the norm for us.

On the first night of our week in Philadelphia we were swarmed with people who were telling us how great an event it was and how much they had enjoyed the show. I kept a watchful eye on all of it, looking for anyone who might be dangerous. Calvin was gracious with the audience, and he loved talking to all of the people who would give him compliments, helpful suggestions or even criticism. There were also those who wanted to join the show. They were people who were either talented or who thought they had a talent. They would pitch Calvin their idea for an act starring themselves and they almost always went away bewildered that the man who ran *Amazing Wonders* was not interested in what they could do.

The final night of shows in Philadelphia arrived. That was a special night for *Amazing Wonders*. The acts were as spectacular in rehearsal as they were during the actual show. The audience was captivated. Everything seemed perfect.

At the end of the show Calvin took the stage.

"Hello, Philadelphia!" he shouted, making sure everyone could hear him.

The reply he received was applause.

"My name is Calvin Valen and this here show has been in my family for generations. I remember... I remember stories my uncle told me of the beginning. Back when *Amazing Wonders* was just a magician and a juggling act, and it didn't even have a proper name. We've come a long way since then. And here we are, once more, in the great state of Pennsylvania!"

More applause. Calvin knew how to work his audience.

"I have been blessed to be a part of this group of fine entertainers. I have been blessed to be able to run such an amazing operation, and it could not happen without each and every one of them. And it definitely couldn't happen without all of you!"

The air filled with the sounds of clapping hands and the obnoxiously loud whistling with fingers which is something I have never mastered despite my powers and annoyingly long life.

"I have to thank all of you. Now, I have some announcements to make about the future of *Amazing Wonders*. My family is not from around here. My family, being in this business never really had a home to call their own, but the majority of my relatives are now living in Ravenwood, Michigan. I am moving the show to that town. We have made deals with the town, and we are going to set up a permanent location for *Amazing Wonders* there. This, tonight, was our final show on the road."

There was less clapping when he paused that time.

"And I can't thank you all enough for being the best audience we could ask for. We are going out on top and moving onto the next phase of this show's life, and I thank you all for giving us the grand finale of audiences. Thank you all! I love you! We love you! Thank you!"

The applause erupted once again, and there was more of that whistling. How do they do that? Centuries of life, and I still can't do it.

The crowd mostly cleared out, but there were those who stayed to offer Calvin critiques and advice. Many wanted him to open the permanent attraction for the show in Philadelphia instead of Ravenwood, but Calvin merely smiled and said that the deals were already made.

We had known his speech was coming as we had known about the Ravenwood deals for two months. Calvin merely needed to finish out his scheduled obligations.

Calvin had a table set up where he sat and talked with everyone who wanted a word with him. Many of our performers did this. Abigail, the pretty, young singer and dancer was there, surrounded by a group of young men. Johnny Lass, her male equivalent was likewise surrounded by women. Others like Ronco the Bronco (that was the name he chose), the show's strongman was talking with people next to Miraculous Mary, our show's magician. I kept an eye on all of them, even Ronco. You never knew what kinds of people these shows could attract.

All night long I had a sick feeling in my stomach. The *darkness*, which had always been there, was deepening. As I stood watch over my friends I began to feel uneasy. I pulled Calvin to the side and told him, but he ignored me. He was with his fans for one last time, and he was going to enjoy every last moment of it. I stayed silent the rest of the night, but all the while there was a familiar and unpleasant aura around us.

2017

"I WAS WONDERING WHEN the show was going to move to Ravenwood," Calista said, looking over the latest pieces of manuscript. "I didn't realize it was on the road for so long."

"We were never anything special," Jasper said. "Compared to other shows. Circuses. We were amateurish at best. But we were usually able to make a decent profit. That's all that really mattered."

"So you didn't have much time in Ravenwood before it all happened," Calista said.

"Not much time at all. Everything that led to the massacre was in motion before we even arrived."

Calista nodded. "Did you meet any of my other family when you came to Ravenwood?"

"Your other family didn't like Calvin too much. Some did, but mostly they thought he was a sinner for what was used in his shows. Girls in low-cut dresses. Magicians pretending to do magic. The Valens were... let's just say they were devout."

"You stayed away from them," she said.

"Yes. Calvin warned me, and I stayed away. I think there were a few that came to my hanging though."

The radio was playing the local news broadcast, but they were saying nothing about the murders in Stetson. Jasper grew tired of hearing about sports, weather, and the economy and turned it off.

"Why do you listen to that so much?" Calista asked. "Last three or four times I've been here you've had the radio on. You don't seem like a music lover."

"Keeping tabs," Jasper said. "I need to know if they're getting close."

"Who?"

"Anyone. The Order. The cops. I killed a small group of witches not fifty miles away from here. They could still find me. If that happens, I'll have to be on the move again. Pick up the book some other time."

A thought occurred to Calista then. "Jasper," she said, "can they feel you like you feel them?"

Jasper nodded. "Some of them. Now and then they will send out hunters to track me down and try to kill me. I always win, and they haven't tried in about forty years."

"So back in Ravenwood," she said, "they could feel you?"

"One of them could," Jasper said. "They'd been watching us for a while. Stalking us. That one though... he was my greatest enemy. He had such a mastery of his own sorcery. I thought there was a chance I might not beat him."

"Who was it?" Calista asked.

Jasper smiled. "You'll find out. I'll get back to work right away."

"So you're at the massacre now?" she asked with morbid fascination.

"Not yet," Jasper said. "Getting close though."

1867

"JASPER, I'M WORRIED ABOUT YOU," Calvin said the day we left Philadelphia. He and I were riding at the rear of the caravan. Calvin should have been closer to the front, but I had fallen behind to be alone with my thoughts and that had brought my friend to the back.

"Don't be," I said. "I'm fine."

"You were saying some strange things back in the city," he said.

I closed my eyes partly in annoyance and partly because the wind was making them dry. I had told Calvin my feeling that something was wrong, and I had explained what I had meant by it. Perhaps it was nothing. After all, a feeling was just a feeling, and I was surely just imagining things. That's what I was telling myself then. I know better now.

"Never mind," I said. "I'm okay. Trust me."

Calvin rode forward to speak with his other workers while I brooded. Despite what I told myself, I could not shake the feeling of *darkness* that was everywhere.

———◆———

TIME PASSED AND THE feeling never completely went away. I had gotten used to it though. I learned to live with it, just as I had for decades already. This feeling was more powerful than the one that seemed to be in every corner of the world, but I could do nothing about it. I stopped bringing it up to Calvin because it just made him worry. Of course, he would worry though. I was an immortal man with strange powers who was feeling something odd in the air. He probably thought I was cracking, and I think on some level I thought I was cracking too.

Audrey Lark, sister to our pretty singing blonde Abigail, was one who took real notice of the difference in me. She and I had been sleeping together for the past two months, and she was suddenly dealing with me rejecting her.

One night when the caravan had stopped to make camp, Audrey and I had a tent to ourselves. When she kissed me though, I was like a stone.

"What's your problem?" she asked, running her hand over my chest.

"No problem," I said. "I just want to be left alone." I talked in a low voice, and my tone was icy. I glanced at Audrey. She was the exact opposite of her sister. While Abigail was blonde, petite and meek, Audrey was a full-figured brunette who didn't know the meaning of the word meek.

"I'm sorry I asked," she said in reply to the cold way I had spoken to her.

"I can't talk about it," I said.

"You've told me a lot of things that you haven't told the others," she said. "Why can't you talk about this?"

I took a deep breath and looked into her big brown eyes. I opened my mouth for a second, and in that second, I was prepared to speak. Then I closed it again. She snorted and turned away from me.

"Don't be angry," I said without much conviction. Feeling the *darkness* again after all of this time had, in a way, thrown me back to that horrible winter morning in 1750. And also to 1819 when I had my second encounter with the Order. It was like everything that had happened since then no longer mattered.

She was wanting to start a fight with me. I know she was, but she decided on a more delicate approach. "Have you eaten anything?" she asked.

I shook my head.

She left the tent without another word. I had planned to stay awake all night to avoid the horrific nightmares that seemed to wait for me in my sleep. I didn't need sleep as much as a regular person anyway. I could stay awake and think. The thoughts that passed through my head were of leaving. I wanted to walk away from *Amazing Wonders* and search out the source of this *darkness*. I knew it was dangerous. The last time I ignored it, two performers ended up dead. I couldn't let that happen again, nor could I leave my surrogate family unprotected. I would see them safely to Ravenwood, then I would being investigating the *darkness*. The thought of getting a taste of vengeance was nearly intoxicating. I yearned for it. I needed it like a drunk needs his next drink. I feared for the safety of my friends in *Amazing Wonders,* but I also dreamed of the things I would do to those who practiced the twisted religion of the Order.

Audrey returned with two big venison sandwiches and two bottles of beer. "You need to eat," she said.

"Thanks, but I'm not hungry." I had found that when something emotionally troubling came my way I could avoid food and drink for weeks without it bothering me.

"Please," she said. "For me."

I smiled. "Sure," I said.

I took the sandwich and began to eat. It didn't taste bad. The beer, on the other hand, was awful.

We ate in silence for a time until she finally spoke. "Calvin is worried about you too."

"Fine," I said.

"What?"

"Fine. I will tell you what my problem is right now though I don't think that you will understand. No one could understand this."

She shrugged. "Try me."

"I feel something wrong in the air," I said. "It's worse than it's been in decades."

She blinked at me. I knew that she was okay with me being immortal, but when I mentioned it to her she always seemed to get uncomfortable. She pressed on though. "It's about your family, isn't it?"

I nodded.

"I remember you said it before," she said. "You felt something in your village when you woke up. *Darkness.*"

"It was everywhere. Thick. I don't know what else to call it and *darkness* is as good a name as any. It's been around for years and years now. I've felt it. It's stronger now."

"Stronger recently?"

"I've felt it since our last night in Philadelphia."

"That is when you began acting strange," she said.

"I told Calvin and he thought I was just imagining things. Going crazy. Crazy old man making up stories. Better to just smile and nod at him."

"I'm sure Calvin doesn't think of you that way," Audrey said.

"It felt like it," I said. "And my dreams... the nightmares have returned." There were tears stinging my eyes. "And they're worse than ever. I'm afraid to close my eyes at night."

I turned away so she would not see me weep, but I began to sob like a child when I felt her hand on my shoulder. The images of my dead family were flashing through my mind. Nothing she could do would make it any easier.

I didn't cry myself to sleep that night, but I seemed to have cried Audrey to sleep, for eventually, when the words were no longer being spoken, and the sobs had turned to sniffs, I heard her snore.

And I had been wrong about her. It seemed that she had understood. Or at least partially understood. I don't think anyone can grasp the full meaning of what I have gone through. That is why I am alone now. I wander the world, striking at the Order when I can, and vanishing into the shadows. It is better that way. It seems that everyone I care about gets hurt in the end.

THE JOURNEY CAME TO an end in Ravenwood. Calvin, using money he had earned from the show, had bought a small farm, and that was where we set up camp for the last time.

"Tents will do for now," he told me, "but eventually I want a whole house built. A house big enough for all the workers to live in comfortably."

"Quite the plan," I said.

"It is, isn't it?" he was happy that day. He had finally stopped moving after living a life on the road. His family was close, and his side attraction was now going to be a business located in one place.

We were in his barn and sitting on a broken wagon as we talked. The door of the barn was wide open and the sunlight shone through.

I was trying to figure out a way to bring up the *darkness* again. I sensed it not only growing stronger but also getting closer. I was afraid for my friends. I felt like I was under that tree full of hanging corpses in my old village.

"Calvin," I said. I had waited for him to stop chatting. The only thing that seemed to shut him up was a jar of water one of the workers had brought him. It was an unbearably hot July day, Calvin splashed half of the water on his face.

"Nasty hot day," he said, laughing.

"Yes," I nodded.

"So what were you saying?" he asked, wiping his wet face with his shirt.

"I have something I need to tell you."

"Is it about that thing you think you've been feeling?"

"The *darkness*. Yes," I said.

"God, Jasper..."

"You remember the stories you were told," I said.

"Yes," Calvin said. "But that was so long ago. 1819, Jasper!"

"It's back," I said. "Trust me. I know this feeling. It's back and it's dangerous."

"But you said you've felt it ever since 1819."

"I have," I said. "But it's getting stronger. Something big is about to happen and it's coming for us."

Calvin said nothing for a while; he just sat and stared. I became aware of my surroundings then. Being uncomfortable tends to make one aware of everything happening around him. I heard the wasps buzzing in their nest near the barn door. I felt the beads of sweat form on my forehead. I listened to the others as they went about making camp. I smelled bacon being cooked. I heard the soft rumble of thunder in the distance.

"Why?" he asked.

"Me," I said. "They're coming after me because of what I can do."

"Bastards," Calvin said. "I won't let them get you, Jasper."

I laughed. "I'm not worried about them getting me. I'm worried about my friends being in the middle of the fight. I know we've been friends for years. You are my best friend. The best friend I ever had. I can't tell you how great it's been being a part of the show."

"You are my best friend too," he said.

"You know all about me and what made me the way that I am. I came from a dark past. My life seemed to end shortly after I turned fifty. First I became a widower. Then my daughter and son-in-law were murdered. Then my baby grandson was sacrificed... And the things that came after transformed me. Now I am immortal. I look younger than fifty now but I am really a hundred and seventy. But long life and strength weren't the only things I got."

"You can sense when these people are near," Calvin said. "That's one of your abilities."

"Yes," I said. "I remember my old village. When I woke up under that burning barn I could feel something awful. Something wrong. I never felt it again until 1819. Then, after that, I felt it constantly, but I could never pinpoint it. It seemed far away until we were in Philadelphia. Then I knew it was closer. It's getting closer everyday. Something's coming, Calvin."

"What if it's nothing but your imagination?" Calvin asked.

"I don't think it is," I said.

"Wait a minute," he said. "Why don't we hunt them down? You and me? If you can feel them near us, why don't we take them on ourselves?"

"I intend to do just that, but I don't want you anywhere near the fighting. Last time I went after them, an innocent young girl was murdered and another performer was maimed. I will not leave the show unprotected. They will strike at me through all of you. I know they will. I intend to kill every last one of them before they can make their move.

Calvin later told me that my eyes seemed to gleam with revenge.

"You are going to go and kill people," Calvin said. "That doesn't even bother you?"

"Not at all," I said. "I've killed them before. I'll kill more of them this time. They're not people. They're monsters."

Calvin fell into silence again. I could tell that I had disturbed my friend, and he did not know how to react.

"Cal?" I said.

"Leave," he said after another moment of silence.

"Excuse me?"

"Leave," he said again. "I think I get it. I can't sit here and judge you on this. I have no idea what it's like to be you. I have no idea the pain that you must go through each and every day. Do you think about it every day?"

"In a way," I said. "I try not to ever think about what happened back then because it's too painful. But it's in the morning. When I wake up and I realize I'm another day older, another day beyond when I should have died, I think of that day in 1750."

"And if you're right and these people are here and they are doing the things that they did to your family... maybe it's right that you should try to find them and stop them."

"I'd like to do that," I said, "but I don't think leaving is the best idea."

"What do you mean?"

"Like I said, they know about the show. They'll be coming here to hurt me through you and everyone else in *Amazing Wonders*. I'll not leave. At least not yet. I want them to try to make their move. When they've done that, and I've stopped them, they'll run. That's when I'll leave. I'll follow them around the world and back if I have to."

He left me in the barn for he had many other things to do that day. The conversation had been easier than I had expected, but it was still difficult. I feared I would do something wrong. I feared I would get my friends killed. It couldn't happen again. I couldn't fail like last time. When the enemies came, and I knew they would, I would have to be ready for the greatest fight of my life.

THE NEXT DAY I was at the general store with Audrey, helping to carry a load of groceries that had been requested by various workers back at the camp. I had two large baskets in each hand.

"You folks from the circus thing that just came to town?" the shopkeeper asked.

"Yep," Audrey said. "Come see our show. We should be having one on Friday though our boss hasn't made any official announcement yet."

"Friday's still a few days away. Maybe he's waiting for the right time." The shopkeeper was a friendly thin man with a horseshoe of black hair around his bald head. He wore a green apron over his white shirt and black pants. "I'd sure like to see it. Been lots of new folks come to Ravenwood here lately. A whole rich family just moved in two weeks or so before you folks got here. Live outside of town on the other end, and now you're all here. I say that the more rich folks who come to town and spend money the better for all of us!"

Audrey thanked the shopkeeper—Glen was his name—and we left. We hadn't brought a horse so I was forced to walk carrying the heavy baskets. Audrey loved to take advantage of my abilities, and I was kind of glad to use them in a nonviolent way. We were halfway back to the camp when a horse rode next to us.

"Hi there," the rider said.

I looked up at him and saw he was clean-shaven and well-dressed. He wore no hat and his hair was oiled back so no stray stands hung loose. His suit looked more expensive than a year of my wages.

"What can we do for you?" I asked.

He looked into the baskets. "Aren't those heavy?"

"I'll manage," I said. I was wondering what this man's problem was. What I carried was my own business.

"Okay. Okay."

There was something wrong about him and I could feel it. The smile and the fancy clothes didn't fool me. When he rode up, I felt it, and looking him in the eye I knew it. He was one of them!

"Clarington," he said. "Cole Clarington."

"Nice to meet you," I said, not giving him my name.

Audrey introduced herself. "And this is..." she began gesturing to me. She stopped speaking when she locked her eyes with mine. I was glaring.

"Are you with that show that just came into town?" Clarington asked.

"We are," Audrey said.

"The *Amazing Wonders*," he said. "A legendary show. Said to have a man guarding it who has great strength and power."

"People say a lot of things," I growled. Audrey shot me a reproachful look.

Clarington laughed. "If I am not mistaken you are showing a lot of strength yourself."

"It's lighter than it looks," I said.

"I'm sure. I would love to see your show soon," Clarington said.

"We'd love to have you," Audrey said.

"Are you in it, my dear?" he asked. "I'd love to watch someone as beautiful as you on stage."

She giggled. I felt my blood begin to grow hot as we walked next to this man.

"When is the show?" he asked.

"Friday," Audrey said.

"I will be there," he said. And then he was off, riding in the opposite direction.

"Bastard," I said after he was gone.

"What was your problem?" Audrey asked, angry that I had been rude to the stranger.

"I'll tell you later," I said, looking around to make sure no one could hear what I was saying. "Something's not right."

I FOUND CALVIN AS soon as we were back at camp. He was busy at work going over plans for the premier show for *Amazing Wonders* in its new permanent location. He was bent over a wagon that was serving as his desk. A rock was his paperweight.

"Problems, Calvin," I said as I approached him.

"Busy, Jasper," he said.

I slammed my hand onto the papers and this made him look at me. "What?" he asked, obviously annoyed that I had interrupted him.

"They're here. Just like I said they would be. The bastards are here in Ravenwood."

"The bad people?" Calvin asked.

"You know damn well," I said. "The feeling that I've been having. The *darkness*. It's here right now, and I think it's been waiting for us."

"Okay. Jasper, I believe that they are here and that you felt all the things that you've been describing. I do. Okay? I have been thinking about it a lot since we last talked."

"Good. Then we're on the same page," I said. "We can do something."

"What would you have me do?" Calvin asked.

"Help me," I said.

Calvin looked me in the eye, then swept his gaze from side to side to make sure no one could hear our conversation and then asked: "Are you going to kill them?"

I didn't answer for a moment and then I nodded.

"You want me to help you kill them?" Calvin asked. "You want me to go to the noose over this? I'm not unkillable like you are, Jasper. I can't just go and do what I want without consequences!"

I said nothing. Instead I approached him, put my face an inch in front of his, looked into his eyes with contempt, and then I turned and walked away.

The anger I felt was not truly at Calvin though. It was anger at the witch cult that had found its way to Ravenwood. I would be doing what I had to do, and I would be doing it alone.

No one could help me.

I HAD MY OWN GUNS. They were packed away with my clothes, and so I found the baggage wagon and took the weapons and strapped them to my belt. I didn't know when these people were going to strike or if they would even bother making trouble for the group, but I was going to be prepared. 1819 could not happen again.

I thought over what Calvin had said. It had taken me off guard when he had said that he couldn't help me. Of course he couldn't. I should never have expected him to kill for me.

The sun was setting and a campfire was lit. The workers were getting ready to help move Calvin into his new house. That was phase one of his plan. The workers would then focus on building their own housing. It would all be located together, and at the center of all this construction would be a glorious stage where *Amazing Wonders* would thrive for decades. That was Calvin's plan at least.

THAT NIGHT, SHERIFF MARLEY rode into our camp flanked by two deputies. The sheriff was an old and tough man of the law. His handlebar mustache was pure white, and he wore a hat the same color. The badge on his coat glinted in the firelight. The men he was with both looked similar to him though they were younger, and I assumed when I met them that they were Marley's sons.

"Who's running this place here?" Marley asked loud enough for all of us to hear.

"That would be me," Calvin said. He walked to where the sheriff sat on his horse and offered to shake his hand.

"I see," Sheriff Marley said. "And what is your name?"

Calvin, realizing the sheriff wasn't going to shake his hand, took it back. This was not a friendly visit. "Calvin Valen."

"Calvin Valen. Related to any of the other Valens around here?"

"My family," Calvin said with a smile.

"Well, Mr. Valen, we've received a complaint."

"About what?" Calvin asked. "We've only just got here. There's no way we could've made any trouble for the town."

"Now, that's just not entirely true," Marley said. "A nice young man. Wealthy. By the name of Cole Clarington. He told me he was threatened by one of your workers."

Calvin glanced at me and then returned his attention to Sheriff Marley. "I know nothing of it," he said.

"That might be," Marley said. "He didn't mention you. He said a man by the name of Gunne threatened to kill him if he ever set sights on him alone. Now, Mr. Valen, I'm sure you understand the situation I'm in. I can't have people threatening each other in my town. This is not like it is out west. We try to keep things civilized here."

"I understand," Calvin said.

"Good. Now I'll have you turn over this Jasper Gunne to me so we can make sure nothing bad happens between him and Mr. Clarington. You don't want there to be any trouble with your show, do you?"

"No," Calvin said. "I don't think so."

He looked at me again, but I was already stepping forward. "I am Jasper Gunne, and I say that Cole Clarington is a lying piece of goat shit."

Sheriff Marley adjusted his position on the horse. "You deny threatening Mr. Clarington?"

"Yes, I do," I said in a whispery voice that sounded a bit too arrogant.

"Then you won't mind coming with me so we can get this whole thing settled," he said. "I don't want any bad blood between people in Ravenwood."

"Fine," I said. *You may not want bad blood in your town, but the feud between me and this Cole Clarington is as bad as blood can get.*

———— ◈ ————

I HAD TO GO to the sheriff's office which doubled as a jailhouse. Calvin had apologized to me before I left. He felt bad about the harshness of his refusal to help me. I told him it was okay and that I suspected this was a trick of Cole Clarington to get me alone. "Maybe he wants to catch me off guard," I said.

I waited for my accuser to come to the jailhouse, and while I waited, Sheriff Marley went on and on about what a great person Cole Clarington was. He and all of those friends of his that had come to town. They had brought a fortune with them, and they had been generous. They bought what they wanted and donated to any who were in need. They seemed the perfect neighbors. I wanted to tell the sheriff what they really were, but I knew that it would sound like lunacy.

"Donated enough for me to hire more badges," Marley said, sipping on some cold coffee. "Yes sir. Good people. Spread the wealth around is what they do. Only been here a few months and already things are looking better for Ravenwood, not that we were bad off before they came."

"How many children have gone missing?" I asked.

The sheriff stopped talking and looked quizzically at me. "What?"

"How many children are missing in Ravenwood?"

"That came out of the clear blue sky if anything ever did," Marley said.

"Not really. Tell the truth. How many?"

"If there are any missing children, it's sheriff's business and not yours. I'll not discuss the town's problems with *you.*"

"I bet they started going missing around the time Clarington and his friends came to town."

"Now see here! I've had just about enough of you and your mouth. You don't come into my office and badmouth someone I consider to be my friend, especially after you threatened him!"

"I threatened no one, you idiot."

"That's it!" Marley said.

I was ushered into a jail cell where I was to be kept until I felt ready to apologize. "Let's see you do something in there," Marley said.

"You have no idea what I can do," I said.

"No weapons," the dense sheriff said. "I searched you myself when you came in. You can just sit here all night if you don't feel like apologizing."

I shrugged. "The cot looks more comfortable than the ground anyway. I'm part of a traveling circus, Marley. I am using to being uncomfortable when I sleep."

"Then maybe I withhold breakfast."

"You do that," I said.

Marley left then. He muttered something about having things to do when he left, and then I was left alone to sit in jail.

I could've gotten out then, but I didn't want to reveal myself and my capabilities yet. Something in my mind told me Clarington was playing a game, and the stupid sheriff was just a piece in that game. He wanted me here for some reason. Did he think I would end up behind bars? Doubtful. What he accused me of doing wasn't worthy of jail time. But maybe he had things he was doing now while I was busy with Marley. My thoughts returned to my friends at the show.

Calvin can take care of them. They try anything with Amazing Wonders and Calvin will send them all to hell.

I sat on the cot and put my head in my hands. The *darkness* was getting thicker and thicker. I felt I might need to escape before the night's end to do what needed to be done.

I am ashamed to admit that I was not thinking of the lives I would endanger or of the lives I could save by getting rid of this cult. I was thinking only of myself and of the vengeance I had only dreamed about. All these years later the wounds were once again fresh and open, and I felt the familiar anger.

Only this time I was not helpless. I was in Ravenwood and I was coming for them. I was not unaware.

———◆———

I SAT ON THAT cot in that cell thinking over what I knew and what I didn't know. The cult was in town. That was obvious. The Order was here. There was guilt there for not having gone after them the way I had meant to decades earlier. I blocked that from my mind though. There was nothing I could have done. They had scattered themselves across the world because they feared me. That's why I could always feel the *darkness*, but I could never determine where it came from. This was all speculation that day, but it seemed the most logical of explanations. And who was this Cole Clarington? Was he similar to Thomas Riden? He played the part well. The town clearly was taken with him. The sheriff loved him. He was the Thomas Riden of Ravenwood. It was happening all over again.

I wondered what his methods were. Would he befriend someone to get close and steal their children? Maybe he wouldn't need that much subtlety. Maybe he would just walk through the door and take whoever he decided to offer as a sacrifice. I suspected he had not only the physical power, but also the monetary power to do as he pleased. The whole town was supposedly enthralled by Clarington and his friends because of their vast wealth.

They were enthralled by monsters.

———◆———

THE DOOR OPENED AND in its frame stood the man I had met earlier that day. Cole Clarington.

"You," I said, glaring through the bars.

"Me," Clarington said. "I must admit that I didn't think you were still around, but I had to know for sure."

"What are you talking about?" I was on my feet then and had my hands wrapped around the bars, ready to bend them and break free and kill this man. The *darkness* was around him like stench on a pig farmer.

Clarington took a step forward. He was young and well-dressed, and he carried a cane that he swung back and forth as he walked. His shiny oiled hair looked perfect, and no doubt he spent a long time on it in the morning. He was rich and elegant, and he was evil. No matter what people in Ravenwood thought of him, he was evil.

"You know who we are?" he asked.

"Some cult of religious fanatics," I said. "Witches. Warlocks. Whatever you call yourselves. You're child killers." I spat in his face.

He raised a gloved hand to his face and wiped away the saliva. "Rude, but expected," he said.

The bars began to creak as I started to pull.

"I am from a group of believers in the eventual world," Clarington said. "We call ourselves the Order. We've been watching you... or rather, we've been watching for you."

"Why?" I asked. I had stopped bending the bars, but I still had my hands on them. I wanted to kill this man, but I was now curious as to why these people were looking for me.

"We know what you are," Clarington said. "We suspected it from day one. Our ancestors came to this country before it was a country. A small village in Massachusetts. You were there. You know what happened." He grinned at me.

I ripped open the bars then. I didn't know that I could do it so fast, but the anger that surged through my body made it easy.

Clarington backed away. He was almost to the door when I was through the bars, and suddenly his smug and arrogant look was replaced by complete horror.

"Wait!" he said, hands raised as if that could protect him. "Wait!"

"Why?" I asked when I reached him. I took him by the collar and brought him to his feet. *I can smash his face with my fist. I can choke him with one hand. Maybe I could even rip his head off. I could open his chest with my bare hands. Maybe I should begin breaking his bones and draw this out.*

"You can't kill me," he said. "We have your woman!"

That made me stop. "Audrey?" I let him go.

"We have her," he said. "If I don't come back, she dies screaming."

"You disgusting, lying…"

"Did you see her today at all before you were arrested?"

I realized then that I hadn't seen her. I had looked for her but she had been nowhere in the camp. I hadn't thought much of it. I assumed she was exploring the town. Lots of our people were doing that. I knew at that moment though, that Cole Clarington was telling the truth.

"Let her go," I said. "This is between you and me. There's no need to hurt her."

"That's fine," he said. "I'll even take you to her. You have to follow me though."

I glared at him again.

"Follow me," he said, "and you'll see her again safe and sound. We won't kill her."

"But don't think you can kill me," I said.

He laughed. The arrogant smile was back on his lips. I smacked it off.

"Don't!" he said, spitting blood. "They'll kill her if I don't come back!"

"I'm not killing you, but I don't want to see your goddamn smile either."

"Fine," he said. "Follow me." He led the way though the door.

"We have been looking forward to this for a while, you know. We don't want to kill you or her. We just want to talk to you."

And so we began the walk to where Clarington and his people were living. No one stopped us from leaving the jail. I think that Sheriff Marley had been paid by Clarington and his friends so they were allowed to do whatever they wanted with me. I think they could have walked in there and put a bullet in my head and the sheriff would not have said a thing. Of course, that would be impossible because a bullet can't kill me, but that's beside the point. These men were allowed to do what they wanted, and therefore, everyone in Ravenwood was in danger.

I would not let what happened to my family happen to anyone else. That was my resolve. But as I walked, I realized that things were dangerously close to resembling the events of 1819.

———◦◦◦———

THE HOME OF COLE CLARINGTON was an apartment above a saloon. I stepped inside of it and noticed that the furnishings were sparse and the floor creaked under our weight as we walked. There were others there, but they were in another room.

"It's small," I said.

"Indeed," Clarington said.

"You look like you could afford better."

"We'll have better soon enough, I think. Got a house that's gonna be built. Until then this'll do just fine."

"Don't like the houses around here?" I asked.

"Not well enough for our family."

"Is that what you call yourselves?" I asked. "Family?"

"Yes," Clarington said. Then he leaned close to me. "We are closer than any blood family in this world."

Once more I thought about killing him.

"There's more than just us in the house though," Clarington said. "We have a vast number of members who are spread all over the world."

"I see," I said.

"Do you? That's good. I hope you'll see things much more clearly now."

Clarington walked to one of the closed doors, rapped on it twice and then returned to the small living room where I was standing. The door opened, the hinges creaking. Audrey walked into the room, three men followed and three women followed them.

"I am a man of my word," Clarington said.

"I'm sorry," I said to Audrey. She appeared unhurt and calm in spite of her circumstances.

"Shall we discuss things then?" Clarington asked.

"You have my attention," I said. I could have killed him then, but any move I made could have cost Audrey her life. I would not attack any of them until I knew that she was safe.

"Good," Clarington said. "Then please, sit."

I sat at one of the seats near the coffee table and Clarington sat across from me. Our eyes locked as I waited for him to begin. Audrey said not a word.

"We have been around," Clarington said, "since almost the beginning of time. We were here before God flooded the earth. We survived because one of the servants of Noah's family was one of us. Then we continued to exist in secret for years and years. We were there when the Israelites were freed from Egypt. We were there when David killed Goliath. We were there when the Spartans fought the Persians. When Rome began conquering the world. When Rome fell. When Christ lived. When Christianity spread. When the Saxons took over Britain. When the Danes tried to do the same. Through the dark ages. Through the modern days. We have always been around. Do you understand what I'm saying?"

I nodded.

"We were around, and yet we were not like what we are now. We are witches. You know this. Not like wiccans though. Our power comes from someone you would call a demon. I personally don't like that name as I think it's a falsehood put forth by the Christians, but that's the only way for you to understand what I am saying. In fact, I would say that the one we worship is our Goddess. Valayra. One day, long ago, a few within the spread-out number of followers and believers thought it would be a great idea if we started to band together like a proper religion. That was the beginning of the Order. It was a simple name, really. We didn't have anything else to call it. We didn't want to attract attention because there were those witch burnings happening, though they killed the wrong ones. We have a plan and a plot that will be executed for decades to come. We want you to be a part of that."

It was when he said that demon's name that a barrier in my memory was cracked.

Valayra.

Blue light. I remembered blue light.

There was something else. Something I couldn't quite grasp. It was blocked out and tucked away. It was coming back to me though.

Valayra.

"After you killed my family?" I asked. "After you cursed me and turned me into what I am? After you kidnapped the one person who makes me happy? You want me to be a part of your order?"

"In 1750, we had a group of our people come to the New World. We wanted to really put things into motion back then, perhaps shape the continent to our image. We didn't though. We killed a few families then. But let me explain why these families were killed.

"There is power to be unleashed by blood. Blood of the inno-cent especially. That's why babies are prized among us and why we will take one as soon as we can get a hold of it. Killing it the way we do unleashes the power, and we absorb it. That's what it all comes down to. Power. They are sacrifices, and they do not die in vain. One day, when we remake the world, all will understand why we did what we did."

"By murdering anyone you want so you can get power?" I asked. "You disgust me. Even now, even after all I thought I knew about you and your kind, you still manag to disgust me."

"Naturally, you'd feel that way," Clarington said. "But you know the power is real, Jasper. You feel it inside of you, right now, don't you?"

I don't know why it surprised me so much that he could feel what I felt. I thought maybe it was a gift only I had. That made me think though. What other abilities did we have in common?

"Let's have some drinks," Clarington said. "Maxwell, get us drinks."

The one called Maxwell stood. He was tall, middle-aged and bald. His eyes seemed black to me and the aura of *darkness* was thick around him like a bad cologne.

"What would you like, sir?"

"A beer for me, if you'd be so kind." Clarington then looked at me and raised an eyebrow.

"Nothing for me," I said.

"Fine," Clarington said.

"As if I would drink with you," I said.

Clarington leaned close to me then and asked: "Have you not been tempted at all, Jasper?"

"Tempted?"

"By what you could do?"

"I don't understand your question."

"By what you can do! You can probably take a bullet. You have powers beyond any normal person, and what do you do with them? You guard some sideshow? You could be a warrior. You could be a ruler of men. If you had the right guidance, you could be the most powerful man in the world!"

"You mean I could use my powers to conquer?"

Clarington looked triumphant and sat back in his chair with his arms folded. "So the thought *has* crossed your mind a time or two?"

"Not too often," I said. "But I have thought of it. I also thought of how foolish it was. I don't want to rule. I just want to die and be with my family again."

Clarington shook his head. "So ignorant. You can't see the big picture."

"Maybe not," I said. "I see things the only way I can. You people killed those I loved and made me what I am today. Because of your people I can never have peace. You are a blight on the world. A curse upon mankind. I despise you. You are worth less than the globs of horseshit sitting in the street right now."

Clarington clicked his tongue. "That's rude."

I saw Maxwell out of the corner of my eye. He produced a knife from his jacket.

"The sun is setting," Clarington said. "We are going to hold a ceremony here one night. Probably not tonight because we'll be busy. But soon after we will offer something pure and innocent to our goddess."

"No, you won't," I said.

Clarington sighed. "If you don't want to do what we ask of you then I can at least give you what you want. You can die and go be with your family if they do in fact still exist in an afterlife somewhere."

I looked Cole Clarington in the eye. Then I looked the one called Malcolm in the eye. I glanced around the room and counted seven others. There were more than just these in this town though. I could feel them. The last person I looked at was Audrey. She was sitting among these monsters, and I felt that there was now no way to get her to safety.

"I'm sorry," I said to her.

I stood, grabbed Clarington by the throat and raised him off of his feet. He dangled in my grasp while the others in the room panicked.

"Drop him!" one of the women shrieked at me.

"Do it now!" a man said. "Or we kill the woman!"

I dropped Clarington and let him fall to the floor. He scrambled to his feet then, his hair disheveled. "Fool! They all want to kill you!" He indicated his companions in the room. "I offer you something far greater than you deserve and you throw it in my face? No. That's not how this happens." He leaned close to me. "You are an abomination. You weren't supposed to exist. You're only here because some halfwit ruined a ritual over a century ago! Do you know what happened after that? They were all killed. You understand? All the people who had a hand in killing your *precious* little family are dead. They were murdered. Hanged in the tree. Their eyes taken. I'm sure you saw. Then the Order fled back across the ocean for fear of you."

I said nothing in response. My jaw was clenched and my hands were balled into fists.

"We got wind of you when we read a newspaper article about some fighter of a man who guards a sideshow. You killed a few people and showed amazing strength. Even had some legends crop up about you. It was obvious to us who you were. That's why we came back to the New World. That's why we are in America. We want you. The things in the past are the past, and the future is going to be so bright that you would be a fool to turn it away. So please, Jasper, let your family rest in peace and move on."

"Move on?" I asked.

"If it makes it any better for you," Clarington said, "Audrey has already moved on."

I looked at her in astonishment. She stepped away from the men who had been holding her arms and walked to Clarington. She put her arm through his.

"You see?" Clarington said, "we're not all bad. Great things are coming. They just come at a price. She understands that. We have talked at length. She wants to be a part of this world we're creating."

"Audrey?" I said.

"It's true, Jasper," she said. "There are wonderful things that Cole has done. Great things. I want to be in that world, and you should be in it too."

"You betray me?" I asked. "I told you all that happened to me. I told you everything and in one day you betray me?"

"It's not that," she said. "You can't see it clearly. You don't hear what Cole is saying."

"I hear well enough," I said. "And I am done listening."

"Jasper..." Clarington said.

I moved fast. The first thing I did was punch Clarington. I can still remember the sound my fist made as it connected with the side of his head. Then Maxwell was on me, swinging a knife. I ducked and jabbed an elbow into his thigh, sending him to the floor. "Who's next?" I cried.

I needed a weapon. Killing them all with my bare hands would have made the task long, difficult and messier than it needed to be. And as much as I wanted my revenge I also wanted it to be over.

There was a scream from Audrey, and there were gunshots. I was shot three times, and each shot drove me across the room. Upon the fourth shot I fell backwards out the window and into the street.

Lying there among the broken glass I gazed up to where I had fallen. I saw the heads of some of the cultists peering out the window. I kept my gaze locked on them as I slowly got to my feet.

"I'm still alive!" I called to them. "Still alive! And I'm coming for all of you!"

"You there, boy!" the familiar voice of Sheriff Marley called. He trotted his horse over and looked down at me. "I thought I locked you up! And you're out here causing problems."

"You let that bastard Clarington take me out of your pathetic little jailhouse," I said. "And now I need your gun."

"Now see here!" he said.

"I'm of no mind for this today," I said. I reached up and grabbed the sheriff by his shirt and pulled him off of his horse. He drew his gun as he fell, and for the fifth time in under five minutes, I was shot.

"That really stings," I said, prying the gun from his fingers.

The sheriff fell and stared at me with a mouth open in terrified surprise. He was focused on the holes in my shirt that were made by the bullets. The same bullets were now lying on the ground somewhere near us, and the only thing they had managed to do to me was to lightly break my skin. It felt like a bad sunburn.

"You're the devil!" he said.

"I'm not the devil, sheriff. You already let him into your town. I'm just going to fix your mistake."

I walked back to the building and opened the front door. I heard scuffling upstairs and the sound of horses trotting behind me. The sheriff's deputies had come.

When I arrived upstairs the cultists were gone. I looked out an open window and saw them scrambling across the rooftops.

"I told you!" I heard one of them shout. "I told you, Clarington!"

"Keep moving!" The voice of Cole Clarington rang clearly over the wind.

I stepped outside and aimed the gun. I fired the five remaining shots, but I only managed to hit one of them and that was in the leg. It served its purpose though since he fell off the roof and landed on his head. The others were unscathed.

That was my first kill that day.

I climbed out the window and ran across the rooftops after them. They were ahead of me, and they managed to drop into one of the buildings and get to the street. I looked down and saw them scrambling to get to horses.

I leapt from where I was and landed in the street. I heard Audrey scream as Cole Clarington helped her onto her horse. He slapped the beast's rear and sent it running away from the fight. That might have been the one selfless thing any of us did that day. In the years that followed I never went after Audrey. I felt betrayed by her, sure, but I never wanted her blood like I wanted the blood of these others.

Clarington was the next to mount a horse, and since this whole adventure had been his idea, he chose to distract me. He charged the animal forward, hoping to trample me.

"Fool!" I yelled, smacking the horse to the side and making him fall face-first into the muddy dirt of the road.

"Bullets don't hurt me," I said as I approached him. "Long falls don't hurt me. Why would a damn horse hurt me?" He was on his feet then, and I punched him in the stomach. It wasn't hard enough to kill.

"You're the fool," Clarington said with a weary voice. "We offer you a kingdom and you spit in our face."

I took him by the throat and held him dangling in my grasp. "Your people killed my daughter. Your people killed my grandson. I can still taste his blood in my mouth. That will never be forgotten, and it will never be forgiven." I began to squeeze his neck. He died there in my grasp.

"Who's next?" I yelled at the others who had been in the room with me when Clarington had unveiled his ideas that I should join him and his cause. I flung Clarington's corpse away.

"None of them," I heard a voice say. And then I felt the *darkness*. It was much more acute than what I felt coming from the group. This was behind me, and somehow it felt worse. I turned and saw a man my height staring at me with cold eyes. He was bald and kept the grey hair on the sides of his head trimmed. He had a goatee that was a matching grey. There was a hat in his hand that was as black as the suit he was wearing.

"Jasper Gunne," he said, "we meet at last."

"And you are?" I asked.

"I'm called Riden. Adam Riden."

I started toward him and just as I reached for his throat he dropped his hat and struck me so fast it seemed a blur. His arm moved and the knife in his hand slashed me across the face. Blood poured freely, and I felt a pain unlike anything I had ever felt. He then shoved the blade into my stomach and twisted.

"Business finished," he said.

And then everything went dark.

2017

JASPER FELL OUT OF his trance. He had been locked in it for hours, and when he looked out the window he saw the early rays of morning light creeping over the treetops.

"Hours," he said. "I've been writing for seven hours at least."

It was the beginning of the end of his story, and it had consumed his mind so much that he couldn't stop until he reached the part of his apparent death. *It had hurt. The bastards knew just what to do and just how to do it.*

Jasper lay on the couch and decided to get a little sleep before Calista arrived to collect the new pages of the story. His dreams were terrifying.

When he woke up three hours later he touched the scar that was still on his face. Every wound he had ever taken from the knives was still visible on his body, and the pain was always in his memory.

Jasper ate his breakfast with a side of eggs. It was two o'clock in the afternoon and the noise of the town was too much to allow him to sleep. Construction crews were working on the road, and the racket they were making decided him on getting up for the day.

Calista knocked on the door as Jasper finished his breakfast. She opened the door without being invited in and waited as Jasper stacked the printed papers from the previous night's work.

"The last chapters are coming," Jasper said.

"Okay then. I've already edited some of what you've written."

"Edited?" Jasper's eyes narrowed.

"I didn't change anything," Calista said. "I simply rewrote a few phrases. Made it all flow a bit better."

"I guess that's fine," Jasper said, opening the refrigerator and selecting a can of root beer.

"Out of drink?" Calista asked.

"I need to get to the store sometime today," Jasper said. "I'm thinking bourbon tonight."

"Then I'll leave you to it," Calista said. She left without another word, taking the manuscript with her.

Jasper walked out behind her a few moments later. He walked to the liquor store, bought some bourbon and a pack of gummy bears. Then he returned to his apartment and to his writing desk.

And he got back to work.

1870

THE BLOOD FLOWED FREELY from my wounds and the sheriff believed that I was dead. I was put into a pine box and buried in an unmarked grave outside of town. Calvin Valen told me later that he had asked where I was buried, but the sheriff would not say. Calvin knew I wouldn't stay dead. He didn't want me waking in a grave again. The sheriff had a grudge though. He thought he was depriving my friends of giving me a proper funeral. That fool was in for a surprise.

The Bible tells us that it took Jesus three days to rise from the dead. I clearly do not have His power. For though I was not dead (remember that first and foremost: I did not die) it took me a week to crawl out of that grave.

During that time, I found myself in a familiar place. The blue glowing world of that strange purgatory where Arthan still dwelled. When I saw him, I immediately remembered everything about my times in this place. It was then that whatever was blocking my mind was removed. I remembered everything about the bluish purgatory from that day on.

"They got you again," Arthan said. That was his greeting. He didn't say hello. He didn't tell me it was good to see me. It must have been good to see me though. He didn't have anyone to talk to when I was on earth.

"Surprised me," I said, feeling like I was talking to an old friend. It was an old friend that I had forgotten about until a few minutes ago. "It's a Riden too. That's who got me."

"Not the elder one, but the younger," Arthan said.

"I'm sorry. What?"

"I've been watching you and them for some time now, Jasper," he said. "There are two Ridens. You've met both now."

"Two?"

"Thomas and his son, Adam."

"Thomas Riden? As in the Thomas Riden from my village all those years ago?"

"The one and the same," Arthan said. "He's learned how to prolong his life. Went for years without a son to carry on the name. That was until about thirty years ago. From what I gather, he wanted an heir in case things go wrong for him in the coming struggles."

"What struggles?"

"With you, of course," Arthan said. Then he laughed at my surprise. "You've been watched for some time. Thomas Riden knows he has to either turn you or kill you. He's betting on you not joining his side though. He knows there will likely be a big fight between you and the Order."

"And when I lose, I end up here."

"With you're old friend, Arthan. Did you understand the dreams I was sending?"

"That was you?"

"It was," Arthan said. "I have limited ways of contacting anyone from this place. That's why I tried to send dreams to you. Since you'd been here twice, your mind should have still been connected to the energies that flow freely through this place."

"They make more sense now," I said.

"Good," Arthan said. "Because I've been doing a lot of thinking, and you are going to need to help me."

"Help you with what?"

Arthan paused for a moment. There was the long cry of a child who was screaming bloody murder. "Another victim of the Order," Arthan said.

"Help you with what?" I asked again.

"I can't leave here," Arthan said. "I haven't left here in eight thousand years. You, on the other hand, can leave here. You've done it twice. When you heal, you'll leave again. I want you to try to remember, though. You haven't been remembering, and that's why I've had to send you dreams. You are my warrior out there. You are my champion. You can take the fight to them. You can hurt these people. You may even be able to hurt Valayra."

I took in what he said for a short time. Then I said: "You want me to fight your war for you?"

"You're already fighting a war," he said, dismissively. "Don't act like you're not. You want to kill them all and bring down their cult."

"It's my own mission. My own vengeance. I'm not doing this for your God."

"Jasper..."

"No! He let those monsters kill my family. He let this happen to me! No! No! I will not fight for Him!"

"And how many more families have died while you've gone around playing bodyguard? How many? It's not about killing the followers. It's about killing the leaders. Killing them at their source. The Ridens. Maybe even Valayra. You're the most powerful man to walk the earth in two thousand years, and you do nothing with that power or potential."

"What can I do?" I asked. "I've done all I can. I searched the world. I've fought them when I've found them, and I still end up here. What more can I do?"

"You can stop feeling sorry for yourself and stop with this foolish vengeance crusade. You can start using your powers as gifts and actually make a difference!"

The dead swirled around us at that moment, glowing purple like they always did. Arthan was still green.

"Look at them all," Arthan said. "This is the legacy of Valayra. This is the pain she causes. I know you probably can't win, Jasper. I know this. Maybe you can give her some pain back though."

"It all seems so pointless," I said. "And I'm healing now. Soon I'll get up and continue the fight. Until then though, I'm stuck here thinking of all the things I want to do to these people."

"You have allies," Arthan said.

"No, I don't. Too many people have died because of me. I'll not have any more die."

"I know," Arthan said. "Like I said, I've been watching you."

"So you understand what I'm saying?"

"Yes. But I've also been watching the Ridens. I know what your old friend, Thomas, wants."

I still couldn't comprehend what he was saying. "Thomas is still alive?" It must have been the eighth time I'd asked that question since he told me.

"Still alive," Arthan said, "and more powerful than ever."

"What did he do?" I asked. "How can he still be alive? Did the same thing happen to him that happened to me?"

"No," Arthan said. "Thomas Riden simply knows the magic involved. He relies on his witches, and they keep him alive, though he forbids immortality for anyone else."

Arthan waved his hand and caused a ribbon of blue energy to form in front of us.

"Watch," he said.

What unfolded before my eyes was indeed strange. This was still the 1870s. Movies were decades away. In fact, in the early twentieth century, when I sat down to watch a movie for the first time, I remember not being able to follow the storyline because I was so reminded of this experience with Arthan.

And so it was that I watched the immortal life of Thomas Riden.

Thomas Riden

THE DAY THAT I was offered up in a botched sacrifice to the demon, Valayra, was also the day that Thomas Riden began his journey to immortality. He had known that something was wrong. Something that happened during the ritual was not right. I watched as Frederick hid my body beneath the floorboards. My dead grandson was on the table. I knew that he would be cannibalized soon and I hoped that Arthan wouldn't show me that. It was bad enough to imagine it. I didn't think I could stand to witness it.

"What did you do?" Thomas asked the man who had betrayed him and stolen control of his followers. "What in Christ's name did you just do?"

"What do you mean?" Frederick asked. "We only did what we came here to do. What we were always going to do. This family was the first of many. The Order rises in the New World, just as your father envisioned."

"My father left you all in my charge!" Thomas yelled.

"And I'm not taking orders from you or your father anymore!" Frederick said.

"You commit treason against your own superiors," Thomas Riden said. "For that, there is no forgiveness."

"I don't need your forgiveness. I will put you in the floor next to your friend." Frederick picked up a hammer and stared at Thomas with a look of pure loathing.

"You've wanted this for a long time," Thomas accused him.

"I deserve it. And I'll be the best thing to ever happen to the faith. We'll establish ourselves in the New World. We'll be cut off from your father, and then, one day, our descendants will conquer his descendants."

Thomas laughed. "You *are* a fool. You realize that, right? You don't have the people to side with you as it is!"

Frederick opened his arms the gesture to all of the others in the barn. "My people are all right here. We've discussed this."

Thomas looked at all of them in turn. "Is it true?" he asked.

"We have discussed it," a woman said, removing her hood. She had a scar above her right eyebrow in the shape of a crescent moon. Her hair was tied behind her head, and her eyes were dark brown.

"Almyra," Thomas said, "why would you betray me?"

"Because she and everyone else agrees with what I offer," Frederick said.

"You've forgotten your place, Frederick," Thomas said. "It is your last mistake."

"Take him," Frederick said. "We won't dine upon the child until the moon is high in the sky. Thomas Riden will have no part of it."

Thomas' hands were bound, and he was taken out of the barn. I watched it all through the cloud in the strange blue purgatory of Arthan. When Thomas Riden was outside the barn, he seemed to be staring directly at me, as if he could see me over a century later watching him through the window into the past.

Thomas closed his eyes then. He made a noise in his throat that was almost a growl. Then the rope binding his hands snapped, and he raised his arms like a reverend praying over his congregation. He turned to his former followers then. They were frozen in place.

"Fools," Thomas said. "I've had complete control over each and every one of you since before we even met. All Ridens have that control. Your blood is mine."

He twisted a hand, and he smiled as his people screamed. Their eyes popped in their sockets, and blood ran down their faces like tears.

"Your friends in the barn are getting the same punishment," Thomas said. "It's a shame, really. My father warned me this might happen. I was hoping to be able to prove him wrong. Now, when I return to England without any of you, he'll know he was right."

There were whimpers and there were pleas. Thomas Riden seemed deaf to both. His people were dead at his feet. He then walked into the barn. My viewpoint followed him. There, I saw that everyone else was dead too, including Frederick. Thomas picked up the dead body of my grandson and made his way to the house.

———

"WHAT HAPPENED NEXT," Arthan said, "was he cannibalized the boy. Ate everything. Ate until he was stuffed and kept on eating."

"Why would I want to hear that?" I asked. If my ghostly form could cry tears, I'd have been bawling.

"Because I didn't think you would want to see it. I've watched it before. That is the moment. The one singular pinpoint in time. That was when Thomas Riden became immortal."

"By eating my grandson?"

"Who was cursed with an abominable magic that was bastardized from the first word of the spell. That one called Frederick was the cause of most of it. You're the cause of the rest."

"How am I the cause of anything?" I demanded.

"Not intentionally. You came back to life though. Your soul was soaked in the powers of the spiritual realm and you returned. That made your blood the blood of an immortal. Thomas Riden dined upon your grandson—flesh and blood—that day. Therefore, it made him an immortal."

The cloud seemed to shift. When the image cleared I was looking at what I assumed was London decades before I arrived seeking out members of the Order. The street looked similar, and I remembered the house where I had thought the leader of the Order had been living.

Unlike the time I was in London, this house was full of people. I saw a fully furnished room. There were couches and chairs before a fireplace, and the portrait above the mantle appeared to resemble Thomas Riden. It was no doubt a relative. My guess is that it was an ancestor of his that was prominent within their disgusting little cult.

There was an old man standing while all others were sitting. He was leaning against the mantle, warming himself by the fire while he held a glass of brandy in his right hand. He looked like the painting and like Thomas. This must have been Christophe Riden.

"You say, my son, that our people betrayed us in the New World?"

"I do," Thomas said. He was one of the men on the couches. They all wore the black robes, but their hoods were removed.

"I remember warning you of such things," Christophe said. "And you would listen not. And now we risked exposure."

"It's the colonies," Thomas said with a wave of his hand. "What could they possibly matter?"

"They matter to me!" Christophe snapped.

"Forgive me, Father," Thomas said.

"Perhaps in time," Christophe said. "I do not approve of how this was handled."

"You mean what I did to them?"

"Yes," Christophe said. "You could have taken care of it in a cleaner way and made your way back home. You could have done this before Frederick defiled our sacred rituals."

"Yes, I could have," Thomas said. "At the time, I made a mistake. I thought perhaps I could reach Frederick. I didn't expect the others to side with him."

"It's done now," Christophe said. "I am just disappointed. You are over forty years old now. I can't keep holding your hand and leading you. I need *you* to be a leader."

"Yes, Father."

"These are my final days. I know this. I feel it. I'll be with our blessed goddess quite soon. I need to know there is someone strong enough and wise enough to lead our people further down the path. Not just to gain power for himself. No. I need someone who will bring us closer to our blessed ascension from the shadows. Are you that person, Thomas?"

"I believe I am," Thomas said.

"And sadly, I think you're not. Perhaps your brother would be better suited for the task."

"Robert?"

"Indeed," Christophe said. "I think he deserves a test."

"He's but a boy," Thomas said.

"Over twenty years old now."

"And a bastard," Thomas growled.

"That matters only to the god of the Christians. Valayra cares not."

"I don't like this," Thomas said. "In fact, I hate it. How can you suggest giving Robert this power?"

"I don't," Christophe said. "But as of tonight, I will amend my will. When I die, Robert Riden will become the High Master of the Order. You will obey him in all things as you have obeyed me. That is, unless you can prove yourself to me before my death. For your sake, my son, I hope that you can."

Thomas Riden stood then and looked his father in the eye. "Don't worry," he said, "I will."

That very night, Thomas Riden proved how sincere he was in his desire to take control of the Order. Arthan showed me images and visions of that night. Everything in the Order changed. The ambition of my former friend on that night would rule the fates of many for decades to come.

When the image cleared again Thomas was standing behind a young man who was on his knees. In Thomas' hand was a kitchen knife. The lad in front of him as bleeding from his throat.

"It is the only way," Thomas said as his brother died at his feet.

He then looked at the other black cloaks who were in the room with him. There were five visible in the candlelight and at least that many shrouded in the shadows.

"My brothers and sisters, are you with me?" Thomas asked.

They voiced their agreement.

"The war begins tonight. It is a terrible war that will not end in our lifetime, I'm sure. Tonight, the Order will be broken, but from the shattered pieces, the New Order will rise stronger and fiercer than anything on this earth!"

There was a cheer from the followers.

"Bring forth my father," Thomas said.

I watched from the purgatory as Christophe Riden was marched into the room where his youngest son had just died. He glanced at the corpse of Robert Riden, but his face betrayed no emotion.

"This is what you wanted, is it not, Father?" Thomas asked.

Christophe Riden shook his head.

"Then what?" Thomas asked. "I am the rightful leader of the Order. I am going to fulfill the will of our goddess. I will do the things that you never could."

"My son," Christophe said. He sounded exhausted. "You are an abomination upon this world. I have seen what is to come. I have seen it in my dreams."

"Then why did you do nothing?" Thomas asked.

"Because I'd hoped you would be wise and stay off of this dark and evil path that you are starting."

"It's the correct path, Father," Thomas said.

"I see your doom and the doom of our Order," Christophe said.

Thomas stepped forward, wielding the same knife that had killed his brother a few moments before. "Then, old man, you did not look far enough."

Christophe Riden was killed in the same way as his youngest son. When the deed was done, Thomas looked from the knife to his followers and said: "Get ready. The war begins now."

<hr />

"YOU SEE?" ARTHAN ASKED. "It all started when your family was killed." He waved his hand and made the vision vanish.

"But Thomas was acting so much different with his father. He was acting like that Frederick."

"Thomas Riden had time to think and time to understand that he agreed with what Frederick had been saying. The difference was that he wanted to lead the New Order himself."

"So that's why I hadn't seen much of them in the last century or so," I said.

"Exactly. You encountered them one time. That was in the midst of the long war that's still being fought among the followers."

"They were testing me. Seeing if I was still alive. Seeing how dangerous I was."

"Yes," Arthan said. "Thomas Riden knew you were still alive, because he was still alive. He's alive now."

"Because he ate my grandson," I said. It all made a dreadful sort of sense.

"You and he are now connected. He ate the flesh and drank the blood of a sacrifice that was done in all the wrong ways. Strange forces were at work then, and they created you. Anyone with your blood is like you. Thomas eating your grandson and finishing the evil ritual was what granted him his immortality. I've been watching it all. I've been waiting for you to return to this place."

"You are going to use me," I said.

"We can fight them. I need you to strike at them and bring them down. I can't fight from here, but you can continue my battle. You can win."

"Each time I've dealt with the Order, I've ended up here. Next time might be permanent."

"Then it's permanent," Arthan said. "But what do you have to lose? Nothing. What do you have to gain? Vengeance."

"I will fight them to my dying breath," I promised. That would be a long fight too. Unless they could find a way to put me in the ground and keep me there.

"Then we have an agreement," Arthan said. "Maybe someday I'll get out of this prison. Then I can continue the fight myself."

"Until then," I said, "let me worry about this cult."

Ravenwood

I WOKE UP IN my grave just as I expected. With a grunt of annoyance I punched upward and broke the lid of the coffin with one blow. I opened my fist and felt the dirt surrounding my hand. I brought my arm back through the hole and punched again and again. I climbed up from the grave until I reached the surface. Then I walked to the Valen Farm.

Instead of knocking on the door in the middle of the night and waking everyone, I made my way to a stream that was on Calvin's property. The water was cold but refreshing. I cleaned the dirt from my skin as best I could. I was returning from the grave, but I didn't want to appear as a ghoul to my friends.

If my previous experiences were any indication, I had been underground for at least a week. I wondered how much had changed in that time. Was Calvin okay? Was the show okay? My friends were left defenseless. Would the Order hurt them?

And beyond the thoughts and concerns I had for my friends, there was also the matter of the missing children.

Calvin had watched me approach the farm, and he had continued watching as I made my way to the stream. I saw him when I returned from the water. He had a cigar hanging from his mouth and a glass of whiskey in his hand.

"I shouldn't be surprise to see you," he said.

"But you are," I replied.

He walked down the steps of the porch and embraced me. "Welcome back," he said.

From that moment until sunrise we talked of what had happened the previous week. I told him all about the experience of being seemingly killed and how I had gone to Arthan's purgatory. I told him the things I had seen there.

"There's more going on that I realized," I said. "Thomas Riden is still alive. The one who was my friend so long ago."

Calvin, in turn, told me of what had happened in Ravenwood. The show had opened up two nights ago for the premier, but attendance was not what we had hoped it would be. There was a stigma attached to the show now thanks to the things that had happened the day that I killed Cole Clarington.

The survivors of that day had not been seen again. It appeared that I had scared them off, though they were the ones who dealt the fatal blow in that conflict. *They know that you don't stay dead, fool!* They were hiding from me. Hiding and waiting.

"Have there been any children missing?" I asked. "Has anyone from town talked about missing children?"

"God, yes," Calvin said in a whisper. He shook his head and then drank the rest of his whiskey. "I hate to think of what's going to happen to them."

"Nothing's going to happen to them," I said. "Not while I'm breathing." I sounded so sure of myself, but I knew that I could easily fail. I had yet to stop the Order from committing any act of evil. I was only ever successful in retribution.

The early morning sun greeted us as we continued our conversation. I told him of how Cole Clarington had persuaded Audrey to join the Order.

"I haven't seen her since that day," Calvin said.

"She's probably dead," I said. "If it's anything like what happened in 1750, they're all dead. If she was with them, she was killed too."

"Killed by Thomas Riden?"

"If it's like it was back then," I said. "But I don't know. Thomas also had a change of heart and mind during that time. And being immortal definitely changes everything."

"I would imagine," Calvin said.

Then I said the thing I had wanted to say all night. I thought that our conversation had been the perfect pretense of it, but it would turn out I was wrong. "Calvin," I said, "I think you should move the show."

"Move it?" Calvin asked.

"Until this business is over with the missing children. I don't want you or the show in the crossfire."

"No," Calvin said.

"You just said that you didn't make as much money as you wanted. There are towns that will pay twice what you made on Thursday."

"No, Jasper," Calvin said. "I can't leave. None of us can."

"Why not?" I demanded.

"I wasn't going to tell you yet," Calvin said. "I didn't know how to tell you. The show has been hit."

"Hit?"

"The children. Arnold and Lilith."

I felt a cold knot form in my stomach. "No," I said.

"They went missing Friday night. That's why I was still awake tonight. I couldn't sleep."

Arnold and Lilith were the two youngest Valen children. They were Calvin's nephew and niece. They had come to stay with Calvin when the show moved to Ravenwood because they wanted to know about their family's sideshow. It ran in their blood.

"That's why you didn't do a second show after Thursday?" I asked.

"All of our energy is going into finding them," Calvin said. "Of course, my brother and his wife blame me. I would blame me too."

"You should blame me," I said.

Calvin shook his head. "I blame the monsters who took them. I want them back. I'll get them back."

"Then why were you afraid to tell me?"

"Because I need you with me. I don't need you charging head-first into this thing. You do that, innocent children are killed. My own family. No. I need you focused and I need you thinking."

I nodded. "I'm with you," I said. I thought of telling him that we would do things my way, but I realized that I was not a leader and that Calvin was more level-headed than I would ever be.

"I'm counting on it," Calvin said. "I've been waiting for you to come back this last week, and I've been watching for you since Friday. I hope that together we can save them. Then I'll move the show."

There was something unspoken in Calvin's words. We would rescue his family, and he would move the show. I knew though that I was not to go with the show once it moved.

I can't blame Calvin though. This was my fault. If I had stuck to my conviction that I was bad for those in my company, the Valen children might have never been taken.

What a fool I was.

"Calvin?" I said.

"Yes?"

"I'm sorry."

And I was sorry. The youngest family of my dearest friends was in the hands of my enemies. And as I stood watching the sunrise, I felt the evil in the air. I felt the *darkness*.

2017

"THAT WAS WHEN YOU started remembering Arthan's Purgatory?" Calista asked. "The third time?"

"Third time's the charm," Jasper said. "Not only did I remember everything of that time, but I remembered the other two times as well. My mind was overloaded with the new memories. It took days to sort through them all. In fact, it might have been quicker if I wasn't going after the twins almost as soon as I woke up from my death nap."

"You had priorities," Calista said.

"Of course I did," Jasper replied. "Those monsters had the children and at least ten more. I had to do something, and I had to do it fast. No one else could."

"Because you felt responsible," Calista said. She was trying to empathize with someone she could not possibly understand, and she was failing.

"It was more than that. It wasn't just because I felt responsible. It was because it was the right thing to do. With my powers, I could help. In this last century there were stories that showed up in comic books. Superhero stories. Now there's movies too. That's sort of the same drive that I had, though I will never call myself a hero. I'll never deserve that title."

"Didn't you save those kids in Stetson?" Calista asked. "That sounds pretty heroic to me."

"And now the cops are after me," Jasper said, "again."

"Again?"

"I've had all sorts of trouble with police since I started this crusade. The cops being after me is nothing new. I want to get this done so I can move on. Hide out in some big city on the streets. I have to wait for one of the sects of the Order to start doing things before I can make any moves against them anyway."

As he was talking, he also cracked open a bottle of coke and poured it into a glass that was half full of whiskey. He took the glass to his couch where he kicked his feet up and turned on the radio.

"Break time," Jasper said.

The news report was the same as it was a few days ago. The FBI was involved in the investigation. Jasper knew what would come of it. The children would have been interviewed by the police, of course. The interviews would have amounted to nothing. No one wanted to admit that a secret order of sorcerers existed. It was a conspiracy theory that even conspiracy theorists avoided. That was part of the Order's magic. They kept everyone in the world in the dark to what they were doing.

Jasper clicked off the radio. He finished his whiskey and then closed his eyes. "You can let yourself out," he told Calista.

She did as he said, taking the latest pages of manuscript with her. Jasper, meanwhile, began to nap. As he slept his afternoon away, he dreamed. The dreams that came now were not the same dreams that had plagued his sleep for the length of his immortality. He had actually grown accustomed to those. No. This dream that flashed through his mind was new, and Jasper woke with a start when it was over.

In the dream he was standing in Ravenwood. He was almost always in Ravenwood in his dreams, only this time it was the modern Ravenwood. The sky was darkening as if a storm was about to begin, but the wind was still. Jasper looked up and saw the sun's rays being overtaken by the unnaturally dark cloud cover. There was something else in the sky too. Something that shouldn't exist.

It was a dragon.

Jasper looked down to the cracked pavement on which he was standing and then up to the crumbled buildings. There had been an earthquake in Ravenwood. It had destroyed the town. People were in the streets. Those that weren't running in panic were looting local businesses.

And then there were the Black Cloaks. They seemed to descend onto the looters like ants on a morsel of food. The silver of the daggers in their hands soon turned red as they murdered everyone without hesitation.

Then, among the chaos and the bloodshed, the dragon landed and looked directly at Jasper. It beat its wings once, and then it started to change. First it shrank down until it was the size of a person, then the wings folded into its body. Lastly, it stood on its hind legs and morphed into the image of a woman.

She was clad in black armor that appeared to be the same texture as her dragon scales. Her face was the only skin exposed, and it was deeply scarred. She was beautiful once. But that was long ago. Before her great battle. The dragon wings that folded into her once again spread out, only this time they were angel wings. Black angel wings.

She pointed as Jasper.

"You," she said. "You are a destroyer. A plague upon my world. You will suffer eternally for what you have done."

Jasper did not respond. He woke in a cold sweat. The time was six o'clock. The sun was going down. Ravenwood was not in ruins. The nightmare was over.

Jasper splashed water from the kitchen sink on his face and then sat down at his desk. It was time to start writing again. The dream was new, but Jasper had an idea that it might have been a premonition more than anything else. Perhaps even a threat.

"Valayra," he said to himself. "She's threatening me. Bitch."

He started writing again. Time was growing short. He needed to finish this tale to get the truth of the Order out into the world.

Time was short.

1870

"THE CHILDREN," CALVIN SAID, "should be at this place." He pointed to a spot on a wrinkled map that he was holding. "The Groban farm."

Of course it was a farm. It had to be a farm.

Calvin had been busy since my apparent death. An advertisement was posted all around Ravenwood offering to help bring the children home.

IF YOUR CHILD IS MISSING, WE CAN HELP.
COME TO THE VALEN FARM AND BE PREPARED TO FIGHT.

"Surprised that the sheriff didn't make you take it down," I said.

"He did. And he tried to arrest me. He failed."

"How did he fail?"

"Because I have the largest group of workers in the whole town, and they stood between the sheriff and me. I also had the support of all the parents who had come to try to find their children. There are others too. Some who haven't lost anyone but just want to help. I think we can make a real stand against these monsters here and now."

"I hope so," I said. "If we can just rescue the boys and girls, I'll be happy. I'll deal with the Order later."

And what Calvin said was true. There were many that came to help who were tired of the lies and apathy of the sheriff and his deputies. The children at least had a chance.

The day began with everyone arriving on the farm. I heard horses and carriages approaching the house. At first, I thought it must be the sheriff's men, but I was delighted to find that I was wrong.

"Friends," Calvin said.

That is what they were. Young men and women and those that were nearing old age. There were at least two dozen that had come.

"Welcome," Calvin said. "There are tables set up behind the house. We'll feed all of you while we talk."

The food I had smelled cooking earlier was already sitting on a wagon in the yard. Some of the cast and crew of *Amazing Wonders* served it to those that had come for Calvin's meeting. Eggs, beans, sausage, bread, and coffee.

While the townspeople were eating, Calvin began to speak. I stood beside him as he addressed those who would be our allies.

"Let's save the children and kill the bastards that took them!" Calvin said. There was a delay before the small crowd erupted in a cheer of bloodthirsty agreement.

"How do we do this?" an old man asked. He was at least seventy, and he didn't look all that strong anymore. I wondered if he would have the strength to lift a gun during the upcoming fight.

"We just do it. It shouldn't be that hard," a younger man said from his seat further down the table.

"Bullets in the head. That's how you deal with them," another said.

"Kill the bastards," another said.

These young people were arrogant and sure of themselves. Of course they were. I supposed many of them were sure of their number. They didn't realize what they had signed up for. I doubt they would have abandoned their children to their gruesome fate if they had known, but it was clear to me that no one knew what sort of evil we were facing. The older generation sitting before me was not joining in with their careless boasting. They may not have known what they were facing, but they knew that it would be a dark day in Ravenwood.

"These people," Calvin said when the noise died away, "are not going to be easy to kill. Not for us."

"They won't be," I put in.

"They have control of the law. That means they have firepower on their side as well as the devil magic I talked about before."

The old man who had spoken before spat. "I don't believe in no devil magic, but I am worried about fighting the sheriff and his men."

"You should be more worried about what the Order can do," I told him.

"I thought you died!" I heard someone call out.

"I don't die," I said. "I just sleep for a while."

The old man stayed on topic. "What is the Order?"

"The Order is a cult of witches that kidnap children and sacrifice them to their goddess before eating them," I said.

There was a stunned silence.

"I don't think Calvin has told you what they truly are because Calvin doesn't even know what they truly are. I am the only one who has experience with them, and that is why I will lead this fight."

'What?" A man stood up and walked toward me. "Why should you lead? Why should we follow you?"

"Because I am the one here who stands the best chance of beating them. I will lead the charge."

"We don't even know you. We know Calvin. We know the Valens. Who do you think you are to give us orders."

"Frank," Calvin said, "please."

"You trust him?" Frank asked.

"I do," Calvin said. "Jasper is the best person to lead us."

Frank was tall and thin. Tired blue eyes looked out from under the rim of his black hat. His clothing matched the color of his hat except for his belt which was brown. A six shooter was at his side.

"You want reassurance?" I asked. "This should prove that I am the one to lead as well as prove that the Order is what I say it is."

"What's that?" Frank asked.

"Shoot me."

"What?"

"Draw your gun and shoot me."

"I'm not gonna shoot you," he said.

"It won't kill me."

"Not gonna happen."

"Fine." I turned to Calvin. "Calvin, will you please shoot me?"

My friend pulled the gun that was inside his jacket and aimed it at me. I opened my shirt to reveal I was wearing nothing the stop the bullet. This was going to hurt, but I felt it was necessary. I spread my arms, and Calvin shot me.

The force of the shot knocked me on my back. The men and women who had come to our aid screamed in horror at the sight of me apparently being murdered on my own free will.

I was on my feet again in seconds. A small drop of blood had formed from the welt left by the bullet.

I smiled at them all.

"How?" one of the women asked.

"It's part of my history with the Order," I said. "I am a lot older than anyone eating here today. My name is Jasper Gunne, and I am one hundred seventy years old."

———◆———

THE INTERRUPTIONS HAD CEASED, and I was able to tell my story. I explained how I was the first generation of my family born in the New World. I told them all of how I had married the love of my life and had a wonderful family. I delved into how I had lost my wife to illness and then how everything had been taken from me by the Order. I tried my best to explain their magic and how it had been mutilated by the evil and vindictive Frederick. I don't think many of them understood what I was saying. Back then, even I had a difficult time understanding it. I knew it, but I couldn't explain it well enough to make anyone else grasp my meaning.

I explained how I had come to live with the Valen family who had been traveling with *Amazing Wonders.* How I had known Melvin Valen and Richard Valen. How Calvin Valen had become my dearest friend. I even talked of the Ridens and how Thomas Riden was thought to still be alive.

"He's coming," I said to them.

It was a war older than the Bible, and it was still being fought. Arthan was a prisoner of that war, and I thought he might have been watching me then. Here I was recruiting new soldiers. I was afraid though. I was afraid I was going to lead them all to their deaths.

"These people have our children?" one woman asked. "The same ones that killed your family? Your baby grandson?"

"The same ones. Descendants of the same ones at least. And Thomas Riden. He is a part of it."

"We have to kill these bastards!" she cried out.

The others either shouted their agreement with her or slammed their hands on the table. I smiled. This time would be different. The last time it was just me trying to stop this evil. This time though... this time I had help.

"We'll save your children and we'll make sure the Order can never do this again," I said.

But I knew that I was not telling the truth. The Order was spread throughout the world. If we stopped them here, they would do the same thing again elsewhere. The fight would be never-ending.

Good thing I'm immortal.

"Tonight, we all go to the Groban farm together," Calvin said. "Jasper leads."

"Why not now?" one of the women asked. The others began shouting their agreement.

"Because Jasper says we have until the full moon, which is two days away. And I want to use the time to come up with the best strategy. If these people are as dangerous as Jasper says, we might end up dead if we try now, and that won't save our children. Promise me, all of you, that you will not go alone and try anything."

There was a murmur of agreement from the people sitting at the tables. It was not enthusiastic, and I wondered just how many were going to break their promise. Back in 1750, if someone had told me to wait when I knew where Richard, my baby grandson was being kept, I would have disobeyed.

Calvin was done with his meeting, and so he and I helped ourselves to beans and bread. The eggs and sausage were already gone. We sat away from everyone else. Calvin was nervous of the coming night of fighting, and he was worried about his niece and nephew. I kept him company as he ate, but I did not try to talk to him.

As we finished eating we heard horses approaching. I looked at Calvin, and he rolled his eyes. We knew who had come. It was the sheriff.

Sheriff Marley was flanked by two of his deputies. They wore white hats with matching shirt and pants. Their stars were pinned to blue vests. Each had two six-shooters strapped to their belts, and each had a hand on one of their guns.

I stayed out of sight, not wanting to reveal myself as being alive until we encountered the Order later that night.

"What do you want, Marley?" Calvin asked from the front porch. "This isn't a good time."

I watched from a window on the top floor of the house. Marley looked at the horses tied to the porch and shook his head. "Got a party here today?"

"Some friends come to help me do something about my missing niece and nephew," Calvin said. "The law doesn't seem to care."

"Listen here," one of the deputies said, "you'll be causing no trouble in our town. You're not getting a mob all riled up over nothing."

"I'll get one riled up over something. Now I suggest you leave while you still can."

"Son of a bitch!" the same deputy cried as he drew one of his pistols.

I heard guns being cocked and knew that I did not have to intervene. *Amazing Wonders* and the people of Ravenwood came to Calvin's aid just as they had before I woke up in my grave.

The sheriff looked side to side at his deputies and then hung his head as if he were sad. "I had hoped to reason with you, Valen. You come to my town. You open your business. We welcome you with open arms. Then you cause trouble."

"I'm doing what I have to do," Calvin said.

"These people are scared enough with their kids missing, and you come here and make them think that the law is responsible. Know this, if you did not have all those people with all those guns backing you up, you'd be in jail like your friend was last week."

Calvin said nothing.

"We're going!" Marley said to his deputies.

And they left.

I NAPPED THAT AFTERNOON. I was unaware of my exhaustion at first, but something was happening to my body. I remember sitting in a chair reading a book, and then, suddenly, I was standing by the window.

Only, that wasn't quite right.

I was standing by the window, but when I turned around, I saw that I was also sleeping in the chair. I was, in fact, out of my body. I raised a hand to my eyes, but I could see nothing. Indeed, I was not even there in physical form. My spirit was free.

Did I just die again?

And then I heard the voice that threatened to confirm my suspicions.

"Jasper?"

It was the voice of Arthan. Not only was I remembering everything from my last trip to his purgatory, but now he was calling my name. I was dead again. What else could it be? I was dead and about to go back to the purgatory. My body couldn't take it anymore. It couldn't stay alive anymore. The unnatural powers had taken their toll. My friends would all die now without me to help. It was all over. The Order would win. I was finished.

"Jasper!"

"I hear you, Arthan," I said.

"Good. I've been calling for you. This was your third death last time, right?"

"Yes. And it looks like I'm joining you again soon."

"Why?" he asked.

"I'm dead here again. I'm looking at my body now. It's all over."

"It's not," Arthan said. *"Look at your body closely. Are you breathing?"*

I moved closer. *"I am,"* I said. *"I don't understand."*

"You will," he said. *"It's taken some time because you're not part of Valayra's Order, but your powers are still waking up."*

"My powers?"

"The more you die, the more powerful you become. You just left your body. You are free to do as you want."

"But what can I do?" I found myself not even questioning the new ability or the fact that Arthan could now speak to me in my spirit form. When you're an immortal with demon powers who can't stay dead, you stop questioning things. I knew that Arthan was right because I could feel a connection with my body.

"You know of possession?" Arthan asked. *"Spirits and demons?"*

"I've heard of it."

"That is what you could do."

Before I could reply I was jolted awake. It was like being startled from a dream. One second I was by the window speaking with Arthan and the next I was in the chair and startled. I thought for a moment that I had only dreamed of my conversation. Then, I sat back, closed my eyes, stayed still for a few minutes, and emerged from by body again. I returned to my body again a second later and opened my eyes.

———◦———

I DIDN'T COME TO Calvin Valen's meetings. I didn't talk to any of the people who had come to get their children back. They wouldn't have been able to help with what I was going to do. If Arthan was correct, I would be able to turn the Order against itself. They would kill each other and I would save the children and no innocents would have to die. It was like a gift from Heaven. These powers would have been so helpful the last time I had encountered these monsters. No matter now. I could do it all myself. I could save every child that had been taken.

Drift away. Leave your body. Do it now.

I was in an upstairs bedroom where I had told Calvin I would take a rest before the upcoming fight. It was planned for nightfall, but I would end it while the sun was still setting.

I practiced. I would sit on the bed, then project myself forward. I would find myself standing at the other side of the room while my body was still seated. I was a living ghost.

This caused me to laugh. The laughter was loud to me, but evidently no one in the house heard it.

I found that it became easier the more I did it. I was still being pulled back to my body, but I could resist the pull by simple concentration. While Calvin was making plans and thinking I was resting, I left the farm and made my way to Ravenwood.

I have reached sixty miles per hour when I run, and I believe I was moving at least that fast as a living ghost. I made my way to the Groban farm at that speed and was there before I even really thought of a plan. I'd only known of its location because of Calvin's map. Making my way there, I noticed how dead Ravenwood was. There was no one on the streets though it was only late afternoon. Was a sense of dread to blame? Perhaps. It wouldn't stay quiet for long though.

If Arthan was right (and if I'd actually heard my angelic friend instead of imagining him) then I would be able to possess the bodies of others. I could turn the Order against itself. If Arthan was right. That was my whole plan. It may not have been a great one, but I doubted the Order would be prepared for it. As I walked through the wall to enter the house I saw that they were preparing for a fight. There were rifles and pistols and ammunition everywhere. They knew that the town was coming for them.

"Why does this Valen not forget us?" I heard one of them ask.

"The High Master says he is Dedran returned," another replied. "That is why he can see through our spells."

"I don't believe in Dedran coming back," the first said.

"You don't have to believe. The High Master believes. Besides, how else can he lead such a group of people against us. It only happens when Dedran is here."

"Or an abomination like the one that was killed a short time ago."

"The High Master says to be ready for him too. He doesn't believe he will stay dead."

"Of course, he doesn't."

"Do I hear blasphemy coming from you?"

"Not at all. I would never speak against my High Master."

"Good."

I didn't understand any of it then. I knew I was the abomination, but what was Dedran? I know the answer now, and it is terrible, but I was utterly confused back then.

The children were in the center of the living room encircled with lit candles. They had the same somber look on their face. They were afraid, but resigned to death. Bloodshot eyes told of tears shed, but now they were too tired or too dehydrated to weep. The bastards in the Order had probably let them suffer in their thirst and hunger.

I looked at the cloaked men and women. Adam Riden was among them. The cloaks they all wore were the same as they had been back in 1750 and again in 1819. I saw knives on the table that were the same jagged blades that had taken the life of my grandson.

Sheriff Marley and his men were in the house. I noticed that the sheriff would not look at the bound children. Maybe there was a piece of good still inside him that rebelled against what he was doing. It is a barbaric and evil thing to do. Kidnapping and murdering children in ritualistic sacrifice. It is something you would think men like Sheriff Marley would fight against. That promise of power though, it is strong and it breaks weak men. I've had allies over the years that have betrayed me because of power promised to them by the Order.

May they rot in hell.

"We have a problem, Riden," Marley said. "I need to see the man in charge."

"That's me," Adam Riden said.

"I mean your pa," Marley said.

Adam Riden rolled his eyes and said: "My *pa?*"

"Yeah."

"You mean my father? What does he have to do with it?"

"He is going to turn my town into a battlefield! I need to talk to him!"

"Your town matters not to us," Riden said.

"It matters a hell of a lot to me!" Marley replied.

"You need not worry," Riden said. "I am going to deal with those who come to stop us, and the goddess will bless our efforts. My father will arrive soon, and your townspeople will see sense. It has been foreseen."

"I don't think they'll see sense," Marley said. "I've been out to the Valen place. They're preparing for a war out there."

"And my people are more than adequately prepared to deal with the rabble," Adam Riden said.

"That's the problem, young man," Marley said. "I was chosen by the people to protect them. I can't have 'em dead in the street."

"But what if these people are working against you?" Adam asked.

"Then we try to stop it without killing!"

"Look around you, fool," Adam Riden said. "We don't need you. We've never needed you. We offered you this chance because your firepower makes things easier for us. You don't care about these people. You're just afraid."

Marley bristled at being called afraid. "Now, see here," he said.

"No. You see here. You're afraid of what's going to happen. You're afraid of being killed before you get your reward. You care nothing for these people. You only care for yourself. If you cared you would not have helped us take all the children. All of them were acquired with your help."

"I..."

"All of these children were brought here to die with your help. Don't talk to me about how you want to spare your people bloodshed. Don't talk to me about how you love your town. You only want to avoid the fight to protect yourself."

From my vantage point in the corner of the room, I heard all of this. There was fear in Marley's eyes. I figure he was regretting his choice now. Surely, the Order had promised him such wondrous power that his ignorant greedy soul could not resist. Now he was paying the price for that power. I looked into his eyes, and I saw tears. He cuffed them away and frowned. His resolve had returned. He was going through with this evil no matter what.

And then I acted.

Going by Arthan's words, I moved to possess Sheriff Marley. I wasn't sure how to do it, I just did what seemed natural. As a spirit, I took control of him. He fought me at first, but soon I had taken his mind for my own.

I opened Marley's eyes. He was still there with me inside his own mind, but he could do nothing to stop me. I felt his fear. I heard him beg me to leave. I even heard him pray to God, the Father. What a fool. As if God would listen to someone conspiring to offer children to a demon in order to gain power.

I was in control.

I made the sheriff draw his gun. I could hear him inside his own head, begging me to let him go. I ignored him. The gun was raised and pointed at Adam Riden. I could see the resemblance of my old friend in his stunned face. He backed away with his hands over his head.

"Mr. Marley," he said, "let's talk this over."

That was the last sentence he ever spoke. I pulled the trigger.

"Kill them!" I yelled with Marley's voice to the other lawmen that were in that room. I didn't know if they would obey me, but if they did, I was hoping to be done with this fight before it could even begin.

Instead of joining in the killing they stood still, clearly not knowing what to do next. The black cloaks made the decision for them as they drew their guns and knives and attacked us. The deputies would die regardless because their boss had killed Adam Riden before their eyes. That was fine with me.

Sheriff Marley was soon riddled with bullets. I kept firing the gun as he died. Three more of the black cloaks were dead. As Sheriff Marley's body breathed its last, I was forced out.

Almost instantly, I was being pulled back to my own body. I had to focus quickly and force myself to stay in that farmhouse. Once I steadied myself, I moved to get back into the fight.

I possessed a black cloak.

The man I possessed was frightened and shocked all at once. He retreated to the corners of his mind just as Marley had done. I ignored his spirit's whimpering and used him to kill the cloaks on either side of him. This was perfect. As soon as the two were dead, my black cloak was cut down.

I repeatedly possessed them. One after another. I took control of a woman and made her jam her knife into another cloak's throat. Then I took control of a man and unloaded his gun on the remainder of my enemies in that room. Soon they were all wounded and fighting each other, not knowing why things had turned the way they did and not knowing who to trust.

They were all trying to survive by killing one another. It was chaos in that house. I had done my job. The deputies were all dead with their sheriff. The black cloaks were half their number now and the other half were locked in a bloody knife and gun fight.

I waited as the killing came to an end. Then, when there were only three left, I possessed them each in turn. I heard their souls scream as I forced their bodies to kill themselves. They slid knives across their throats, spilling blood onto the floorboards.

And then my spirit was standing amidst the bloodied corpses of my enemies. I felt relief as I realized that the fight was over and the children were safe. There would be no battle in Ravenwood that night.

We had won.

2017

J ASPER GUNNE WAS SMOKING a pipe when Calista came by with the edited pages of his finished manuscript. She opened the folder, took out the finished file, then replaced it with the new pages he had typed in the last couple days.

"Smoking kills," Calista said.

"Not me," Jasper replied.

His eyes were closed as he smoked. He hadn't bothered to greet Calista when she arrived, and he remained seated and unmoved

"What's wrong?" she asked.

"Nothing," Jasper said. "Just remembering things. Bad things."

Instead of replying she read over what he had written. "Strange," she said when she got to the part about his soul leaving his body to possess others. "That whole spirit thing kind of comes out of nowhere."

"That's how it came for me," Jasper said.

"But it's so sudden."

"It's because of the dying thing. I had to die three times to get the powers I have now. It wasn't until the third time that I even remembered Arthan. The third death was my spirit's awakening. I became two beings then. A flesh being and a spirit one.

"It says Arthan spoke to you."

"He did," Jasper said. "We still speak sometimes. Even he can't see everything that happens though. For a while he talked to me during my long fight against the Order, but now he's silent. Been silent for a few decades."

"Maybe the Order is all dead," she said.

"I hope so. Except for the few small groups of them I still find. It might be why I can't feel the *darkness* the same as I used to. Maybe I did kill them all."

"Yeah," she said. Then she slid the papers back into the folder. "I have to get going. I'll edit these a bit."

"Okay," Jasper said, standing as she left. "I think I'll get back to work, actually."

"See you tomorrow or the next day," she said.

When Calista was gone, Jasper sat at his computer, puffed on his pipe, then began writing again. Within a minute his mind was thrown back to the year 1870 and the aftermath of his bloody supernatural battle.

1870

THE CHILDREN WERE REUNITED with their parents that same day. I returned to my body, and raced back to the Groban Farm to release them. I didn't bother with questions as I bolted out the door. I ignored the people who were sitting in the yard, preparing to fight. There was no time to waste.

"It's okay," I said when I arrived at the farmhouse where so much confusing carnage had just played out. "I'm here to help you. Your parents sent me."

The children were shaking. Some were sobbing while others were attempting to maintain their composure. These brave boys and girls stared with clenched jaws and tears running down their cheeks.

I reached out to feel the *darkness*, but it was miles away from us that day. The leftover fading energy was coming from the corpses of my enemies. I had been successful in defeating them, but it had taken a toll. I was exhausted.

As we walked back to the Valen Farm, I had to keep myself focused. I felt as if I could pass out from exhaustion. It was the price of my spirit leaving my body to fight. I would need rest soon.

No one stopped us. I didn't expect they would. Most of the town was gathered near the Valen Farm, preparing for a battle that was already won. The people who would have given me problems were dead. I knew that this wasn't over though. Thomas was still out there. We were going to meet again. I could feel it.

It was a slow walk back to the Valen Farm. It would have been slow without having to worry about leading the children. I was weak. Too weak. The cost of this new power that I had used to its full potential was a physical drain. If I had stayed out of my body much longer, I knew that I would have ended up in Arthan's Purgatory until I could recover.

I can only do that when I absolutely have to.

It was worth the exhaustion though. I'd saved innocent blood from being spilled. But how many more would die now because of my actions? The Order was not a group that was defied. They would be coming. Valayra would demand it.

When we arrived at the farm, it was midday turning into evening. I heard a gun shoot off. It was a signal that someone was approaching. Then, soon after, the front yard filled with the parents of the children that had been taken.

I dropped to my knees and let the children run to their families. They ran, shouting for joy, and the parents embraced them, crying tears of relief and happiness.

"HOW DID YOU DO IT?" Calvin asked me in a sharp, angry tone. The gratitude that the parents seemed to be feeling was not to be found in my friend.

"I used a new power. One that lets me leave my body and possess other people."

"You possessed them?"

"The black cloaks. Yes. First it was Sheriff Marley. I made him start the fight. Then I possessed his men and then moved onto the black cloaks. I made them kill each other.

Calvin shuddered at the way I was calmly talking about these things. It was nothing to me. I just had a new power. I had killed those who were my enemies. I had enjoyed it. There was no guilt to be felt. I fear that I am desensitized to this sort of violence now. But maybe that's a good thing. I don't need to deal with a conscience on top of my eternal war.

"Do you realize how dangerous that was?" Calvin asked. "The children could have been killed."

"My way was less dangerous than yours," I said. "You wanted to lead half the town to the Groban Farm and have a battle. How many do you think would have died then? My way was better. I didn't know if I could do it or not, so I didn't bring it up. When I did do it, I made sure that I finished the job before coming back. Our enemies are dead, and the children are safe. What more do you want?"

Calvin had nothing more to say at that moment. He walked away in one direction and I went in the other. I needed to rest. I couldn't deal with him now. I knew what his problem was even if he didn't. Being strong or fast or even being able to take bullets was astonishing, but it was something he had known I could do since he was a child. Leaving my body and possessing others though, that was a level of strange he was not ready to fathom. It was unnatural. Even I could accept that. I wasn't going to apologize for it though. The monsters in the Order of Valayra made me the way I am, and I will always use those curses/gifts to make them regret it.

———◎———

I WAS A HERO in Ravenwood following the events of that day. I remember being awoken in the early afternoon two days after I had saved the children. I had been sleeping a lot to recover from the fight. I had spent nearly sixteen hours asleep before being roused, and I was still physically exhausted. It would be a week before I felt normal again.

"What is it?" I asked Julia, one of our actresses. She had shaken me awake, and I was startled to see her in my room. "What's wrong?"

"Come outside, Jasper," she said.

I sat up and stumbled to the door wearing only my pants. I reached out to feel the *darkness*, but it was far away. I held the railing as I descended the stairs - sure that my legs would fail me. When I made it to the front door, Calvin opened it for me. Then, as I stepped onto the porch, I looked across the faces of a crowd that had gathered in front of the house.

They all began to clap.

I stood in awe as the town showered their adoration not only on me, but on *Amazing Wonders* as well. The cast and crew of the show gathered around me, and we all took in the praise of the town we had helped save.

"Take a bow, Jasper," Calvin said, standing next to me. "You've earned it."

And so I took a bow. We had won the love of the town. We had saved the children. The black cloaks were as dead as the corrupt sheriff and his men.

Yet I felt that it was not over. Somewhere out there, Thomas Riden was still alive. I didn't know what he would do next, but I knew that I was tasked with stopping it.

———◦◦◦———

I DRANK FOR FREE at the tavern from that day forward. The town loved me, and everyone involved with the show. When I refused to become a sheriff, the job was offered to Calvin. He refused it too.

"*Amazing Wonders* is my job," he told them.

I spent most of my days meditating. I searched for a point where I could feel the black cloaks. They remained elusive. I could sense Thomas Riden, but I could not locate him. I knew he was coming at some point. You might wonder why I didn't leave. It's because I knew I had endangered the town. This was the place where Thomas knew I had last been seen. He would come with all of his power.

A sheriff was elected a month after the death of Marley and the black cloaks. Sheriff Warson. He was a good man, but stubborn. I remember he always woke up early and went to sleep late. He would be seen walking the town with a scowl on his face. He was looking for trouble, and he expected it to begin soon. I personally warned him of what was coming, though I spared him the details about myself and the things I had done in my painfully long life.

It was a cool breezy morning at the Valen Farm when I sat with Warson on the porch, sharing a pot of coffee with him.

"This is a fine piece of land out here," Warson said, wiping coffee from his white handlebar mustache.

"Third generation," Calvin said from behind us. He had come out with a fresh pot to join us.

"You don't farm it yourself though," Warson said.

"No. Use the land for my other business. My uncles were the farmers."

"I knew them," Warson said. There was a hint of disdain in his voice. Warson was one of the people in Ravenwood that had objected to a sideshow being established permanently in the town. "Good people. One of them was even my friend. Once."

"Sheriff," I said, bringing the conversation back to the reason I had invited him here, "we need to talk about the things that happened in this town. We need to talk about Marley, his men, and about what's to be done when the black cloaks return."

"The black cloaks? You mean the rich people that came to town, bought everyone's trust, then kidnapped all the children."

"There are more. Many more. And they are coming. They are coming to this town, and we need to be ready."

Warson sipped his coffee and looked out to the field that was left without crops this year. The tents were taking place of the vegetables. In a year's time, Calvin hoped to have new barns in that field to house his show.

"Gotta say something," Warson said. "I don't much like you people. It seems trouble started when you all came to town."

"That's unfair," Calvin said.

"Is it? Only going by what I saw."

"And what did you see?" I asked.

"First there were no problems out of the ordinary. Then you folks show up. A week later, we have a pile of dead bodies."

"That wasn't us," I said. "It was all them. We saved the children from those monsters."

"And you're a damned unnatural son of a bitch, if I do say so," Warson said. "You expect me to believe that someone like yourself just happened to show up when all this was happening? No sir. I'll tell you what I believe. I believe you're a part of it. I don't know how or why, but I believe that you are not to be trusted."

I had expected some of the people in Ravenwood would think this way, but they had all shown me such adoration since I had saved their children that Warson's attitude surprised me. Rather than get offended though, I tried to see it from his side. I probably wouldn't have trusted me either if I was him.

"Jasper has a link to the black cloaks," Calvin said.

I closed my eyes in annoyance. I didn't want to spend an afternoon telling my story to the new sheriff. I only wanted to warn him of what was coming for the town.

"A link?"

"Jasper can feel them. He can sense where they are in the world. He says they are moving fast toward Ravenwood. You should take his warning seriously."

"Oh, I'm taking it all very serious," Warson said.

"So what are you going to do?" Calvin asked.

"Prepare," Warson said.

"Did you see the power they had?" I asked.

"Power?"

"The power they had. The power they used. Did you see it?"

"I don't know what you mean."

"Exactly," I said. "You don't. You weren't there. They have some sort of power like demons and devils. They will use it. Something's different now. Something's wrong. I think Thomas Riden means to punish this town."

Without hesitating, he gave me his answer to the problem I had presented. "The Lord Jesus Christ will protect us."

That was the end of the conversation. He finished his coffee with one final gulp, nodded to Calvin, then walked down the steps, untied his horse, and rode back to town.

"Things will get ugly," I said to Calvin. "If you mean to stay in Ravenwood, you need to be prepared. Guns. Bullets. Arm everyone. Something bad is on the way."

"Is it going to be worse?" Calvin asked.

"I don't know. There's a change in the *darkness*. I know they mean to come to Ravenwood. I don't understand it though. Why? Because we stopped them from the mass sacrifice? That doesn't make sense. They should be going into hiding. That's why I'm nervous. They are coming here instead of running."

"I'll stand with you, my friend," Calvin said, "until the end. Together. You and me. Killing these monsters."

And there was a hint of bloodlust in his voice. That was good. He would need that. There was something else too. When he talked of fighting against the black cloaks with me, he seemed to have a sense of purpose, and it was enough to get him excited. It was similar to the way he would discuss new acts for the show. Ever since the day I'd saved the children, Calvin had not been enthused in any way about *Amazing Wonders*. He was done with that life. He had seen the horrors that most never realize exist. It made entertainment a shallow way to live a life. This was a true purpose.

Calvin Valen was my greatest friend and my greatest ally. He stood beside me without the powers that I had been cursed/blessed with. He stood by my side against the hordes of shadowy evil that secretly crept across the face of the earth. I loved that man like a brother, and that's why I have never forgiven myself for his death a decade into our crusade. He could have had a happy and normal life if he had stayed away from me. In fact, many associated with the show would have been better off if old Melvin Valen had not taken me in.

I bring nothing but pain to those I love.

2017

 A GREEN TRUCK PULLED into the parking lot of the apartment complex. Jasper noticed it but didn't pay much attention. He was still lost in his own thoughts. He had come outside to sit on the steps and look toward the town that had been built on the ashes of the original Ravenwood. The memories were vivid. The dreams were horrific. Everything he had experienced back then was in a way more real to him than even the present day. The feeling of *darkness* was growing stronger and more defined. Something at least equal to the horrors of 1870 was on the horizon and Jasper didn't know what to do about it. The things he had done last time had made it all so much worse. He had won, but there had been a price to pay. A price too great. He was still staring toward the town when the man in overalls, a black flannel shirt and a blue baseball cap stepped in front of him.

"Hello, there," he said.

"Hello," Jasper said, looking at his visitor. Immediately he noticed there was a resemblance to his old friend, Calvin Valen. He understood then who this man was.

"Jacob Valen," he said, extending a hand.

"Jasper Gunne," Jasper said, shaking his hand. He stood.

"I know," Jacob said. "That's why I'm here. Will you walk with me?"

Jasper shrugged. "Lead the way."

They walked in silence for a time. Jacob led him down some side roads that led to an old dirt road. Once on that road Jacob began to talk. "Calista is my daughter. She's been writing a lot of stuff lately, and it all seems to be about you, Mr. Gunne."

"We are working on something," Jasper said.

"I need to know," Jacob said, "if you are just making crap up or if you really believe in all the garbage that she has been writing down."

Jasper was not surprised by this reaction. He had not expected everyone to believe his story. Maybe no one would believe it. It didn't matter to him. He wanted his own account of what had happened in Ravenwood to be available to the people of the world. He wanted to try to disprove the ludicrous legend of the Monster of Ravenwood.

"I think you know about our family and our stories," Jacob Valen said.

"And what if I did?" Jasper asked.

"I would say that you're trying to make a quick buck."

"I don't need a quick buck. I have more money than probably anyone you know, not that it matters."

Jacob shrugged. "I don't know what you want or why you're doing what you're doing, but I'd ask you to stop. Too many people bother us as it is. Ghost stories. People want to hear the old tales. They come up with records of what our family did a hundred or so years ago, then they make a circus of us for a while."

"I don't intend to do that," Jasper said. "You won't believe me, but I *am* Jasper Gunne."

"I'm not a gullible man," Jacob said.

The two continued to walk. It was clear that Jacob Valen didn't know what he had meant to accomplish with this visit. He had only felt compelled to say something to this supposed charlatan that was claiming to be from their family's past.

"My daughter's a grown woman," Jacob said, "and a successful writer. She can do what she likes. I just don't want her getting mixed up in something bad."

"And I'm something bad?"

"I think you know what I'm saying," Jacob said.

Jasper shook his head and stopped walking. The sun was setting, and the mosquitoes were swarming, though none would bite him. Jacob Valen looked uncomfortable and it was clear to Jasper that there was something he wanted to say but was too afraid to say it.

"You think me a fraud," Jasper said.

"That is exactly what I think," Jacob said.

Jasper nodded. "Fine. I'm going to prove I am who I say I am."

"You're what?"

"I'm going to prove it to you."

"Listen, I'm not here to buy what you're selling. I just want you to know that I know you're a fake. Don't fuck with my family, and we'll be okay."

Jasper ran down the road then. He ran faster than any normal man could run and yet he still didn't reach his top speed. Then he turned around and ran back toward Jacob Valen. Jasper saw the old man try to move out of the way, but it was too late. Jasper would have run into him if that was his intent. Instead he leapt over him.

"Holy hell," Jacob said.

Jasper landed, squatting with his hands on the ground. He picked up two rocks, stood, twirled, and hurled them at the trees. They dented the trunks.

"How could I do that if I'm not who I say I am?" Jasper asked.

Jacob waved a finger in his face. "You?"

"Me," Jasper said. "I am the one your family has talked about for over a hundred years. I am the one that your ancestor called brother."

"Jasper Gunne. That's your real name?"

"It is. And I would never do anything against your family, sir. I love your family as if it were my own, though I have not met any of you since Calvin died."

Jacob Valen, once again, seemed to not know what to say. No one ever knew what to say. This man had thought Jasper a charlatan. Now he was finding out just how wrong he was.

"You want a drink?" Jasper asked.

Jacob nodded. "I don't usually like the stuff, but I could use one now."

Jasper led Jacob back to his building. He ignored the neighbors gathered near the door who were talking with one another and blocking the way. He pushed past them, leading Jacob into his apartment.

"Whiskey or rum?" Jasper asked.

"Whatever," Jacob said. "Not much preference."

Jasper poured two shots of rum. He took one and handed the other to Jacob.

"So how did it all start?" Jacob asked after his shot was gone.

"You'll have to read our book," Jasper said. "Not to be rude, but it's all very painful for me to remember, and I have already put it down on paper. You can read it if you want."

"I might have to do that."

There was a knock at the door and then it opened. "Jasper, I'm back with more revisions." It was the voice of Calista Valen. She didn't bother waiting for Jasper to answer the door. She never did.

"Dad?" Calista said, looking at Jacob. "What...?"

"He came to see me," Jasper said. He got up and walked back to the kitchen, taking Jacob's shot glass with him. He refilled the glass and his own and then poured one for Calista. "He thinks me a fraud."

"Not anymore," Jacob said.

"I showed him some things," Jasper said, handing Calista her shot and returning to the couch where he handed Jacob his second.

"You *were* reading my book, weren't you?" Calista asked her father.

"Yes," Jacob said. "I was worried about you. Now I'm more worried than ever actually."

"Why?" Calista asked.

Jacob shook his head. "It's all still too new to me. I can't wrap my brain around any of it."

"I'm real," Jasper said. "That's what you really wanted to know, wasn't it? If I was lying?"

Jacob nodded, then let out a nervous laugh. "Yes," he said. Then he shook his head. "No. Yes. I don't know. You're real. But I don't want you to be real."

"Thanks," Jasper said. "I also wish I was never born."

"That's not what I mean," Jacob said. "If you're real then the people who made you are real too."

"The Order," Jasper said. "They call themselves the Order."

"And what are they?"

"You really want an answer?" Jasper asked.

"Yes," Jacob said. "Are they all dead?"

Jasper shook his head. "I can still feel them, but I can't locate them anymore. I don't know what it is. Somehow they are able to throw me off. I don't know. I feel them, but finding them... it's impossible."

"And you've been at this for over a century?"

Jasper nodded. "It used to be a bit easier to track them down. I guess it was only a matter of time before they figured out a way to outsmart me."

"But who are they?" Jacob asked.

"They are a secret society of witches and warlocks," Jasper said. "Not like wiccans or the characters in books or movies. These people worship a devil that they call a goddess. They offer the blood of the innocent to that goddess, and through the ritual they are given the *power*. It's a kind of magic."

"And they kill little kids to do this?" Jacob asked.

"Yes," Jasper said. "Without hesitation or thought. They say that they are offering the children to Valayra. That is the name of the devil. Supposedly Valayra is wrapping them in her arms and they are becoming a part of her army. Not just children though. Sometimes they kill adults."

Jacob began shaking his head again.

"All of it seems absurd," Jasper said. "Absurd until you see me and my powers."

"So what are you then?" Jacob asked. "How many kids had to die to make you?"

"Only one," Jasper said, remembering once again the blood of his infant grandson and the taste of it in his mouth. Try as he might, he would never forget that taste. "The warlock botched the ritual. Included me in it out of cruelty. It was my own baby grandson who was sacrificed. I tried to stop it. The things that were done... If the warlock had done what he was supposed to do then I would have died with my family that day, but he didn't. That's why I am here standing before you now. I became something else. And I could think of no better way to use my powers than to try to kill every last witch or warlock out there that is doing the same things to children and families all over the world."

When Jasper had finished his short speech there was silence. Neither of the Valens knew how to respond to what he had said. Jasper sat in an old armchair that was losing its stuffing. He wondered absently how many more times he would sit there. He hadn't meant to stay in Ravenwood for long. Once the book was finished, he figured he would move on. But maybe not. Maybe the Order was indeed coming back. Ravenwood held meaning for the followers of Valayra. If they came back, Jasper could deal with them directly. It was a frightening thought. 1870 all over again. It would have to be different this time though. There was already too much blood on his hands.

"Do they know you're still alive?" Jacob Valen asked.

"What?" Jasper said, pulled from his own thoughts by his guest's voice.

"Do they know you're still alive?" Jacob said again. "The witches?"

Jasper shrugged. "I don't understand them all too well. It's not like a religion like Christianity or Islam or Hinduism. They don't all follow one set core of beliefs." He scratched his chin. "Their doctrines and traditions are passed down with little written record. Think of it as legends and tall tales. Oral history, they call it. That's how they pass down their beliefs. Some know about me. They are small groups that make up a big one, see? Some know about me and some don't. I've met both kinds. I'm sure there are some out there that know all about the history and battles against me, but there are probably just as many that don't even realize I exist."

"Really?" Calista asked.

"I met one that told me he thought I was only a myth," Jasper said. "He believed that for about thirty more seconds until I bashed his head into the pavement. There is no mercy for these child-killing assholes."

Jacob stood, looked at his daughter and then at Jasper. "I would just like to shake your hand, sir," he said.

"That's quite all right," Jasper said.

Jacob walked to him and extended his arm. "I mean it," he said. "I'm sorry about earlier. I hope the friendship you had with my grandfathers can continue."

"I hope so too," Jasper said. He shook Jacob Valen's hand and then watched as the old farmer left. Calista nodded at Jasper and then followed her father out the door. There were no new pages of manuscript that day. She had nothing to collect.

How odd that I should come across the Valens again, Jasper thought, and not for the first time since he had met Calista. If not for the fact that he abandoned Ravenwood and *Amazing Wonders* after the massacre, Calvin may never have had children, and there would not have been descendants to befriend Jasper now. He remembered that day after the massacre. He remembered meeting Calvin after the hanging that had failed. His friend had wanted to go with him but Jasper had refused. After some arguing, he had relented and then crept away in the middle of the night before Calvin could notice he was gone.

It was a hard life. I made the choice out of the love for our friendship. I couldn't bring that violence on him.

But that hadn't worked. Calvin had become a part of it anyway. Tears formed in Jasper's eyes at the memories of the last moments of his old friend's life.

He wiped his eyes and turned his attention to his computer. It was time to write.

1870

SHERIFF WARSON WAS STILL suspicious of me and of *Amazing Wonders.* I remember standing at my place next to the stage and looking out at the crowd who had gathered for opening night. There, in the distance, on horseback, was Sheriff Warson.

Calvin's show was a hit with the town. The money poured in from the crowd who had come to be entertained. And entertained they were.

Dancing girls began the set. They were followed by a mock duel between two dwarves. The little men stood on the stage and drew their guns. With a loud pop, the one in black fell over and the one in white bowed to the crowd as the winner. The show rolled along with singers and more dancers. There was a juggler and a magician. The second half of the night was a small play that Calvin had written himself. It was a good night for the show, and we hoped that it would only get better.

But things wouldn't get better. I felt the *darkness* coming. It was closing in on us, and I didn't know what to do besides let it come. I took comfort in the fact that Sheriff Warson seemed to understand that the problems of the town were not over. He was watching. I doubted he would be swayed as easily as his predecessor. I remember thinking Warson would be a good ally when things got bad.

But would they get bad? That was what I wasn't sure of. I had killed the cultists who had been in Ravenwood, and I felt confident I could do it again. I thought the chances were good that the fight wouldn't last too long.

The main problem was Thomas.

I wasn't sure I could kill my old friend. If he was immortal like I was, he would be unkillable.

He ate my grandson.

I'd been considering my own existence and that of Thomas Riden's since I learned he was still alive. He was connected to me in the most grisly of ways.

My grandson's blood had been poured down my throat, and Thomas Riden had eaten his flesh.

ONE NIGHT LATER, Calvin and I were at the tavern. We were throwing back whiskey and not paying for any of it.

"Let me buy you another," a voice would say as soon as our glasses were empty. I would tap my glass and it would be filled. It was a good night for the most part.

"I'm glad we can do this," I told my friend. "Gotta get all the good times in before the Order gets here."

"You keep saying that," Calvin said. "Maybe they'll run and hide."

"They're coming."

I was more than sure now. The dreams had gotten worse. It seemed I was connected to Thomas Riden's mind. I could even sometimes see through his eyes. They were on the road we had travelled so many times. They were getting closer to Ravenwood. The only thing left to determine was when he would arrive.

"If they do come," Calvin said, "we'll help you. Not just the show, but the whole town. They'll meet their end here."

"I hope that I can handle them before it comes to that," I said.

"The spirit possessing thing?"

"Exactly."

"Could work," Calvin said. "But if this guy who's leading them is like you, things could go wrong."

"Maybe you should practice trying to kill me so you can be ready to kill him."

"Taking off your head might work."

"Might."

Calvin and I laughed then. Brothers in arms looking toward a coming battle. I loved that man like a son and like a brother. He was the last and best friend I ever had.

———◦———

ALL AT ONCE, the next day, my sense of the *darkness* was clouded. I could feel it, but I could no longer discern the path along which it was moving. I woke at around nine thirty, and I did not feel the Order. I thought something might be wrong with me. Perhaps the alcohol from the previous night had shrouded my senses. I tried to reach out and feel them, but it was useless. In the space of about ten hours, they had vanished.

"Calvin!" I yelled, leaving my room and running down the stairs. Calvin was at the breakfast table with a hand on his head.

"Bad morning, Jasper," he said. "Guess that means it was a good night."

"Calvin," I said, "we have bigger problems than your headache."

"What?" he asked with a somewhat slurred voice.

"Problems. I lost them. I lost the Order."

———◦———

TWO HOURS LATER Calvin and I were walking through the woods near his property. The breeze was cool on that July day. The sky overhead was growing dark with storm clouds.

"Jasper, I think you're not seeing this the right way."

"And what way should I see it?"

"You say that the feeling you have now is the one you've had for a hundred years or whatever?"

"Yes. Recently it was clearer, but now it's back to being blurred. It's like they vanished and went back into hiding."

"Maybe they did."

"That doesn't make sense. They were coming here. I saw it. I felt it."

"Maybe they were coming, but they found out what you did here. Maybe you scared them back into hiding."

"It doesn't feel right," I said. "And if I did, that means they'll still do what they've been doing. More will die. I thought I had the chance to end it all here in Ravenwood."

"A wasp might sting someone who goes near it," Calvin said. "But isn't it better to leave a wasp nest alone?"

"These wasps aren't stinging. They're destroying lives."

"That they are," Calvin said. "But what can you do now, Jasper? It's as you said. You can't feel them anymore."

Calvin was right. There was nothing left for me to do. My link to them was severed. It was over.

And so over the next month we went on with our lives. I was, in a way, devastated, but I was also relieved. For all of my talk about killing the bastards as soon as they came to town, I was not sure I could kill Thomas Riden. It may sound cowardly, but I was used to fighting against those that were weaker than me. I didn't want to fight someone who was just as strong as I was. Don't get me wrong. I would have fought him. I would not have run away. I just wasn't confident I would win the fight.

THAT WAS SUPPOSED to be the end of it. The Order has receded into the shadows. Weeks went by, and *Amazing Wonders* planted themselves firmly in the town. Ravenwood recovered from the violence it had endured, and it looked forward to better times.

I was forgetting about my vengeance again and focusing on my job and my friends. I wanted to seek out the Order, but with my sense clouded, it was impossible. Calvin helped keep things in perspective for me, and that allowed me to enjoy myself in Ravenwood.

Calvin was happy. His wife was pregnant again, and he could not keep himself from giddiness. That was something I admired about my friend. Many would be cautious to be optimistic in Calvin's situation. The first child was lost due to miscarriage and the second had died on the road when she was a year old. Anyone else would be afraid to be happy, but Calvin would not let past tragedy cloud the future.

He was a wise man, and I should have followed his example.

———⊕———

I REMEMBER WALKING to the river after I finished helping Calvin build a fence around his yard for his dogs.

I went to the river alone, stripped naked, and dove into the cool water. I did not swim for a long time. In fact, I doubt I was in the water for more than five minutes. I made my way to the riverbank after cooling off and started putting my clothes back on.

"Hello, Jasper." I heard the voice of Thomas Riden cut through the air like an arrow. I turned swiftly and saw my old friend standing there with a smug smile on his face. "I see you've been well," he said.

I couldn't believe what I was seeing. Thomas Riden. He was standing there watching me. He hadn't aged a day since 1750, and now he was there, dressed all in black and smiling. He did not wear a black cloak like so many others in the Order did. He was dressed in a black suit that looked more expensive than the wages of the entire cast of *Amazing Wonders*. He reminded me of Cole Claring-ton for a moment. The Order was wealthy and its leaders evidently liked to flaunt their riches.

I moved forward without thought and grabbed my former friend by his neck. He laughed as I lifted him.

"Are you going to kill me, Jasper?" he asked with a voice strained by the pressure I had on his throat. There was a smile in his eyes.

My mind and reason returned to me, and I lowered him to his feet. "How?" I asked.

He shrugged.

"I don't think I can kill you," I said. "And I think you know that." I couldn't feel his presence there. Here he was, the deepest well of all *darkness* and evil, and I could not feel him in front of me.

"Everything I thought I knew about you was right," Thomas said. "How marvelous."

"What are you talking about?"

"I suspected that you were still alive," Thomas said. "Ever since I realized that I was stronger and faster than ever. And that I no longer got sick."

"And that was because you ate my grandson, you sick piece of..."

"Yes! How did you know that?"

"I watched you," I said. I forced my voice to betray no emotion. I would not have him see my sadness and anguish over the memory.

"It was a terrible thing that happened back then," Thomas said. "Terrible. I punished everyone involved."

"Except yourself," I said.

"You remember what happened," he said. "I was betrayed. They took the side of that mongrel, Frederick, and were planning to kill me."

"Then you killed them all. I know. I saw their bodies. Eyes cut out."

"It was a nice touch," he said.

"You didn't do it for me," I said. "You did it for your own damned pride."

"You're right. I tried to get you to listen to reason, but you refused. Later though, when I figured out that things were different with me, I thought of an old prophecy. You're that prophecy, Jasper. You're *the* prophecy."

"What?"

"The Order is old. Ancient. Older than anything else in the world. We were even here before the Flood. Did you know that?"

I glared at him in response.

"Of course you did. You've learned a lot about us since that unfortunate day in 1750. You know what we believe. You know why we do what we do."

"You're monsters," I said. "Monsters who've killed thousands, maybe millions of people and children. It ends now. I swear it."

"Jasper, Jasper," he said. "Let's walk."

"I think I'll stay where I am," I said.

He closed his eyes in annoyance. "Fine," he said. "I come to you in friendship."

I laughed.

"It's true," he said. "Friendship. The friendship we once shared."

"The one that led to my family's death, you mean?"

"Jasper," he said. "I am sorry. That was not my doing. I tried to stop it."

"They still died."

"Yes."

"And now you're doing things like that again and again to innocent people."

"Sacrifice, Jasper. All who are offered are welcomed into the loving arms of our mother."

"They are robbed of their lives so you and your other monsters can have power," I spat at him.

"It's not like that. All of the deaths. All of the pain. It was for a reason. There is a deeper purpose."

"The only purpose that exists is the one I have," I said. "You made a big mistake that day. Your man, Frederick did. I am between the worlds now, Thomas. I have been to the purgatory of Arthan. I have spoken with him. His war has been renewed."

Thomas took a step backwards.

"I have come back to the world for one thing. Vengeance. I have waited years. Decades. A century and more. I have waited to repay to you what you did to me."

"Jasper..."

"I have killed your followers. Three times now I have come across them. Three times I have killed them. It's not enough. It couldn't be enough. But you? You were there. You were the reason that the evil came to my family. You were our friend, and you betrayed us. I will not forgive this. I will not forgive you. I will kill you and everyone that you love."

"To what end?" Thomas asked.

"Personal satisfaction," I said.

"You're a fool! I would think that all this time alive would have shown you the bigger picture. I guess some people are born ignorant, and they stay that way."

"Bigger picture? You're a bunch of devil-worshiping monsters."

"The end of your world is coming, Jasper. It's coming, and I'll be the one who brings in the new era. That's the true big picture. Everything is going to end, and we will stand on the ashes of the world. The Order. The true faith. The children of Valayra."

"You're not going to see the end of the world," I told him. You're not even going to see the end of the night."

And then I struck him, backhanded, across the side of his head. Thomas fell to the ground. I grabbed him by his throat again. This time I wouldn't let him talk. This time I wouldn't let him go. This time I would squeeze his throat until his life was gone. I held him high, against the sunlight. His body shaded me as I began to choke him.

And then I felt a sharp pain in my shoulder. I looked down and saw that one of those damn daggers had stabbed me. The blade was still there, and the wound was already gushing blood.

I dropped my old friend, and he ran. His horse was tied up not far from where we were, and by the time I had my hand on the open wound, Thomas Riden was galloping away.

I tried to staunch the wound, but it was to no avail. I had to get back to the farm and warn Calvin. Our worst fears had just come true.

———◦———

I STUMBLED BACK TO the farm, moving far slower than I wanted to. By the time I arrived at Calvin's door the wound had begun to close. I had lost a lot of blood though, and I was weak.

I struck the door three times, and a few minutes later, Calvin opened it.

"We're in trouble," I said.

"Jasper, you look pale."

I fell then. If not for Calvin catching me, I'd have fallen on my face.

"What's wrong?" Calvin asked.

"Gotta get to town. Warson. Thomas is here. They're here."

"Thomas?"

"They're here!" I screamed.

"Okay. Fine. Did they do this to you? Of course they did this to you."

"Get to the sheriff," I told him. "I need to rest and prepare. I'm going to try the same thing I tried last time." I sat against the wall with my hand clasped over the cut.

<hr />

CALVIN LEFT WITHIN MINUTES with two pistols strapped to his hips. I made my way to a bed, and there, I lay on my back with my eyes rolled back. It took some concentration, but I left my body, and my spirit was gliding through Ravenwood. I tried to feel the *darkness*, but it was as clouded as before. Thomas probably had a way to throw me off their trail. Ravenwood was small enough though. I would find them eventually.

I saw Calvin walk into the jail to speak with Warson. I moved on. It was early evening then. I was arrogant in spite of the wound I had taken. I honestly believed I could kill them all without even getting out of my bed. I believed it would be over within minutes of finding Riden and his followers.

I was wrong.

I searched for hours, the sun setting lower and lower as I tried to find my enemies. A few times I saw Sheriff Warson and his deputies riding through town and knocking on doors. Calvin was with them. They were preparing for battle.

Good work, Calvin, I thought.

All at once our time in Ravenwood seemed to come full circle. I had a feeling that night that this would be the end of my life there. I put the thought out of my mind and focused on the grim task at hand.

The Groban Farm was the first place I looked. I doubted I would find them there, but I checked it anyway. Of course, it was empty except for broken furniture and the bloodstains on the floorboards.

I then remembered the road on which I had seen Thomas and his people traveling. It was the same one that we had used when we had come to Ravenwood. Maybe they were still there. Maybe they had a camp.

I drifted across the fields surrounding Ravenwood to find the road. When you're a living ghost, travel is faster than horseback could ever be.

I drifted high above the trees so I could see further. As I continued to drift across the sky, I saw them. They were camped a mile from Ravenwood on a small patch of pasture.

I dropped to the ground and drifted into the camp. It was larger than the group that had been occupying the Groban Farm. I saw Thomas there, standing on a stump so that he was elevated above everyone else. I also saw that everyone had weapons on them. Not just guns. Swords. Knives. Axes. They were preparing for war.

Thomas cleared his throat and then spoke with a voice that seemed to carry itself effortlessly through the air.

"Sons and daughters, all," he said. "This is a great day for not just me, not just for the Order, but for all of mankind. Today we will take a piece of what is needed for our holy cause. The world is weak, and we have found a place that will allow us to bring devastation to the blasphemers. I ask you all once more: do you believe?"

They all shouted their agreement with him.

"Do you believe in what we are doing?"

They shouted their agreement again, and this time, some of them raised either their weapons or their fists.

"I am old and weary of this world. I've been here far longer than any of you have. And I have fought. And I have struggled. And I have sacrificed so much. My own father's life blood was spilled by my very hands. It was all for a purpose. Glory be to Valayra, our goddess. Glory be to her. The days of the Christ Child are at an end. We will bring about their end. Valayra!"

"Valayra!" the followers shouted back.

"Valayra!"

"Valayra!"

"Valayra!"

"Valayra!"

I'd heard enough. I dove into the body closest to me. I was a young woman who held a pistol in her hand. After a second of struggle, I locked her into the back of her own mind and took control. I raised the gun and shot the person next to me.

There were shouts of surprise from all of the cultists. Then, in the chaos, I pointed the gun at Thomas, but he turned to me and held out his hand. Suddenly, I could not move the woman's fingers to pull the trigger. I could do nothing.

"Hello, Jasper," he said.

And then, to my horror, I was forced out of the woman's body. I hovered in place between the formerly possessed woman and the man I had tried to kill.

"Leave her be," Thomas said.

"Lord, she killed a brother." I did not see who had replied.

"No. Indeed she did not. It was the abomination. Jasper Gunne. He is here right now."

"Where, lord?"

"I have his soul in my very hand," Thomas said.

He turned around and entered a tent. He was there for a few minutes while I struggled free myself from his grasp.

Arthan, help me, I said with my thoughts, but there was little help to be had from the imprisoned angel at that time.

Thomas emerged from the tent and held a round bottle with a flat bottom and a corked opening. He popped the cork off of it and grinned at me. I don't know if he could actually see me, or if he just knew where I was because he was holding me in place.

"I hoped you would come," he said.

Then I felt myself being pulled into the bottle. My spirit shrank and was contorted until it fit through the small opening. Then Thomas shoved the cork back into the throat of the bottle.

And I was trapped.

2017

"THIS STORY JUST KEEPS getting weirder," Calista Valen said after she had read over the newest batch of papers Jasper had written.

"I know," Jasper replied.

"You were in a bottle? Like a genie?"

"That's the guy who grants three wishes, right?"

"Yeah."

"I was trapped there, but not for too long."

"But how did it work?"

"Magic. This whole thing is about magic. The Order is the oldest group of sorcerers that's ever been. When people finally stopped believing in magic, they had perfected it to being as easy as breathing. I don't even understand their magic, and I've been researching it for decades."

"So Thomas Riden knew how to stop you?"

"He did," Jasper said. "It was a painful experience. After a time, your body starts to pull your soul back. That only happened once I was healed though."

"Healed?"

"I was stabbed, remember?"

"I actually forgot because of the whole soul in a bottle thing."

"When I am stabbed by one of their blades, the wound actually hurts my spirit. Poisons it, a bit. Once my spirit is out of my body, my body heals fast. That's also how Thomas got me."

"What do you mean?"

"You'll read about it in the next batch of papers."

She nodded. "So I take it you were furious when you got out?"

"Nothing could stop me once I was free."

"And nothing has stopped you since then either." It wasn't a question. She merely stated a fact.

"Nothing ever will," Jasper said.

He poured a cup of coffee for himself and offered one to Calista.

"No, thank you," she said. "I'm going to edit this and get back to you."

"Fine then. I'll just keep writing."

"Good. I am dying to know what happened next."

Soon Calista was gone and Jasper was back at his computer. He cracked his knuckles, drank his coffee in one burning gulp, and went back to work.

"My soul in a bottle," he said with a smile on his face. "Thomas really thought he had me."

1870

I TRIED TO MOVE through the glass and through the cork. Somehow the bottle had me trapped. I felt like Arthan stuck in his purgatory.

No. I couldn't afford to think like that. There was a way out. I just had to find it. *Patience. Wait. Thomas will want to gloat. Wait for your opportunity.*

I was terrified for the town and terrified for my friends. It didn't help that I couldn't see out of the dark glass. I didn't know if the black cloaks were still sitting around their camp or if they had gone to Ravenwood. I bounced around in the bottle like a trapped fly. I felt the pain of my body calling me back. I tried to let it happen, but I still couldn't get through the glass.

Soon enough though, Thomas began speaking again. This time he was not making a speech to his people. He was talking to someone privately.

"Jasper Gunne's in here," he said with a laugh, shaking the bottle.

"That person you sent us to kill?"

"Yes. The one who would have killed you if I hadn't told you to come with us later."

"I might have killed him," the other man said.

Not likely, I thought to myself.

"I should have come first," Thomas said. "I should have. I take responsibility for that failure. It was a stupid decision. I thought they could find him. I thought they could even handle him if they had to."

"They bought off the town though, right?"

"Yes," Calvin said. "The town was bought. The sheriff. The mayor. Problem with that though is those fellows are dead. There's a new sheriff now. I met him earlier, and he told me to get out of his town. Not a very charming fellow."

"So it was all for nothing?"

"No," Thomas said. "We're going to make this whole town pay for rejecting us."

"We are?"

"The skies will blaze tonight. Everyone will die. Then we will be able to work on opening the gate."

"You know for sure the gate is here?"

"It's here. Valayra's hellish purgatory is on the other side. We can bring her to the world. It's all here in these charts and maps. Centuries of piecing it all together. Here. In America of all places. Michigan. I knew that it was in the New World."

"I don't understand it, lord," the young man said.

"You shouldn't understand it, lad. But you're my disciple. That means that one day you will understand. When the war in Heaven was being fought, this was the place where Yahweh sent Lucifer and his followers."

"To America?"

"No. To Earth. There was nothing here but a black pit. That's where they went. Then, Yahweh created Earth around it."

"You said Valayra wasn't one of Lucifer's followers."

"She wasn't. She was a rebel all on her own. Had armies fighting in Heaven before being defeated. And imprisoned."

"So she was thrown out of Heaven with Lucifer?"

"Yes. And Lucifer found his way through the newly created world. There are doors to the prison where they were all sent.

That's how he and his demons get to do what they do."

"And he's our enemy."

"Yes. Lucifer is our enemy, just as the Christ Child is our enemy."

"And Valayra has been stuck in her hell for as long as Earth has been here?"

"Yes. That's where she is. Her time is coming. I can hear her now. Talking to me. Whispering. She wants to come forth."

"We're going to let her out?"

"The children we were going to sacrifice should have been enough to bring about the amount of magic needed. The town betrayed us. Now we will kill them all and bring our goddess to us anyway."

"With their blood? The blood of everyone in Ravenwood?"

"I tell you this, my lad," Thomas said, "none of them will survive this night."

I then heard Thomas laugh and say, "good boy." I was puzzled for a moment until I heard the sound of a dog panting.

"Why the dogs, lord?" Malcolm asked.

"They'll be used tonight after we attack the town. They'll hunt down and kill any man woman or child trying to escape."

"So we take them now?"

"No. We'll leave them here with the hunters. When the sky is orange, they will release them. I don't want my puppies killed in a crossfire."

"Very well, lord."

"It's almost sundown," Thomas said. "Let's ride."

From my bottle I heard the group of black cloaks mount their horses and ride away. In a span of ten minutes they were gone except for the three left to guard the dogs. My friends were about to be attacked, and there was nothing I could do except wait in the bottle.

———◦———

ANOTHER TWENTY MINUTES passed before I let out a scream of frustration. I knew nothing could hear me, but I let it out just the same. I was angry, and I needed a release.

And then I heard the hounds bark.

I wonder.

I screamed again. Louder.

The dogs barked and howled. I heard the men left to guard them trying to get them to stop. They weren't sure what was happening, because they couldn't hear me. Only the dogs could.

I screamed again and again and again. The dogs were going out of their minds with fright. I screamed one last time, and one of the dogs charged into the tent and toppled my bottle over.

The dog barked and attacked the bottle. One of the men approached the dog. I think he grabbed the dog's collar, and in the struggle, he accidentally kicked the bottle.

It bounced on the grass and then smashed into a rock.

Suddenly I was free. My spirit escaped the bottle, and I looked upon the dozen dogs and the three men guarding them. I moved to possess the man closest to me, but then I felt my body pulling me back.

I was too weak to resist.

I returned to my body.

———◦———

WHEN I OPENED MY eyes I was in my bedroom. I sprung to my feet and ran down the stairs. I found Mary (one of the dancing girls and a cook) in the kitchen.

"Where's Calvin?" I asked.

"He hasn't come back from town, Mr. Gunne," she said. "Things are getting bad out there though. We've been hearing things."

"Things are about to get worse," I said. "Keep the doors locked and keep yourselves armed."

"Where are you going? You could barely stand a few hours ago!"

"I'm going to end this before it gets started," I said.

I ran toward Ravenwood. I could already hear guns being fired and screams filling the air. Thomas Riden was beginning his massacre. I leapt to cover more distance. I knew I had to be fast. Everything was coming down to this night. I had been a fool. I thought they were all lunatics. Crazy. Of course they were crazy. I didn't think they had the kind of power that Thomas Riden apparently had. If not for him being able to catch and imprison my soul, I would have thought he was doing no more than empty boasting. But that night, I knew that at least he believed he could bring their goddess to the earth. Whether he would succeed or fail did not matter. He believed he had to kill everyone in Ravenwood to get what he wanted.

It was time to use my powers for something good.

I heard more gunshots. I leapt further and further. I made it into town just in time to see black cloaks riding down the street and vanishing into an alley. I wanted to attack and fight, but I knew that was risky. There were too may blades around that could hurt me, and if I was taken out, everyone would probably be dead by morning.

I made it to the jail without being attacked by a cloak. That was good. I didn't want them to know I was free of the bottle until it was too late.

———— ·◎· ————

I LEAPT ONTO THE nearest building and ran across the rooftops. I looked down to see where my enemies were going and how they were moving. They had gathered around the saloon, and thrown down wagons as shields. I watched as the black cloaks exchanged fire with the people in the saloon. I figured that's where Calvin and Sheriff Warson were.

I dropped behind the building and entered from the back. The sheriff and his men were indeed there, as was Calvin. My friend was the first to spot me.

"Jasper! You're okay? You're healed?" He left his position near the window and walked over to me.

"Fine now, Calvin. It didn't work. Not like last time."

"Gunne," Warson said. "Glad you're here. We need all the men we can get."

"There are more than what's out there," I said. "At least sixty people. They want to kill everyone in Ravenwood."

"God, why?"

"Their leader, Thomas Riden, says the town betrayed them. They will use all your deaths to open up a door to hell and bring their demon goddess here."

I could tell that I had lost Warson. In fact, I'd lost all of them. Calvin was almost with me, but even he was confused.

"It doesn't matter. All that matters is that they want to kill everyone. Everyone! We need to fight back."

"That's what we're doing," Warson said.

And then the shooting started again.

"I need a gun," I said. I walked into the kitchen and chose two knives that were used for cutting meat. I made sure they were secure in my belt. "I said I need a gun!"

"Here," one of the deputies said. He handed me his pistol.

"Thank you. I'm going out there."

"And doing what? You'll get yourself killed," Warson said.

"No, he won't," Calvin said.

I then left the saloon the same way I entered, taking a bottle of whiskey with me as I went. Once I was on the roof I opened the bottle and began drinking. It was sundown now. The black cloaks were terrorizing the streets, people were screaming and running for their lives, and the only resistance to all of this was cornered in a saloon where they were spending their ammunition too rapidly. I had two knives and a gun with six bullets. I took one more drink.

"Damn waste of whiskey," I said. Then I looked down, saw Thomas Riden, and threw the bottle at his head. It connected with a satisfying cracking sound. My old friend fell over, a hand pressed against the side of his head.

I stepped forward and fired the gun. Each bullet found a mark, and before my enemies could get away from danger, I had killed six of them. I threw the gun at another and hit his shoulder. He screamed in pain as his shoulder bones splintered from the blow. I smiled and drew my knives. Holding one in each hand I leapt from the roof and landed in the midst of the black cloaks.

Despite killing six and wounding a seventh there were still eight others there including Thomas. Fifteen then. Fifteen had cornered the town's law. Three others were back at the camp with the hounds. That left forty-two to run free.

"Jasper," Thomas said. "You got out."

I glared at him and then moved. I moved faster than the men and women in black cloaks. Their bullets hit me and made me feel as though I were being stung again and again by angry hornets. I ducked beneath a blade as a cultist tried to slash at me. I used the steak knife to cut through his bowels. He cried out in pain as he crumpled to the ground. I then leapt over the heads of my enemies and brought my boot down on another cultist's head. She made no sound as she landed on her back. She was likely knocked out. I finished the job with one quick stomp on her forehead.

"Jasper!" Thomas yelled.

I caught his arm as he slashed at me and I elbowed his face. I turned my attention on two more attackers and ducked under their swinging arms, rolled, and stood, imbedding my knives in their throats.

Another still hadn't figured out that a gun was not going to work. He shot me again. The stinging annoyed me, so I grabbed his arm, pried the gun from his fingers, then slammed the pistol against his head. I used the last two bullets in that gun to kill Thomas' other two followers.

Then it was just me and Thomas Riden.

My old friend was staggering to his feet. He spat blood and touched his broken nose. "It's been a long time since anyone has hurt me," he said.

"I plan to hurt you a lot more tonight."

"I'm sure," he said with a smile.

"Call it off and ride away," I said.

"Now why would I do that?" he asked. "My people are killing

everyone in Ravenwood right now and doing it for the glory of the goddess. Why would I call it off?"

"Because you can have me if you call them off. I won't fight you. You can put me back in the bottle or figure out how to kill me. That's what you want, isn't it? You want me dead?"

"I want you to be my friend," Thomas said.

"That is never going to happen again," I said.

"So you'll come with us willingly? Be our prisoner? Until we figure out how to kill you, that is?"

"Yes," I lied.

"That's a tempting offer. There are those within the Order that have wanted you dead since they figured out you were an abomination."

"You can give them their wish. Just spare Ravenwood."

"Oh, Jasper," Thomas said. "This is such a good offer. I'd be a fool to pass it up."

"Then we have a deal?"

"Of course not," Thomas said. He then raised his arm and suddenly it was like I had been blown away by a gust of wind. I crashed into the overturned carts and ended up in the street.

"What?" I asked, getting to my feet.

"We'll handle this now!" Thomas said. He slashed toward me with his knife, and though I was at least ten yards from him, I felt the blow sting my cheeks like a whip. "I have no time to waste on your foolish promise. It was just coincidence that you were here this day. We have been preparing this for a long time."

"Thomas, there are innocent people in this town."

"They will all be welcomed into the arms of our holy mother. Now stand aside or die."

"I am not standing aside."

Thomas sighed. "I'm sorry, old friend. I had hoped you would see reason and help me recreate this world."

"You killed my family," I said.

"Simpleton," Thomas said.

And then (I swear that this happened, though I've never seen anyone do it again) Thomas' hands ignited. Fire ran back and forth across his fingers. He threw it at the saloon, and the building was instantly engulfed in orange and red flames.

"Calvin!" I yelled.

Thomas slashed at me with his knife again, and the force knocked me to my knees. I looked up and saw him charging at me. I ducked out of the way of his stabbing knife and caught his leg. I stood and tried to slam his body against the ground. He caught himself with his hands though and flipped onto his feet, kicking me in the teeth as he did.

I rushed at him then, using my strength and speed to propel me faster than Thomas could possibly move. I reached him, broke his right arm, then, as he screamed in pain, I picked him up to break his back over my knee. As I lifted him though, I crumpled to the ground. I had been a fool once more. A knife was stuck in my leg.

Thomas coughed as he staggered to his feet. He clutched his broken arm to his chest. "Easy and predictable," he said. "Damn, that hurts."

I grabbed the hilt of the knife and began pulling the bloody blade from my leg.

"I have another," Thomas said, reaching into his coat and pulling another knife from his belt. "I think it might end now."

And then I heard a shout and a gunshot. I looked up and saw that a group of people were riding toward us. They were led by a man who had attended a few of our shows, though I never got his name. There were half a dozen all-in-all, and they were riding fast. Thomas cursed and ran into the burning saloon.

I stood, feeling a great amount of pain in my hip. "Thank you," I said to the six when they had stopped.

"Not a problem, Mr. Gunne," he said. "We've been fighting the bastards where we can. Hank Barter's my name."

I shook his hand. "How bad is it?" I asked, knowing the answer.

"Pretty bad. There were almost twenty of us when all this started. We keep losing men. We won't last much longer."

Hank was a man of about fifty years of age. His thin hair was grey, and his face was streaked with dirt. There was blood running down his arm from an open wound. He had been shot, but the stubborn bastard was ignoring his own pain.

"The town's burning," he said, tears in his eyes.

"Yeah," I said. I looked behind me and saw that the fire that had all but engulfed the saloon had spread to the other buildings. It was no ordinary fire though. It was from the very dark powers that had created me. Rain had begun to fall, but the fire spread in spite of it. This was the end of Ravenwood.

"Jasper!" I heard my name called by Calvin Valen, and my spirits rose. I turned and saw him running toward me. We embraced.

"How?" I asked.

"We were already gone when the bastard set the place on fire," Calvin explained.

"Took the chance you gave us to get away," Warson said. He walked to Calvin's side with his surviving deputies. "Hell of a mess you got us into, Gunne."

"It wasn't me," I said. "They would have come here anyway. I just happened to be in the way."

"I doubt it," Warson said.

"Never mind," Calvin said. "What's done is done. We need to fight back. We need to save the town."

"Easier said than goddamn done," Warson said.

"I have more guns," Hank Barter said. "Back at my shop. Lots of weapons. Need more people though."

"Calvin," I said, "you and the sheriff try to get as many people to fight as possible. We make a stand, and we do it soon. Meet back at the Groban Farm."

"Why there?"

"It's close," I said. "And we will be away from the fires. They might attack though, so be ready."

"Okay," Calvin said.

"Hank," I said, "take me to your shop. I need guns and bullets."

"You can take your pick of whatever you like," Hank said.

"Good. Because what I don't take, I need you to get to the Groban Farm."

"I can do that."

"Won't work," Warson said. "They'll see what we're doing and kill us all."

"Not if they're busy trying to killing me," I said.

Warson looked as though he were about to say something else, but then he decided to keep his mouth shut.

"Right," I said. "The Groban Farm."

"That place is gonna be torn down when we're done with this," Warson grumbled.

As I rode with Hank Barter and his people, I reflected on how the Groban Farm had been central in this conflict. First it was where Thomas Riden's people had established their temporary home. Now, after expelling the black cloaks, we were making a stand against a larger number of them on the same farm.

It hadn't been my intent. It just seemed the most natural place to meet after we got everyone together and armed them. Meet outside the town and then take it back. That was all we could do. We had to make a stand against them on that night.

I hated to admit this to myself back then, but the thing driving me the most was fear. Fear that not only was Thomas Riden going to butcher every man, woman and child in Ravenwood, but that he was also going to open the gate to his demon goddess. If Valayra came to Earth, everything would be over.

WE ARRIVED AT HANK'S SHOP. He did indeed have weapons. Rifles, pistols, shotguns, knives, and even a few hatchets, axes and tomahawks.

"Take your pick," he said. "Not too worried about making a profit no more."

"Good," I said. I strapped a gun belt to my waist with a six shooter on each side. I then lined the belt with knives. I took two tomahawks in my hand, and then I headed out the door.

"That's it?" Hank Barter asked. "That's not much firepower."

"Take all you can back to the farm. We'll need it. I'll be okay."

Within seconds I was on a rooftop overlooking the burning town. All of my years of rage had brought me to this night. I had once again met my one-time friend who had betrayed me so long ago. All of the demonic power in the universe could not have helped them that night. I was ready to kill. They thought they were hunting the weak. The fools. The black cloaks had just become my prey.

I heard the horses before I saw the riders. It was a group of five. I leapt from my position on the roof and landed in front of them. The horses stopped and neighed. I wasted no time. I struck one horse across the throat, and its rider was thrown as it fell. I then buried the tomahawk in the thrown rider's skull. I pried it free and then attacked the remaining four.

With ease I leapt over one of the riders, chopping into his back as I did. I left the tomahawk in him and sought my next victim. They were riding away now. I threw the tomahawk and it lodged in the skull of one of the fleeing black cloaks. I then drew my guns and fired two shots. Each hit their target.

I heard more shouts and screams as the fires around me burned more fiercely. I had to find Thomas Riden. I hoped that if I could beat him or subdue him that I could end this madness.

I walked up to the two men I had shot off of their horses. One of them was still alive. He groaned as I put my hand on his neck.

"No," he said. I saw that the bullet had hit his shoulder.

"Where's Thomas?" I asked.

He shook his head.

"Tell me," I said.

He shook his head again.

"Everyone's riding around and killing," I said. "The people of Ravenwood have run, but you're all still here. Why? What's Riden doing? How is he going to bring Valayra to Earth?" I put pressure on his shoulder wound and made him cry out.

And still he would not talk.

I put my hand on his collar bone. I felt it between my thumb and trigger finger. I smiled at him again and then I pinched the bone and heard it break. His screams were louder than anyone else's that night.

And then he passed out.

"Damn," I said. I punched his face as hard as I could, leaving a dent of broken bone and bruised, bleeding flesh.

Where was Thomas?

I leapt onto the rooftops again and ran across the ones that were not yet on fire. The heat from the blaze was strong. The fire raged on in spite of the storm that should have killed it.

I stayed perched on the roof for a time, trying to reach out and feel the presence of my enemies. They were nowhere and everywhere all at once. Thomas had masked their presence somehow. I ran across the rooftops again, not able to see anyone. The fire was spreading though. Ravenwood would be gone by morning. The sun completely set as rain began to fall. Thunder roared and lightning flashed across the sky.

But in the street there was silence.

"Where? Where? Where?" I kept whispering the question to myself.

I continued moving across the rooftops in my rain-soaked clothes. My silver hair had come free of its tie and it hung in front of my face like damp curtains. I swept it back as I ran.

And then I heard the screams.

And the gunshots.

———◆———

I LOOKED OVER MY shoulder and saw in the distance that the Valen farm was in flames. I ran back toward the farm. It should have been empty. Calvin told them all to flee. There should be no one there.

As I approached, I saw that my friends had not obeyed Calvin's orders.

"No!" I screamed as I watched those I had lived with and worked with try to leap out of the top floor windows. One woman prepared to jump, but a bullet was put between her eyes. Another tried to jump anyway to escape the flames that had engulfed the house. It was the same sort of fire that was now ravaging the town.

"Riden!" I screamed his name as a challenge. "Riden! You piece of horse vomit! I'm right here, you coward! You heretic! Face me!"

Thomas Riden appeared from within a group of black cloaks that backed away from him as I approached.

"Hello, old friend," Thomas said. "That last bout we had sure was fun, wasn't it?"

"Let them go," I said. "These people have done nothing to you."

"They'll be enfolded into the everlasting embrace of our mother," Thomas said.

"You're mad," I said.

"You're a simpleton."

We circled one another, neither of us wanting to make the first move in the fight. I was burning with rage, but I had to keep it in check. If I allowed myself to let go and fight with blind emotion, I would be in Arthan's purgatory before the storm was over.

"You think you're special?" Thomas asked me. "You're not special. There have been people like you over the last eight thousand years. There have been a few. We have learned to fight you. We also learned to take your powers and use them against you. How do you think I was able to block your senses? Couldn't find us, right? You couldn't see us with your sense unless I wanted you to."

"How many?" I asked.

"You're the seventh," he said. "I've taken some of your power. I thought all those years ago that Frederick, fool that he was, had created another abomination. I dined upon your grandson after I killed all of my people. It turned out I was right. I don't have the same power as you, but I can do things that most people cannot do. With all the power that runs through me because of our blessed goddess, I am more than you could dream of being. She has showered grace upon me, and I will do her will."

"You will die trying," I said.

And Thomas laughed.

I charged at him, throwing all of my might into my punches. He ducked out of the way and struck my chest with a blow that would have broken the ribs of a normal man. I caught his arm as he pulled it away and slammed my elbow against his biceps. He groaned in pain and that told me that he was not quite as unbreakable as I am.

He grabbed my neck and pulled me forward. I landed face-first in the mud and rolled over just as Thomas stomped on my head. He tried to stomp on me again, but I caught his shin and made him lose balance. Then I was on top of him, throwing all of my power into the punches I rained on his face.

Thomas caught my fist and flipped me onto my back. He was on his feet within a second and running. "It's been fun, Jasper," he said as he ran from me.

I moved toward him and that was when I saw that the other surviving black cloaks had rounded up the survivors of Ravenwood, including my friends from *Amazing Wonders*. They were gathered together in the yard. Hundreds of people held in place by a circle of men with guns.

"Don't do this," I said to Thomas.

"Come another step closer and they'll all burn," he replied.

"Okay," I said. "Let's just talk."

"We were talking," Thomas said. "Then you attacked me."

"Fine. Let's stop fighting Just leave. Leave this town and never come back. I will let you live."

"That's not an acceptable offer," Thomas said.

"If you kill these people," I said, "I'll kill you."

"If I kill them, their blood will open the gateway."

"There is no gateway," I said. "This is all a lie!"

"Then it's a lie that's powered both of us, Jasper! I believe with all my heart that my goddess is waiting for me to unleash her. What happens then? I serve at her side, a ruler over this world answering only to Valayra."

"If she was so powerful," I said, "she wouldn't need rituals to come to the earth. She would just arrive herself. She's nothing more than a fallen angel. A demon in the shadows. She's no goddess."

Thomas spat at me and then turned away. I followed him. He was headed for his people, probably to rally them again to bring a new attack on Ravenwood.

But he stopped.

From where I was I saw why he had stopped. A whole mass of people were marching toward us, guns and knives in hand. Calvin and Sheriff Warson had not obeyed my orders. Instead they had come back to Calvin's farm where their enemies waited.

The ones on horseback arrived first. They charged at the group of black cloaks, emptying their pistols into the bastards as they rode. Suddenly it was slaughter and madness everywhere.

Thomas joined in the fight and I followed. Calvin's house was now forgotten, though there were no survivors. I had a feeling that this angry mob of people was all that was left of Ravenwood. I leapt into the brawl myself.

"Ravenwood!" I yelled. "Kill them all! Every black cloak dies!"

I struck my enemies with my fists, with knives and with their own guns. It was a bloody and gruesome massacre. A big man stood in front of me. I punched his groin, and he fell to his knees. I then drove a knife into his eye. I spun and sliced into the neck of another man with that same knife. Then I turned and threw the knife at one who was a bit further away.

The black cloaks were diminishing in number but so were the brave men and women trying to avenge Ravenwood. Thomas was handling that.

"We are close!" I heard Thomas yell. "Bless us, goddess!"

I fought harder in my attempt to get to Thomas once again. I needed to end this now, and the only way to do that was to remove my old friend from the battle. I hacked my way across the black cloaks, killing with unnatural speed and efficiency, but soon I was out of weapons. My bullets were gone, and the guns I had used as clubs had been discarded. My tomahawks and knives were buried in the bodies of my enemies. I saw that Thomas was still armed with a darkblade.

When he saw me, he smiled through his weariness and attacked me. We grappled with one another. I caught his arm, and he switched the knife to his other hand and slashed at me. I dodged it and tried to steal the knife from him. I thought that if I could get a hold of it, I could use it to kill him. If his powers were similar to mine, his weakness might be similar too.

Thomas threw me back into the fight, and then he seemed to vanish. "Damn!" I yelled. I then looked to my side and saw a gun aimed at Calvin Valen's head. I looked down, saw a rock, picked it up and threw it at the shooter's head before he could take the shot. The shooter was dead before he hit the ground.

Calvin looked up and saw me and walked toward where I was standing. The black cloaks were retreating. The townspeople were chasing them.

"It's a bloodbath," Calvin said.

"I thought you were waiting at the Groban Farm," I said.

"Couldn't wait. We heard what they were doing here at my place. We made a decision."

"I'm sorry, Calvin. I should have went to find them I should have taken the fight to them."

"They were coming here anyway," Calvin said.

I looked into my friend's eyes and saw they were red with tears. He was trying to keep it together, but he was nearly overwhelmed by the loss he had suffered.

"I need to find Thomas Riden," I said. "If I kill him, we can end this now."

"How can you kill him?" Calvin asked. "I saw the way he fought you. He's the same as you."

I squatted next to a black cloak. There was a dagger in her hand, but I didn't want that. I drew the darkblade from her belt. "With this," I said.

And then I heard the loud and harsh voice of Thomas Riden thundering over every sound on that bloodstained battleground. I turned to see Thomas levitating over the charred ruins of the Valen farmhouse. His hands were outstretched, and he was reciting an ancient prayer in the long forgotten language of the Order.

"He's calling for Valayra," I said. "If he does that, she'll come to Earth."

I took the darkblade by the tip and leapt. Once I was level with Thomas, I threw the blade at him. His eyes were closed in prayer, ushering the dead souls of Ravenwood to his demon goddess so she could feed and gain the strength to enter the world. He never saw the blade coming.

As I landed I saw the blade strike him. It broke his concentration, and he fell into the smoldering remnants of the Valen house, a darkblade in his side.

"Got him," I said.

———◦———

CALVIN AND I FOUND TWO of the show's horses that had survived the fight so far. We mounted them and then rode through Ravenwood, delivering our vengeance against the black cloaks. Calvin screamed in rage and agony as he killed with bloodthirsty joy. If he could have tortured and killed every single one of them, it would not end his pain. I knew that from experience. But Calvin was gone now. Lost in his own lust for vengeance. I helped him.

The town of Ravenwood was ashes before we finished hunting down the black bloaks. The only survivors were a handful of people, Calvin, myself and Sheriff Warson. For all of our efforts to save Ravenwood, the town was essentially dead.

2017

"THE TOWN WAS essentially dead," Calista Valen said as she read over the end of what Jasper Gunne had written.

"No monsters," Jasper said. "No creatures. No dragons or anything like that. Just a group of witches and two men with too much power fighting to the death."

"Did you guys kill all the black cloaks?" she asked.

"We did," Jasper replied. "Rode through the ashes and killed every last one of them."

"And that was the end of the Ravenwood Massacre?"

"Not exactly," Jasper said. "More happened."

"More?"

"The story's not done yet. There's still some things that happened in Ravenwood that I haven't covered."

"Your hanging?"

"Yes," I said.

"Did my family survive? I mean, of course they survived. I'm here. You didn't mention them though."

"There were a few people that managed to escape the chaos. The Valens were among them. They got away shortly after it began."

"But Grandpa Calvin still went away with you on your crusade?" she asked. "Wouldn't he have stayed behind with his family?"

"Calvin's wife blamed me and blamed him. She told him to leave and never come back. His children were forbidden to see him, and he was no longer welcome in Ravenwood."

"But he's buried here," Calista protested.

"Yes," Jasper said. "Calvin was buried here. I sent his body back to his home. His sons were grown by then, and I learned in a letter that they had saw to burying their father properly, much to the anger of their mother."

Calista put the papers down and sipped the herbal tea that Jasper had made for her. Jasper was once again struck by how similar she looked to his old friend, her ancestor, Calvin. It was like writing for a ghost.

"Was Calvin as great a man as you made him seem in this story?" she asked.

"He was the best man I ever knew. The bravest. The kindest. The strongest. He was better suited for my powers than I was. He might have been able to make a difference."

"You don't think you've made a difference?" she asked.

"Not in the least," Jasper said. "What have I accomplished? My friends are dead. A bunch of black cloaks are dead, but the Riden family is still alive. Hell, Thomas is planning something now. I can feel it."

"Thomas didn't die then?" she asked.

"That's the end of the story that I intend to write," Jasper said.

"The darkblade didn't kill him?"

"There's more to tell," Jasper said. "That's all I'll say until I get it down on paper."

"My father will want to read it," Calista said.

"Strange how quickly his mind changes."

"He's been watching the news a lot lately," she said.

Jasper glanced at her. "What does that mean?"

"You haven't heard?" she asked. "Something about an old book from the Bible being found in a cave in the Middle East."

"I hadn't heard. No television."

"It's called *the Book of Angels*."

"What does that have to do with anything?" Jasper asked.

"The book talks about the second devil," she said. "Valayra."

Jasper slapped a hand to his forehead. "It makes sense now! That's why I've been feeling them making their moves."

"Because of a lost Bible book?"

"Exactly," Jasper said. "I don't think that this book was lost. They knew where it was. It was meant to be found now."

"I don't understand."

"They wanted the world to learn about Valayra. They are going to try again. They're going to try and bring her to Earth."

"You think so?"

"I know they are. This is how they work."

"What are you going to do then?"

Jasper drummed his fingers on the countertop for a moment. "There's nothing I can do yet. I have to wait for them to make a move and then go to them." Calista's news of *the Book of Angels* seemed to slide all the pieces of information into place. Jasper immediately had the full picture of what was happening.

"When do you think they'll make their move?" Calista asked.

"Tomorrow? A decade from now? I don't know. But it's coming, and it's going to be bad. Things have gotten ugly in my personal war against the Order, but they've been quiet for the past twenty years or so. I've only run across small groups broken off from the cult. This though... Thomas Riden is going to lead the charge once more. And if I had to make a guess, I'd say they're coming back to Ravenwood."

Calista's eyes flashed with alarm. "Why?"

"Because that door is supposedly here. If he wants to summon his goddess, he has to go to where there's a door. I only know of three places on Earth where the doors are said to be, but the one in Ravenwood is the easiest to get to."

"So he'll be coming here. Do you think he'll destroy the whole city?"

"Not this time," Jasper said. "I won't let him."

"You think you can stop him? What about his fires?"

"I will kill him on sight. I think I can kill him at least."

Calista said nothing for a while. Then, without another word, she left the apartment. Jasper noticed she left the fresh pages of manuscript behind. Jasper opened a bottle of whiskey and sat down once more at his computer. There was nothing to do now except wait. He knew that. If the bastards were going to "discover" *the Book of Angels*, he could make sure his accounts were recorded properly. He felt that the world was about to change.

"Come out and play, Thomas," he said as he began typing. "Our game's not over."

1870

THE MASSACRE WAS OVER. Ravenwood was ashes, and its people were dead. Calvin reunited with his family, and there were tears of joy on his face. That wasn't to last.

"I blame you," his wife said as he hugged her close to his chest.

"What?" Calvin asked.

She pushed away. "I said that I blame you."

"This wasn't my fault," Calvin said.

"Yes it is!" she said through her sobs. "It's your fault for letting that monster live with us! It's your uncle's fault! It's your damn grandfather's fault!"

"Julia..."

"No!" she screamed. Then she pointed at me. "Get away from us! Get away from our family and stay away, you monster! You demon!"

I admit that I was hurt, but I understood her pain. While her children had survived, many of the friends we'd all had in *Amazing Wonders* had died in the massacre.

"Give her time," I said to my friend.

As I walked through the remains of Ravenwood I felt the eyes of every survivor following me. They blamed me just as Julia Valen blamed me. This was an unfair accusation. Calvin had been right. Thomas Riden and his people were going to come to Ravenwood anyway. It was just luck that we happened to be there at the same time. Without us, the town would have been swallowed whole by the *darkness*, and many more would have died. Maybe it was more than luck. I don't know. God and I are not exactly on speaking terms at the moment, but maybe He had a hand in it. If He did, I hope that He is still watching now. I think we're going to need the help.

Sheriff Warson, on that day, personified the misplaced anger of the survivors of Ravenwood. He rode next to me and drew his gun, cocking it. "Stay where you are," he said.

I looked up at him and then at the gun. "Is this what you want to do, Warson?" I asked. "After I helped defend your town?"

"You brought this evil here," he said. "And for that you'll stand trial."

"Your last sheriff brought it to you. I just helped fight it." I started walking again.

"I said to stay where you are, boy!" Warson growled.

"I'm at least a hundred and ten years older than you," I shouted back to him. "Don't call me boy."

And then he shot me.

I spun and touched the back of my head where the bullet had hit. A welt was already forming. *Perfect.* I looked at the sheriff and shook my head. "Did you notice anything about the way I fought last night?" I asked.

"I don't know how many it will take to bring you down," Warson said, drawing his other pistol, "but I'll keep trying until one of us is dead."

"You're being foolish," I said.

"Come with me and this goes no further."

"I'm leaving," I said.

"Not before you answer for your crimes against Ravenwood, you're not," Warson said with angry contempt in his voice.

I heard a gunshot and then watched as Warson's horse fell

dead, throwing the sheriff as it fell into the road, a bullet hole in its head.

"No one kills you but me," Thomas Riden said as he stumbled toward me. His clothes were burnt and torn. He was clutching his side where the darkblade had struck him. He hadn't been in the ashes of the Valen house when Calvin and I looked. I figured he may have escaped. I wasn't expecting to see him again that day.

"Thomas," I said.

"You have ruined it all," he said, stopping a few yards from where I stood. Sheriff Warson scrambled to his feet and moved to a safer distance. He had seen what Thomas and I were capable of in a fight. "I would have made a new world. I would have ruled at the right hand of my goddess. Do you understand? You have kept me from my destiny. All these years preparing and waiting. My own immortality. You wasted it!"

He charged at me then. I braced for his attack and caught him as he lunged at me. I threw him to the ground and punched his wounded side. Thomas howled in pain and then delivered a powerful kick to my stomach that threw me off of him. I landed about ten feet away.

"I don't know how I'll kill you," Thomas said, drawing a darkblade from his charred coat, "buy I'm going to try."

He was still fast and strong in spite of his wound. He slashed at me, and I caught his arm. He dropped the knife and caught it with his other hand. He then struck me across the face, and as I recovered, stabbed deep into my shoulder.

I broke away from him, cringing as the darkblade left a fresh wound. I clutched my shoulder and felt the blood gushing. He attacked again and again. I dodged his attacks instead of fighting him off. I needed to wait until I had an opening. I was afraid that if Thomas wounded me again, I would be sent back to Arthan's Purgatory, and then he would turn his vengeance toward the town's survivors.

Thomas was frantic though. He was wounded and angry, and he wanted his vengeance to be finished. I don't think he had any idea what he would have done once I was dead or after he had killed everyone that had helped stop him just a few hours earlier. He was maddened with a helpless rage because of his failure to his goddess, and I personified that failure.

We were reduced to brawlers in what was left of the street. Nothing more. The powers we had used only hours before were meaningless now. The darkblade had done its work. We were almost human then in our level of strength. I wondered if Thomas would go to Arthan's Purgatory if I managed to kill him, or if he would simply die.

I stooped and picked up a clump of dirt as Thomas charged at me again with the knife. I ducked as he swung the small blade and threw the dirt into his eyes. He yelped and put a hand over his eyes and swung his weapon madly as I danced beyond his reach.

"You should not have done what you did," I said. "You should have remained our friend. My family's blood is on your hands."

He wiped the dirt from his eyes and squinted toward me. "Your family? Your family would be dead by now anyway!"

"You denied them their lives so that you could play with a *darkness* you cannot understand, nor control."

"I understand it!"

"It failed you!" I shouted back at him. "It failed you and you failed it! It's over, Thomas! Now, you'll pay for what you did to my family!"

I backed toward the nearest of the burnt buildings and waited for him to attack me. The survivors of Ravenwood, including the Valens, were all gathered to watch this fight. This was the true end of their nightmare. But how would they ever forgive me?

I stooped once again and picked up a piece of charred wood. As Thomas came at me with the *darkblade*, I used the broken plank to defend myself. One blow of the *darkblade* broke the feeble plank in two. I moved in closer to Thomas, felt him bury the *darkblade* in my stomach. I grunted as my one-time-friend twisted the knife. And that was when I saw my chance.

Through the pain, I saw that Thomas relaxed a bit, feeling as though he had won. In that split-second, I drove the jagged end of the broken wooden plank into his right eye. The screams that Thomas made that day still ring in my ears, and I admit that they can still make me smile when I think on them.

"Bastard!" I snarled, staggering towards him. Thomas, weakened by the blows from the *darkblade* was more vulnerable than ever, but if he had been a normal man, he would have been dead instead of on his knees trying to remove the sharp piece of charred wood from where his eye used to be.

He looked up at me in time to see the *darkblade* slash at him. His throat was opened on the streets of the town he had burned. I dropped the *darkblade* as I watched his blood run freely. I could still feel him though. He was still there.

But he was beaten. The fight was done. I probably couldn't kill Thomas Riden. That was fine. He couldn't kill me either. But perhaps everyone would be safe. I thought of how I had to instruct them to do something with his body. I had an idea to wrap him in the strongest chains and bury him in a coffin full of heavy stones. All this went through my head as I turned to face the town that had been ready to kill me.

And then Sheriff Warson hit me with the butt of his rifle.

⸻◦⸻

I WAS HANGED later that day.

When I woke I was still in pain. I tried to reach my hand over to put pressure on my stomach wound, but I found that I was handcuffed. What was worse was that I was unable to break the cuffs. The *darkblade* had done its work.

I remember looking out into the crowd of angry faces and thinking they all had no idea what had truly transpired here. I had done what was necessary, and without me, they would have been dead along with their friends and family. I hadn't saved the town, but my actions had saved the few survivors. I was the reason there were survivors.

Despite my weakness, the noose did not break my neck. The crowd jeered at me as I choked. I dangled there for a short time while they threw rocks at me. It didn't matter. The humiliation of being hanged was bad enough. I had indeed fallen.

That was when Sheriff Warson put a bullet in my head. If I had not been so weak, that bullet would have probably glanced off my skull and left only one nasty welt. But I was weak, and that meant that I was instantly in Arthan's Purgatory.

———◆———

"THAT *WAS* A BATTLE," Arthan said when he saw me. He embraced me and clasped what would have been my arm in my spirit body. They orange light that glowed off of him seemed to grow brighter as we talked.

"I lost," I said.

"No. You won more than you know."

"Ravenwood was destroyed."

"But Valayra is still trapped," he said. "You might not have saved Ravenwood, but you saved the rest of the world."

"So Thomas spoke true?"

"He did," Arthan said. "Don't expect him to stay down too long. He's already been in and out of here."

"He'll heal just like me," I said.

"Not just like you. He's not the same. He's different. But he has other plans. We need to be ready."

"Other plans?"

"I've been watching all of it," Arthan said. "You had a lover, didn't you? Someone named Audrey?"

"She turned on me. Went with the Order."

"No," Arthan said. "She was with them from the start, but she could mask her spirit from you."

"What do you mean?"

"Thomas was able to disguise his whole group and throw you off," Arthan said.

"Yes."

"Because there have been people like you before. Thomas

looked through all of the lore of the Order to learn how to work your powers against you."

"I don't understand though," I said. "If Audrey was part of the Order all along..."

"Yes?"

"Why did she and I become lovers? What was there to gain?"

"Jasper," Arthan said, "the truest fight is coming and it's coming soon. Audrey is pregnant."

"Impossible," I said.

"Possible," Arthan said. "There are ways. Thomas Riden knew them too."

"You mean it's possible for me to have children?"

"No. Well... yes. In a way. A deep, dark magic has to be used. I have seen what they were doing. The children that were born were unnatural and powerful."

"Children?"

"She bore twins," Arthan said.

I was too astounded to say anything in reply to Arthan for a while. While I stood in silence he waved his hand and showed me Thomas Riden's other plan.

"The girl is the one who we need to worry about," he said. "Her brother was sacrificed on the highest altar of the Order shortly after they were born. She took his essence into herself. She will be just as strong as you."

Arthan then left me with my unfortunate information. My daughter was born. I watched her through the blue mist into the world of the mortals where she was sleeping in a cradle. My daughter. With my powers. Raised by my enemies.

No.

"Arthan," I said, "I will not let this happen."

"What will you do?"

"I'm going to find her."

And that was the end of our conversation, for I was forced out of Arthan's Purgatory as my body was close to mended.

MY BODY HEALED AND forced the bullet out of my head. When I woke in my latest grave a week after my hanging I felt rested and ready to return to the land of the living.

Calvin Valen sat atop a horse near my grave. He was wearing his black Sunday clothes and his best white hat. He was watching as I clawed my way out of the dirt. He tipped the hat toward me as I finally unearthed myself.

"You're going after them, aren't you?" he asked.

I nodded. "Who buried me?" I asked.

"Some grateful folks in town," Calvin said. "Buried you so no one would do anything else to you. I didn't stop them. It meant I would know where to look for you when you woke up."

"I see," I said.

"Julia threw me out of our house. Doesn't want the children near me anymore. It's just me, my horse and these goddamn clothes. I look like a travelling preacher man."

I laughed.

"So I have nothing left to live for here in Ravenwood," Calvin said. "Not the town or my family. Not the show. I'm coming with you."

I did not argue. In fact, I thought it would be nice to have some company.

"Where to first?" Calvin asked.

"Let's head east. We need to find a ship to take us to England."

"Climb on and let's go," he said.

"I think I'd rather run," I replied.

And so we left what had once been Ravenwood, Michigan. Calvin rode his horse and I ran beside it, keeping up all the while. I will never forget Calvin Valen. I wish he hadn't come with me back then though. He should have tried to make things right with his wife. My crusade was going to lead to nothing but pain.

And still Calvin stuck by me the whole time.

I did not tell him then about my supposed daughter born to

Audrey within the inner circle of the Order. I did not know how to even approach that subject. We could discuss it on the boat. This new mission of mine was no longer one of vengeance. It was one of rescue and redemption.

I would keep my failure in Ravenwood in my mind forever so that I would not repeat it. I couldn't fail again. Too many people were counting on me, and they did not even know it.

My immortality now had purpose.

AUTHOR'S NOTE

ANGRY TEENAGE REBELLION is a strange thing. I remember writing a story for English class when I was sixteen. I'm sure you reading this remember those assignments. They were always about dull topics. I had to write a story about camping, and being who I am, I made it violent. It was my way of making the task bearable. The problem was that it was a school assignment, and the violent story was even worse because I went to a Christian school. Thirteen years later, I realize that I was being stupid when I wrote that story, but back then, after being scolded and threatened with detention and forced to rewrite the entire assignment, I was seething with rage.

I spent weeks afterward with a notebook that I carried everywhere. Inside that notebook was my secret project. I was writing a story for myself. It involved a super-powered man who was fighting a satanic cult. I wrote two of these stories, and I only let a few of my friends read them. They were about thirty hand-written pages, but they were my way of fighting back against what I saw as the school censoring my "artistic freedom." In my youthful ignorance, I saw these turning into hit graphic novels. I even started to script one, but I cannot draw, so the idea fell as dead as Richard Gunne. *(Too soon?)*

Now, thirteen years later, I have released an updated and revised version of that old project. *Massacre at Sundown* is the beginning of a trilogy that will tell of the struggle between Jasper Gunne and the Order of Valayra. I am excited to have this first volume completed and released. This is unfinished business for me. It is the oldest idea for a book that I can remember that I have not abandoned. It has crept back into my mind again and again, and I am happy that after numerous false starts, I am finally on the road to completing this project started by my angry sixteen-year-old self.

I want to thank Miranda Fry for editing this book. She had a keen eye, and did not hesitate to point out things that needed correcting. I want to thank my mother, Rebecca Evans, and my brother, Michael Evans, for listening to my continuous prattle about this book since I began writing it. I also want to thank my talented and poetic friend, Tiffanie Valdez, for her input and for helping spur my creativity through our poetry exchanges.

This is just the beginning. The real story of Jasper Gunne and the Order of Valayra will unfold in *Day of the Devil.*

–September 19, 2017

ABOUT THE AUTHOR

Matthew David Evans is a novelist, short story writer, and poet from Sturgis, Michigan. His first novel, *Prophets of the Otherworld*, was published in 2011. *Massacre at Sundown* is his second novel, but it will not be his last. He is currently at work on a follow-up book called *Day of the Devil*, as well as a horror project set at Christmastime called *Grim Tidings* which he has written with his friend, Lee Webb.

matthewdavidevans.com

www.ingramcontent.com/pod-product-compliance
Lightning Source LLC
Chambersburg PA
CBHW071254170626
46809CB00001B/213